THE BAYOU BULLETIN

The Fabulous Jax is Back for Good!

Jacqueline "Jax" Delacroix, eldest daughter of newly appointed federal judge Justin Delacroix, has returned to Bayou Beltane after spending most of the past ten years in Europe where she pursued a successful career on the Grand Prix riding circuit. "I intend to raise and train the best event and dressage horses in the South," she said when asked what her plans were now that she's retired from active equestrian competition.

A world-class horse-woman, Ms. Delacroix won her first novice level event at the tender age of seven and continued to take top honors through all levels of competition during her high school days. The Fabulous Jax, as she soon became known in the international press, reached the pinnacle of her equestrian career during the 1996 Summer Olympics in Atlanta, taking a gold in Individual Dressage and helping her team to a silver in the three-day event.

Ms. Delacroix will be residing at the family's Riverwood estate, where her twin brother, Beau Delacroix, manages the racing stables. "We're all very proud of Jacqueline's success, of course," says Charles Delacroix about his granddaughter's return to the family fold. "We're even more pleased she finally decided to come home."

Candace Schuler is acknowledged
as the author of this work.

ISBN 0-373-82565-X

EVERY KID NEEDS A HERO

Copyright © 1998 by Harlequin Books S.A.

DELTA JUSTICE

Every Kid Needs a Hero

CANDACE SCHULER

Harlequin Books

TORONTO • NEW YORK • LONDON
AMSTERDAM • PARIS • SYDNEY • HAMBURG
STOCKHOLM • ATHENS • TOKYO • MILAN
MADRID • WARSAW • BUDAPEST • AUCKLAND

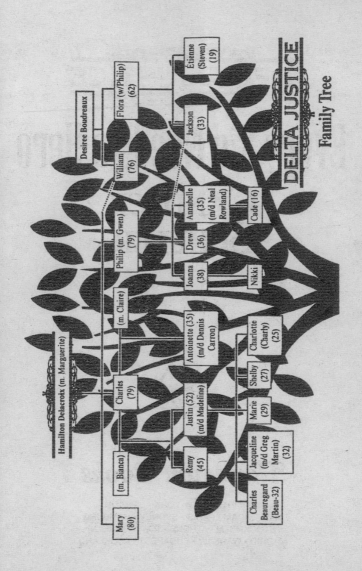

DELTA JUSTICE

Family Tree

Hamilton Delacroix (m. Marguerite)

Mary (80)

(m. Bianca)

Charles (79)

Remy (45)

Justin (52) (m/d Madeline)

Charles Beauregard (Beau–32)

Jacqueline (m/d Greg Martin) (32)

Marie (29)

Shelby (27)

Charlotte (Charly) (25)

Antoinette (35) (m/d Dennis Carron)

(m. Claire)

Philip (m. Gwen) (79)

William (76)

Desiree Boudreaux

Flora (w/Philip) (62)

Joanna (38)

Drew (36)

Annabelle (35) (m/d Neal Rowland)

Jackson (33)

Étienne (Steven) (19)

Nikki

Cade (16)

CAST OF CHARACTERS

Jacqueline "Jax" Delacroix—Eldest daughter of Justin Delacroix and world-renowned equestrian, back in Bayou Beltane to breed event horses.

Matt Taggart—Large-animal vet, widowed with two children, **Amy** (7) and **Jeff** (9).

Beau Delacroix—Jacqueline's twin brother, who manages the racing stables at Riverwood.

Charlotte (Charly) Delacroix—Member of the New Orleans police academy, injured in the line of duty and recuperating under the care of her sister Jax.

Katherine Beaufort—An adopted woman in search of her past, led to Bayou Beltane by fascinating journals belonging to her great aunt.

Annabelle Delacroix—Philip Delacroix's youngest child—a divorced single mother and true Southern belle who befriends Katherine.

Dear Reader,

When the idea of participating in a multi-author series was first proposed to me, I thought it sounded intriguing—and just a little bit intimidating, too. I'd participated in other projects like this before, but nothing quite so complicated and involved as DELTA JUSTICE. Scary though it was, the idea—and the opportunity—was just too delicious to pass up. Take one compelling, carefully guarded family secret with the potential to change lives, add a cast of passionate, interesting characters and the quirks and creativity of twelve authors... Well, it was an offer I couldn't refuse! The experience of writing *Every Kid Needs a Hero* was as interesting and exciting as I'd thought it would be—well worth the sleepless nights it cost me. I hope readers feel the same way.

All the best,

Candace Schuler

P.S. Special thanks to Jennifer Platt, D.V.M., for all the answers she provided to my innumerable questions, especially about the treatment of colicky horses. Any mistakes made in the veterinary procedures described are strictly my own.

CHAPTER ONE

MATT TAGGART COULD HEAR the screaming as soon as he turned off the engine, silencing the rumbling of his Chevy van and cutting Sheryl Crow off in mid-lament. Shrill bursts of equine excitement pierced the relative calm of the stable yard, the sound high-pitched and wild, full of impatience, passion and fury. It could only mean one thing.

He turned to the small, fair-haired child wriggling around on the passenger seat beside him. "Amy, honey," he said, reaching over to help her unfasten her seat belt, "why don't you run on up to the big house and see if Ms Raison has any of those big ol' sugar cookies you like so well."

Had they been anyplace else but Delacroix Farms, Matt would have never presumed on the housekeeper's hospitality without some advance warning, but everybody knew Odelle Raison doted on children. There were always sugar cookies in the glazed ceramic pig sitting atop the big, shiny refrigerator in the kitchen, even though there hadn't been any children in residence at Riverwood since Justin Delacroix's youngest had gone off to college. Matt had no doubt of his daughter's welcome.

Despite the lure of sugar cookies, Amy didn't want to go up to the big house.

"I want to see the horses, Daddy." Her plump bottom lip curved out in the suggestion of a pout. "You said I could come with you to see the horses."

"I said you could see the horses after I finish my busi-

ness with Ms Delacroix,'' he reminded her. That hadn't
been exactly what he'd said, but it was close enough.

"But I won't get in the way of your business. Honest."
Amy looked up at him pleadingly, her eyes as big and blue
as her mother's had been, with the same little flecks of
white in the irises. "I'll be real quiet till you're finished.
You won't even know I'm there."

"I'll know," he said mildly, doing his best to ignore the
guilt induced by her wide-eyed gaze.

At any other time, he'd have let her tag along behind
him, trusting her to stay close and stand quietly—just as
she'd promised—while he examined two of Jax Delacroix's
prize-winning mares for signs of impending labor. Amy had
watched him examine a pregnant mare before. She'd
watched him apply poultices and lance abscesses, and had
even witnessed the birth of a foal without turning a hair.
But he knew what he'd just heard, and there were certain
things a seven-year-old child shouldn't see.

"It will distract me from my job if I have to worry about
you getting stepped on," Matt said to his daughter. He got
out of the van, came around to her side and swung her
down to the ground, then nudged her toward the house.
"You go on now, honey. I'll come up and get you when
I'm finished. You can see the horses then."

Amy held her ground. "But, Daddy, nobody will step on
me. That's silly. 'Sides, Bear said he'd let me ride Rocky
next time I came with you an' he might forget if he doesn't
see me," she added anxiously.

"He won't forget. And if he does, I'll remind him." Matt
lifted his hand from her shoulder and gently cupped his
daughter's chin, stopping her before she could form another
protest. "I promise you'll get to ride Rocky before we leave
today, okay?"

She stared up at him, a doubtful expression on her face.

"Cross my heart," he said, acting out his words, which

caused the keys he still held in his right hand to jingle against his chest.

"W-e-el-ll..." She sighed loudly. "Okay."

"And it's Mr. Bearclaw, remember?"

"But everybody else calls him Bear."

"Everybody else isn't seven years old."

"But—"

"No more buts, young lady." He squeezed her chin lightly, waggling her head back and forth, and let her go. "I swear, one of these days you're going to 'but' me to death." He tensed slightly, realizing what he'd said as soon as the last word left his mouth, but Amy just giggled.

"Oh, Daddy, you're so silly."

Matt let out his breath. "Don't forget to say thank you to Ms Raison when she gives you a cookie," he called after her as she turned and dashed up the path toward the house.

Another disaster diverted, he thought, thankful that his daughter wasn't as sensitive to every ill-chosen word as he was. The child psychologist had been right; children were stronger and more resilient than most people gave them credit for. Both of his kids were making the inevitable adjustment to their mother's death better than he was. But then, they weren't racked with the guilt of a million what-ifs and if-onlys and might-have-beens. His children's love for their mother had been simple, honest and innocent; their grief at losing her was the same. His love for his wife had been...complicated. His feelings about her death were complicated, too. And there was something about the woman he was here to see that complicated those feelings even more.

Not that there was anything between him and Jax Delacroix, nor had there ever been, but, damn, there were moments when he wanted there to be!

Not that he was ever likely to get what he wanted in that regard, he thought, tucking the keys to his van into the pocket of his jeans as he headed across the stable yard toward the breeding paddock. She hadn't given the least little sign that she might be receptive to any advances he might make—and he wasn't about to make any, anyway—but a man could dream. A little. Now and then, when it didn't interfere with the rest of his life or his responsibilities.

Jax Delacroix was the kind of woman it was easy to dream about. Tall and candle slim, with dark hair, creamy skin and the bone structure of a prima ballerina, she was as pretty as a cool spring morning. Well, all the Delacroix women were pretty, if it came to that, but there was something about Jax Delacroix since she'd come back from Europe that made her stand out from the rest of them. Maybe it was the air of sophistication she wore like an invisible cloak. Or the cool, crisp elegance of her movements and manner. Town polish, his mother would call it, and Matt thought that was part of it. Maybe a big part of it.

He and Jax had attended the same high school—in a town the size of Bayou Beltane there wasn't but one—but, pretty as she had been even then, he couldn't recall having given her more than a passing glance.

He'd danced at her wedding the year after high school, but everybody who was anybody in St. Tammany Parish had been invited to celebrate what was generally described as the social event of the year. He'd been dating one of the bridesmaids back then, a cute little redhead named Cissy, so he hadn't been pining over the unattainable bride, as beautiful as she had been in her wedding satin and lace. Truth be told, he'd barely spared her a glance after the ceremonies were over and the dancing began; Cissy had been more than enough to occupy the full attention of a healthy twenty-year-old male.

He'd been away at college and embroiled in the soap

opera his own life had become when he'd heard about Jax's divorce from Greg Martin.

Over the years since college, he'd followed her career just like everyone else in Bayou Beltane as she'd made a name for herself as a world-class equestrian, heaping even more fame on Delacroix Farms in the process. And, of course, like nearly everybody else in the parish, he'd been glued to his TV set during the '96 Olympics when she rode to a gold medal in individual dressage and helped her team to win the silver in the three-day event.

When rumors began circulating through the horse world about her proposed retirement from active competition, he'd half expected to hear that she'd married some duke or earl and settled down someplace in Europe, where she'd spent most of the last ten years. But she'd come home to Bayou Beltane instead, wrapped in that intriguing air of mystery and sophistication.

And *now* he was interested.

And he didn't want to be.

His wife had been dead less than a year.

"WHOA, THERE, LEAR. Settle down, fella." Jax's voice was soft and soothing as she crooned to the excited horse. Her slender hands were strong and steady on his leather lead. "Your lady love isn't quite ready for you yet, big boy." She yanked sharply, pulling the chain beneath his chin tight enough to get his attention but not so tight as to inflict an injury of any kind. "So just settle down."

The horse continued to prance at her side, snorting and calling to the mare, pawing at the ground in his eagerness, kicking out with both back feet now and again in frenzied excitement. King Lear was a well-behaved gentleman in most circumstances, but at the moment it was all Jax could do to keep him under control. She thanked providence for the years of riding and the weight-lifting regime that kept her muscles honed, and yanked on the shank lead again, reminding the stallion who was boss.

"Steady, boy. Steady now," she crooned, and cut her eyes at the three men gathered around the mare in the shade of the open, three-sided breeding shed, trying to hobble her without getting the stuffing kicked out of them or losing a hunk of flesh in the process. If they survived Red Magnolia's flashing hooves and snapping teeth, they certainly wouldn't survive the tongue-lashing Jax intended to dish out as soon as her attention wasn't occupied with controlling a lovesick stallion.

The mare was supposed to have been hobbled *before* her eager suitor was presented to her. The hobbling wasn't to force her to accept him if she wasn't ready to be mounted, but to keep her from hurting him—or herself—when she was. Both horses were expensive, pampered athletes, weighing more than a thousand pounds apiece, and the breeding process could, and often did, get violent. Left to do it on their own, one or the other of the animals would likely come away from the experience with more than a few scars—and even one scar on either satiny hide was one too many.

Just then Red Magnolia struck out, quick as lightning, sinking her big, square teeth into the shoulder of one of her handlers. The man shouted in pain and surprise and jerked away, falling back onto the seat of his jeans and the palms of his hands. Red Magnolia laid her ears back flat and went after him, ripping her lead out of the hands of the man who was supposed to be holding her. The man on the ground scrambled backward like a crab, evading the furious mare by rolling under the lowest rung of the wooden fence. Red Magnolia squealed in victory at routing her enemy, the piercing sound mingled with frustration at having allowed him to escape her. She wheeled around and charged the other two handlers.

One of them got a grip on her lead, but with only one hand. She jerked him around like a puppet on a string. The other employee, a young stable hand who'd had hopes of a future at Delacroix Farms, just stood there, his back against the far wall of the shed, looking terrified.

King Lear reacted to all the ruckus by rolling his eyes back in his head and trying to rear. Jax hauled down on his lead with both hands, pulling the chain under his chin tight, and skimmed her gaze over the line of faces bordering the paddock fence.

Where in the hell was Bear?

She was strong, but she only weighed a hundred and twenty pounds—no match for fourteen hundred pounds of sex-crazed stallion. Lear was about to pull her arms out of their sockets. If the situation didn't change for the better in the next two seconds, all hell was going to break loose.

Out of the corner of her eye, she saw someone vault over the fence, and for a second thought it was the handler who'd been so ignominiously driven from the paddock a moment ago. But the man was too big and too blond to be who she thought he was. He rushed straight at the mare's head, grabbing her halter in both hands and dragging her nose down to the level of his chest, using his full weight to keep her there. The position made it impossible for Red Magnolia to rear and difficult for her to bite, but she could still use her back feet to inflict damage on anyone unwary enough to come too close. Everyone else backed off, out of harm's way, until the mare was under control.

She made a few more token protests, trying to buck and kicking out with her back feet, but in a moment her tantrum was over. She snuffled into Matt Taggart's flannel-covered chest, blowing hard through her nostrils, her ears cocked attentively as she listened to the soothing flow of words he was pouring into them. With a nod, he silently instructed the handlers to fasten the hobbles on her legs. Docile as a kitten now, her attention focused on the man at her head, the mare stood quietly while the two men quickly restricted her ability to kick, then backed slowly away.

As soon as Red Magnolia calmed, Lear calmed, too. Jax let up on the lead, reducing the pressure on his tender nose, reaching up to rub his neck in a soothing motion. The stallion tossed his head, throwing her hand off, and called to the mare, his upper lip curled back to better take in her scent. The mare whinnied in answer, the sound an unmistakable invitation.

It was time to get the show on the road.

Matt took a step back, letting go of the halter and holding the mare by her lead, as Jax brought the prancing stallion forward. She led him toward the mare at an angle, toward her head, letting him approach Red Magnolia as he would in the wild. The mare turned her head and touched her nose to the stallion's. The two animals blew softly, exchanging breath, engaging in the "conversational" first step of equine courtship. The stallion snorted in sexual excitement and struck out, pawing the ground. The mare nickered in return, ears forward, unalarmed by his display of machismo.

Jax took her first easy breath since she'd entered the paddock and realized that the horse hadn't been properly prepared to be bred. She smiled, aiming a grateful look at the man whose quick action had saved the day.

He smiled back, a corner of his mouth quirking up in a sexy little grin. The look in his eyes was warm, appreciative and very male, making her feel suddenly very female.

Her own smile widened for a moment in automatic response to the approval in his eyes, before she remembered. Matt Taggart was married, wasn't he? So why was he looking at another woman as if he'd like to drag her into the nearest empty stall? And why did Jax suddenly feel as if she might not object all that much if he did?

She looked away quickly, confused and annoyed, stumbling slightly as she backed the stallion away to reposition him for his second approach. Red Magnolia sidestepped nervously.

"Easy there, sweetheart," Matt murmured, his voice low and husky, his lazy Louisiana drawl as noticeable as the power in his wide shoulders.

Jax ignored him, unsure if he was speaking to her or Red Magnolia, and turned her attention back to the horse on the end of her lead. Lear made his second approach with more delicacy than he had his first, his long neck stretched out, making snuffling noises as he tickled the mare's shoulder with his velvety nose. She returned the brief caress, signaling her interest, letting him know she wouldn't mind if he came a little closer. The stallion squealed and nipped her lightly, a little love bite of equine affection. She nickered in return. The stallion sidled closer.

He had a full erection now, and was quivering with eagerness, but the mare had not yet signaled her full readiness to be mounted. This part of the courtship ritual could take several minutes more as the mare decided whether to accept or reject her suitor. The process could be hurried along, of course. Red Magnolia was hobbled and, theoretically, couldn't do any damage if she objected to the pace at which the breeding was accomplished. But many a mare had been known to blast that theory to hell and back if she was pushed too far, too fast, and Red Magnolia had already demonstrated her willingness to make a fuss if things weren't exactly to her liking. Besides, whatever any other breeder might do, Jax just couldn't bring herself to force any mare to accept a stallion against her will. If she refused to stand for breeding, there was usually a reason. They could always try again later when she was more receptive.

The spectators at the fence were silent now, the air heavy with anticipation as they all waited for Red Magnolia to make up her mind. Jax stood by the quivering stallion, her hands on the lead, her lashes lowered in unaccustomed shyness, fighting the urge to look up and meet Matt Taggart's gaze again. She could see him out of the corner of her eye, standing as still and steady as a rock, and knew he was looking at her. She could feel the touch of his gaze with every nerve in her body. If she looked up, she'd be staring straight into his heated blue eyes.

What she should do, she knew, was to nip his presumption in the bud. She should lift her lashes, stare directly into his eyes and give him one of her patented Is-that-all-you-have-to-offer-I-couldn't-be-more-bored looks. She had withered the amorous intentions of more than one man that way. There had been that Italian Grand Prix rider she'd met in Paris who'd wisely decided she probably wasn't worth the trouble after being subjected to it. Not to mention the Austrian count at the embassy who had, thankfully, never managed to work up the courage to proposition her after she'd sent him just one coolly amused glance.

She'd fended off some of the most determined, not to mention degenerate, pleasure seekers in Europe; it should be a piece of cake handling one good ol' Louisiana country boy with a bit of extracurricular slap-and-tickle on his mind.

She had half lifted her head, intending to put Matt squarely in his place, when Red Magnolia whinnied and snaked her head around, lightly nipping her suitor on the neck. Lear snorted and tossed his head in response, nearly yanking the lead out of Jax's hands. He'd repositioned himself without her noticing, nudging the mare's flank with his nose, inching around to her hindquarters.

Jax tightened her grip on the lead, cursing under her breath, and forced the stallion back a few steps. She knew better, dammit, than to let her attention wander during the breeding procedure! Inattention on the part of the handlers was the main cause of injury to both horse and human.

But no harm had been done this time. Red Magnolia was leaning toward the stallion in unmistakable invitation, her tail raised and held to one side, her hind legs spread in the breeding stance. The muscles under her sleek red hide were quivering just as much as the stallion's.

Jax led him forward for the final approach, laying the lead line over the mare's rump as a signal that he could now proceed as nature intended, and stepped back to the very end of the lead, letting him mount. She looked up and away, averting her gaze from the wildly copulating horses in an instinctive effort to give them some privacy. Her gaze met Matt's over the mare's shoulders, just as King Lear surged forward and gently clamped his teeth on the mare's neck, holding her still for his attentions.

In a flash, the world narrowed down to only two. The squealing, thrusting horses disappeared. The line of stable hands and trainers standing at the paddock fence melted away. The cool February morning turned as hot and steamy as a July day, making the air too thick to breathe.

Jax tried to, anyway, dragging in a double lungful of air through suddenly dry lips. Her heart began to beat heavily in her chest, thudding against the fragile wall of her rib cage, further impeding her breathing. She could actually feel each labored breath sloughing in and out of her body. She could feel the blood pounding through her veins, too, every pulse point throbbing to some wild beat. She could hear it rushing past her eardrums, drowning out everything but the silent message in his deep blue eyes.

I want you.

Jax's hands tightened on King Lear's leather lead as she tried to look away and found she couldn't.

What was the matter with her?

This was Matt Taggart. She'd known him in a casual

way all of her life. They'd gone through school together. He'd played on the same football team as her twin brother, Beau. She'd seen Matt around town nearly every time she'd come home for a visit, often with his wife and those two cute kids of his in tow. And never in all those years had he ever looked her way. Nor she his, for that matter.

Since she'd moved back to Bayou Beltane to raise and train dressage and event horses, she'd consulted with him a handful of times about the condition of one or the other of her animals, but that had been the extent of their interaction. And never once had there ever been a hint, not a *hint*, of what was in his eyes at this moment.

So why now?

He was a married man, for God's sake!

Why was he looking at her the way Lear had looked at Red Magnolia, as if there was only one thing on his testosterone-soaked mind? And why was she looking back as if she were considering him the same way Red Magnolia had considered the stallion before she accepted him?

The horses finished before she could find the answer. Lear grunted and backed off of the mare. His front hooves struck the dirt of the paddock with a thud that shook the ground under Jax's boots. Red Magnolia curved her neck and looked around as if to see what all the commotion had been about.

The frenzy was over.

The spell was broken.

Almost.

The heat in Matt Taggart's eyes hadn't cooled one iota.

Jax tore her gaze from his with an effort, summoning a stable hand with the lift of an eyebrow. "Take Lear back to his paddock," she ordered, not bothering to add any instructions for his care. Anyone who worked at Delacroix Farms knew how to care for a champion stud, or they didn't work there for very long. "And you—" she zeroed in on the young stable hand who'd plastered himself against the wall of the shed to avoid Red Magnolia's fury "—take over for the doc...." She met Matt's eyes again, swallowed convulsively and looked away. "Take Maggie back to her stall," she said, giving the boy a chance to redeem himself. "I'll be along later to check on her."

She turned away without waiting to see if he had obeyed her instructions.

And without making eye contact with Matt again.

She felt a hand on her arm, stopping her before she'd taken two steps. She turned her head and looked up into Matt Taggart's face.

Seen close up, he was even more compelling than she had realized. His face was lean and narrow, the jaw and brow bones strong and pronounced, softened only slightly by the sun-streaked blond hair falling over his forehead and waving untidily over the tops of his ears. He had a thin, jagged scar—the kind you got from getting kicked by a horse—running from the bottom right corner of his mouth to just under his chin. The lips above it were full but finely molded, sensuous but not weak. His nose was a bold slash of bone, suiting the rest of his warrior poet's face. And his eyes... His eyes were a clear, piercing blue. Not cool, as blue eyes usually were, but hot as lasers. They bored into hers, full of speculation...anticipation...questions.

Jax shook her head slightly, refusing to answer them.

"Have dinner with me," he said, ignoring her silent protest. His voice was low and inviting, the Louisiana drawl as sweet and tempting as honey poured over hot buttermilk biscuits.

Jax reacted to it the same way Red Magnolia had and for just one breathless second let herself be tempted.

Then she stiffened and took a quick breath, drawing herself up to her full five feet, seven inches, tilting her head back to look down her nose at him. "You'll have to find someone else to do your tomcatting with, Mr. Taggart,'' she said, her soft cultured voice and cool gray eyes dripping ice. "I'm not the least bit interested in helping you cheat on your wife.''

CHAPTER TWO

"HEY, SIS." Charly Delacroix carefully turned her head against the arm of her sister's plush, tufted velvet Victorian sofa as Jax slammed through the front door of the small cabin they were currently sharing. She'd learned that moving too precipitously sent stabbing pains through her head. That's what came of getting yourself shot; it tended to limit your mobility for a while. "What's the matter?"

"Nothing."

"Yeah, right." Charly hit the power button on the remote control, tossed it on top of the untidy pile of magazines, empty soda cans and candy wrappers already cluttering up the polished surface of her sister's genuine Louis XVI coffee table, and slowly shifted to a sitting position, using her good arm to push herself upright.

Jax in a snit was bound to be more interesting than "Regis and Kathie Lee" or reruns of "Melrose Place." And Charly had had enough of lying on the sofa and feeling sorry for herself, anyway. Recuperating was boring the hell out of her. "Something's the matter. I can tell. I'm a trained investigator."

Jax eyed her sister for a minute, considering. At twenty-five, with seven years difference between them, Charly was the youngest in the family. She'd been twelve when Jax got married, barely fifteen when she fled to Europe to try to get her life back together, so they didn't really know each other all that well as adults. But they *were* sisters. And Charly had stayed in St. Tammany Parish while

Jax had been off gallivanting all over the world with her horses in tow. Not to mention the fact that she was a police officer. Charly would know things.

"How long has Matt Taggart been cheating on his wife?"

Charly sat up a little straighter. "Excuse me?"

"Matt Taggart. The vet," Jax added when Charly continued to stare at her as if she didn't have the faintest idea who or what Jax was talking about.

"I know who Matt is. I've known him all my life, same as you." Charly ran a careful hand through her short cap of shiny black hair, mindful of the small, neat row of stitches behind her right ear. She cut a quick look at her sister out of eyes that were almost the same cool gray color as Jax's. "What makes you think he's cheating on his wife?"

"He came on to me."

"Matt did? When?"

"Just now. We were out in the breeding paddock with O'Brian's Red Maggie and King Lear, and there was a little dustup with the horses." She waved one hand dismissively. "It doesn't matter," she said, in case Charly thought to ask what kind of dustup. "Matt jumped into the middle of it and kept it from getting out of hand, and then, when it was over, he..." She waved her hand again, less dismissively this time, her long, slender fingers fluttering helplessly as she searched for the words to describe what he had done, and the way it had made her feel. "He asked me out to dinner," she said, although that wasn't the half of it.

"Matt asked you out to dinner?"

Jax frowned at her sister. "That's what I said, isn't it?" she demanded, wondering if Charly's head injury made her slow to grasp things, or if she had always been that way and Jax hadn't noticed it until now.

"Are you going to go?" Charly asked.

"No! Of course not!" But, oh, something in her wanted to. She ruthlessly pushed the ignoble feeling aside. She would never knowingly get involved with a married man; it was immoral to even think of inflicting such pain on another woman. "I don't date married men."

Charly began to chuckle.

Jax's frown turned into a glare. "What's so funny?"

"Oh, honey, Matt isn't cheating on his wife."

"But he—"

"His wife's dead."

It was Jax's turn to look as if she didn't know what was going on. "Dead?"

Charly nodded and pressed her fingers over her mouth to still the bubbles of laughter that threatened to erupt. It wasn't Livvy Taggart's death that was funny, of course—that had been deeply tragic for everyone involved—but the look on Jax's face was priceless.

"Dead?" she said again, trying to take it in. "When? How?"

Charly sobered. "About a year ago now. But she was sick for a long time before it happened. Ovarian cancer was what I heard."

"Oh, my God," Jax said, and put her hand over her eyes as if stricken by the news.

"I'm sorry, Jax. Did you know Livvy?"

Jax shook her head. "It isn't that. I never even met her." She peeked out at her sister from between her fingers. "It's... Oh, God," she said again, and dropped her hand. "I told him he'd have to find someone else to do his tomcatting with because I wasn't interested in helping him cheat on his wife."

Charly's laughter rang out this time, rich and unrestrained. She had to press her hands to the sides of her head to keep it from exploding, but it was worth it. "You didn't!" she squealed, suddenly a teenager again, talking about boys with one of her sisters. "You did! Oh, my God! What did he say?"

"Nothing. I walked away before he had a chance to say a word."

"What are you going to do now?"

"Avoid him for the rest of my life?" Jax suggested.

Charly cocked a knowing eyebrow at her. "By running off to Europe again?"

"It's a thought," Jax said, wondering just how much Charly knew about why she had run off to Europe in the first place.

The Delacroix as a whole weren't a particularly chatty family. Their secrets and scandals tended to be hidden from anyone not directly involved in them. Charly had been little more than a kid when Jax's tangled personal affairs had sent her running for a place to hide, so it was doubtful she knew the whole truth about what had happened. But she was shrewd, and what she didn't know, she could probably guess. After all, she wasn't a kid anymore.

"I don't think running would solve anything this time," Jax said. It certainly hadn't before. "So I guess I'll just have to bite the bullet and apologize for jumping to insulting conclusions."

Charly pushed back the knitted afghan that covered her legs and made a motion as if to get up off of the sofa. "This I gotta see."

Jax waved her down. "You get back under that blanket and hush up before Odelle hears us and comes down here to skin me alive for getting you riled up. You're supposed to be resting quietly. 'Head injuries aren't anything to be messing with, Missy,'" she said, imitating Odelle's scolding drawl.

Both women glanced out the front window toward the big house, neither of them doubting for a minute that Odelle Raison was capable of doing exactly what Jax had accused her of. The housekeeper had ears like a cat, and she'd been looking after all of them since Jax and her twin brother Beau were babies. To the youngest generation of Delacroix, Odelle Raison appeared almost omnipotent.

"It's almost time for your lunch," Jax warned. She leaned down and drew the afghan back up over her sister. "Odelle will be bringing it down from the big house soon, and if she even *thinks* you've been breaking any of her rules, she'll have you out of here and tucked up in your old bedroom so fast it'll make your head spin for sure."

Charly wrinkled her nose at the mention of lunch. "Chicken soup," she said, but she settled back down on the sofa without further protest.

There was nothing Odelle would like better than to have Charly up at the big house where she could fuss to her heart's content. Which was why Charly had chosen to take Jax up on the offer of her sofa while she recuperated. She hated to have people fussing over her; it made her cranky.

"I'm sick to death of chicken soup," she groused. "If I have to eat one more spoonful, I'm going to sprout feathers and start clucking. I want a hamburger from the Dairy Queen. With a large order of fries. And a chocolate shake. Double thick. Or a bowl of Rick's jambalaya," she said, referring to one of the specialties of a favorite Bayou Beltane restaurant, "with lots of big, spicy hunks of andouille in it."

"I'll see what I can do about that next time I'm in town," Jax promised. "In the meantime..." She reached out and plucked the telltale pile of candy wrappers off of the coffee table. "I'll just get rid of these before Odelle sees them."

She dumped the candy wrappers in the trash can under the sink, pulling a wet coffee filter full of used coffee grounds over them to further obscure the evidence of her sister's abysmal eating habits, then brushed her hands together and headed for the front door.

"Hey, Jax?"

Jax turned with her hand on the doorknob and glanced back at her sister.

Charly gave her an impish smile. "You gonna go out with him if he asks again?"

"HEY, JAX, WAIT UP!"

Jax slowed, then stopped, turning her head to smile at her brother, Beau. Of all the people she'd missed while she'd been away, she'd missed her twin the most. They'd not only shared their mother's womb for the first nine months of their lives, they shared the same coloring, the same cheekbones, the same fiercely competitive spirit and the same deep love and appreciation for the Thoroughbreds that populated the barns and pastures of Delacroix Farms.

There was nothing she wouldn't do for her brother. And if he wanted her for something, then her apology to Matt Taggart could wait.

"Did you need me for something, Beau?"

"Good ol' Travis sent us another high roller from Texas. This one's looking for a nice little Thoroughbred for his wife for her birthday," Beau said gleefully, all but rubbing his hands together at the prospect.

"And you need me because...?" she asked as she fell into step beside him.

"He's narrowed his choice down to two, but he wants to see a woman ride them before he makes a decision."

"Last time I looked, over half your hot walkers and exercise boys were girls."

"But none of them are Olympic medal winners," Beau reminded her.

"Oh, I see." Her left eyebrow rose. "You want window dressing."

"I want the best dressage rider in the world to show off my horses' paces."

"Is this Texan's wife going to use the horse for dressage?"

"Nope."

Jax pulled up short beside her brother. "Well, then, why is he wasting his money on a trained dressage horse? A good solid pleasure horse sounds more like what he needs."

"Nope," Beau said again. "His sweet Sue Ellen has her li'l heart set on one a them thar dress-age horses, jus' like in the Olympics," he said in a thick West Texas drawl. "'Sides—" he looped his arm over his sister's shoulders to propel her along beside him "—it's his money to waste, and he's apparently got plenty of it. Travis wouldn't send us a piker."

"If I'm going to show off a dressage horse for this customer of yours, why are we heading for the track instead of the training ring?"

"Bear's got dibs on the ring this afternoon."

"Bear? What for?"

"He promised to give Matt Taggart's little girl a riding lesson."

"Oh." Jax tried to ignore the little spurt of guilt—and guilty excitement—that name brought her. She should be down at the barn right now, apologizing to the poor man for the terrible thing she'd said. But if his daughter was having a riding lesson, it could wait; he'd be hanging around Delacroix Farms for a little while longer. Jax looped her arm companionably around her brother's trim waist. "Let's go see this rich Texan of yours."

Unlike their sister Shelby's fiancé, Travis Hardin, who looked like every woman's fantasy of the stereotypical Texas cowboy come to life, Beau's prospective customer fulfilled another Texas stereotype entirely. Big, brash and loud, his hand-tooled cowboy boots shotgunned on the outside of his trousers, he was the epitome of the nouveau riche pseudo-cowboy with more money than taste. He had an open, honest face, a straightforward manner and firm handshake.

Jax liked him immediately.

"Well, this surely is a pleasure, Ms Delacroix," he said, pumping her arm up and down as if it were a well handle. "It surely is. Why, my sweet Sue Ellen is going to be tickled to death, jus' purely tickled to death, when I tell her that her new horse was once rode by the fabulous Jax Delacroix, winner of two Olympic medals for the good ol' U.S. of A."

"Why, thank you, Mr. Osgood," Jax said, surreptitiously flexing her fingers when he released her hand. "I'm flattered."

"Ain't no flattery about it. It's the dang pure truth, is what it is. And the name's Ollie. Never did care for that Mr. Osgood stuff."

"Ollie, then." Jax nodded her head graciously and lifted one hand to gesture toward the two horses that stood saddled and waiting to be led onto the track. "Do you have a preference as to which one I ride first?"

"Nary a one, Ms Delacroix." He waved his meaty hand at the horses. "Ladies' choice."

Jax checked the tack of the nearest horse, a solid chestnut gelding with a freckled stripe down the center of his nose, making sure everything was secure and adjusted to her liking. Sensing Beau behind her, she lifted her left foot, silently requesting a leg-up instead of using the stirrup to mount. Swinging her right leg over the horse's back, she settled into the saddle as gently as a feather, gathered up the reins and signaled for one of the nearby stable hands to open the gate to the track.

After warming up both herself and the gelding with a

slow, easy lope around the quarter-mile track, she pulled him up in a straight stop in front of Beau and the cowboy from Texas, tipping her head to them in acknowledgment before she put the horse through his paces.

What followed was an equestrian ballet. Jax started the horse off with simple school figures, turning him right and then left in a figure eight, first at a walk, then at a trot, then at a slow canter, at both collected and extended gaits. She shortened and lengthened the horse's stride as necessary, showing off the animal's ability to make smooth transitions from gait to gait and his willingness to turn in either direction.

From there, the horse and rider progressed to a counter-canter and flying changes, slightly trickier work that demanded a horse to change his leading fore and hind legs in midstride.

They finished off with some lateral work, the high, mincing sideways movements that most people pictured when they thought of dressage. The gelding executed each move beautifully, giving Jax everything she asked for and more, performing with the grace and style of a well-seasoned, well-trained athlete. Jax stroked his neck to let him know she appreciated his effort and dismounted, handing the reins to a stable hand as she turned to the other horse.

The second animal was a showy blood bay mare with a black mane and tail and no white on her at all. She tossed her head as Jax mounted, straining at the bit and immediately trying to turn the easy warm-up canter into a full-out gallop. Jax held her back for a moment, just to remind her who was boss, then let her have her head. She was still dancing, her gait high and mincing, as Jax calmly gathered her in, using the pressure of her legs against the mare's sides and the position of her hands on the reins to communicate her will to the animal.

They went through the same routine, step by exacting

step. Only another experienced rider would have noticed or appreciated the combination of strength, skill and concentration involved in making the second routine look as flawlessly effortless as the first. Jax ended with a little flourish designed to take advantage of the mare's high spirits and bouncing step, turning her in a brief series of showy spins and quick steps that would have done credit to a cutting horse.

"Well, Ollie," she said as she slid off of the mare and handed the reins to a waiting stable hand, "what do you think?"

"That was purely beautiful, Ms Delacroix," he said admiringly. "You ride like you was part of the horse. It was jus' purely beautiful."

Jax acknowledged his praise with a slight nod and a pleased smile. "Which one do you think your wife might like? Buster Brown, here—" she smoothed her hand over the gelding's muscular neck "—is the more consistent performer and his temperament is probably more suited to a beginning rider. He knows what he's doing and has a lot of patience. Lady Macbeth is a bit harder to handle, I'll grant you, but she really sparkles in the ring. And you've always got the option of breeding her later when she's out of active competition." Jax flashed him a smile. "We might be able to arrange a discount on King Lear's stud fee for her, if you're interested."

Ollie Osgood was definitely interested. And undecided. He lifted his pearl gray Stetson by the brim with one hand and scratched the top of his head with the other, all the while looking back and forth between the two horses. "Well, hell—beggin' your pardon, ma'am." He slapped the hat back on his head. "I'll jus' take 'em both."

Beau shot his sister a grin, giving her a thumbs-up sign behind Ollie's back.

MATT TAGGART HAD NEVER been so insulted in his life. Tomcatting! Cheating on his wife! Just who the hell did she think she was, making those rash assumptions about him and his life? She'd cast aspersions on his honor, that's what she'd done, and no Southern male worth his salt took that kind of thing lying down! He was tempted to hightail it after snotty little Ms Jax Delacroix and give her a piece of his mind, except...

Except she'd nailed it smack dab on the head. Cheating is exactly what it felt like he'd been doing back there in the breeding paddock.

He hadn't been with another woman since Livvy's death. He hadn't been with Livvy, in the biblical sense, for nearly six months before she died. She'd been too sick. Too frail.

Strangely enough, he hadn't really missed the sex. There were too many other things going on in his life to worry about it—things that made sex seem unimportant. His children needed comforting and reassurance. His wife, while she was alive, needed his support and care. So he'd relegated his sex drive to the back burner and forgotten about it. It had never been very important between him and Livvy, anyway, not after the first heady flush of passion in the beginning of their relationship. And that, he was now convinced, had been mostly youth and rampaging hormones.

His hormones hadn't been on a rampage in a good long while, since well before that awful day when Livvy was diagnosed with ovarian cancer.

All during her long illness, while he'd been weighed down with fear and worry over her condition and the stress of trying to keep everything as normal as possible for Jeff and Amy, the good ladies of Bayou Beltane had kept him and his family supplied with homemade gumbos, tuna-noodle casseroles and prize-winning cakes and pies. Along with the steady stream of food had come offers to take the kids for the weekend, or do the grocery shopping, or see that the house was cleaned. After the funeral, those welcome gestures of neighborly aid and comfort occasionally expanded to include unspoken—and sometimes even verbal—offers of more. But not one had been enough to rouse his sleeping sex drive.

He'd known the women making them nearly his whole life. They were nice women, for the most part. Some of them were even sexy. But they hadn't interested him that way before, and they didn't now. Not even Cissy Mickleson—divorced for the second time and more than willing to end his long sexual fast—had succeeded in stirring his interest.

But Jax Delacroix had.

He'd taken one look at her—at her smooth, creamy skin and her dark, lustrous hair; at all that life and vitality, that beauty and promise; at that intriguing sophistication and elegance that was so much a part of her—and his sleeping libido had perked right up and taken notice. While he'd been real glad to know he wasn't dead from the waist down, after all, that interest wasn't something he planned to do anything about. At least, not in the foreseeable future.

And then he'd found himself standing across from her in the shade of the breeding shed, their gazes locked on each other, with two frenzied horses screaming and plunging in the throes of physical ecstasy between them and sex permeating the air like perfume. And he'd suddenly wanted Jax—right then! right there!—more than he'd ever wanted any woman before. He'd wanted to drag her down in the dust of the paddock and do to her what King Lear was doing to Red Magnolia. He'd wanted it that primitive, that raw.

Thank God he'd somehow managed to refrain from stating his desire so directly.

"Have dinner with me," he'd said, and her eyes had turned hot at his request...his *demand*.

For just a moment—an endless, thrilling, terrifying moment—it almost looked as if she might say yes. Then her eyes had turned ice cold and she'd shot him down with a few scathing words.

Because she thought he was married.

He wondered what her answer would have been if she'd known he wasn't, and then hastily pushed the idea aside. Married or not, he wasn't ready for another relationship. Not with her. Not with any—

"Ah...Matt?"

He nearly jumped out of his skin, startling the heavily pregnant mare that had been half drowsing under his careful examination. She shied away from him, bumping into the side of her stall.

"Easy there, now, sweetheart," he soothed, using the excuse of needing to calm the mare to keep from looking at the woman who'd suddenly appeared at the stall door as if he'd conjured her out of thin air. "Easy, Peg."

It took a moment or two for the mare to settle down again and begin nibbling at the flake of grass hay in the wall-mounted hayrack in front of her. When she did, Matt was forced to look up and face the focus of his reawakened desires.

She stood at the entrance of the stall, her body obscured from the waist down by the heavy wooden door, her hands folded together and resting on its top. She wore a tailored white shirt, open at the throat, the cuffs neatly turned back on her slender arms. Her hands and wrists were bare of jewelry except for the small, utilitarian watch on her left wrist. Small, shiny gemstones—opals, he thought—glimmered on her delicate earlobes, reflecting the light from the overhead fixture. Her dark hair was pulled back in some kind of intricate braid, but little wisps and tendrils had worked themselves free to drift over her forehead and in front of her ears. Her lashes were lowered, shielding her eyes. Her cheeks were flushed.

"How…" Matt had to stop and clear his throat. He felt like a gawky, hormone-driven sixteen-year-old trying to talk to the high school prom queen. "How far along is she?"

"Who?" Jax murmured, without looking at him.

"Peg."

"Oh." Jax lifted her lashes, her eyes flickering toward his. Their gazes met, locked for a second, then skittered apart. "Three hundred and thirty-eight days."

Matt nodded, as if he'd actually taken in her words. "When did the foal drop?"

"Ah…five…no, six. Six days ago," Jax answered, and then, before he could ask another question, she plunged ahead with what she had come out to the foaling barn to say. "About what happened in the breeding paddock, I—" She could feel the blood heating her cheeks and knew her face had turned a rosy pink. "I just wanted to say I'm sor—"

"Forget it," he interrupted, cutting her off before she could make the apology and embarrass them both. But it was too late. His cheeks were nearly as red as hers, the fire creating a ruddy glow under his tan. "There's nothing for you to be sorry for."

"Yes, there is," Jax insisted. "In the first place, I didn't even thank you for what you did. One of the horses or handlers could have been badly hurt if you hadn't taken such quick action."

"Somebody else would have jumped in if I hadn't."

"But somebody else didn't. You did. And then I… And then you issued a perfectly civil invitation and I—"

"Civil?" He'd come across as *civil?* He'd felt like a crazed beast. A sex-crazed beast, intent on claiming his mate. Apparently that hadn't been obvious in his tersely worded dinner invitation. Thank God.

"Yes, and I...well..." Her clasped hands tightened atop the stall door. "I'm sorry about your wife, Matt," she said simply, knowing no other way to say it. "I didn't know."

"There's no reason you should have known. You weren't even in the country when it happened."

"Well, yes, but...I'm sorry, anyway. I hope you'll accept my apology."

"Apology accepted," he said, wondering if he should make one of his own. Was a man required to apologize for what he'd been thinking? No, better not. It was probably wiser to keep his thoughts to himself in this case. "Let's just forget the whole incident ever happened, okay?" *In about a million years!* "It's over and done with."

"Okay," Jax agreed, wondering if that meant he wasn't going to ask her out again. Wondering, too, what she'd say if he did. As attractive as he was, Matt wasn't really her type—he had kids, for one thing. But, still, she would have liked the option of making up her own mind about whether or not she would go out with him. "It's forgotten."

Matt deliberately turned his attention back to the mare. "How's her temperature been?" he asked.

"Steady," Jax said, watching him as he resumed his examination. "It hasn't varied more than .3 degrees in weeks."

Matt nodded and moved to the horse's right flank, quietly, so as not to alarm her again. He laid his left forearm atop her rump, snugging his upper body against hers to minimize the danger of being kicked in the event she had any objections to what he was doing. His left hand lay on her back, forward of the croup. There was a curved, horseshoe-shaped scar starting just above his wrist and extending upward, across his hand—another memento of the years he'd spent working around horses—but no wedding ring on his finger.

Jax wondered if that was significant. Had he taken it off when his wife died? Had he never worn one? Or, like many people who worked around livestock, had he merely left it off while he was working? She was squinting a bit, trying to see if there was a paler mark on his finger to indicate which it might be, wondering with a part of her mind why she even cared, when the movement of his other hand caught her attention.

He held his right hand flat against Peg's distended belly, fingers splayed, palm slightly cupped, making small, soothing circles. He slowly maneuvered it down and under her in the direction of her udder, patiently sliding it back up her side each time she showed the least sign of becoming nervous or restive, showing her she had nothing to fear from his touch. The steady, rhythmic motion had a lulling, hypnotic quality—one that affected Jax as well as the mare.

She felt herself swaying forward, leaning toward him the way the mare leaned into his touch. When he finally maneuvered his hand under Peg's belly, gently scratching the itchy place between the two halves of her udder, the horse gave an audible sigh and closed her eyes. Jax sucked in her breath to keep from doing the same thing.

He had good hands, strong and capable, with long, blunt-tipped fingers and a fine sprinkling of golden hairs across the backs of them. And they moved so gently over the mare, so surely and knowingly. Jax had no trouble at all imagining them moving over a woman like that. Moving over her.

Gently.

Surely.

Knowingly.

"Isn't any milk, yet."

Jax blinked, yanked out of her fantasy by the realization

that he was talking to her. "Ah…I'm sorry," she said, struggling to make sense of words she'd only half heard. Something about milk…? "I didn't quite catch what you said."

"As far along as she is, I would've expected some show of milk by now," Matt said. "How long since she bagged up?"

Oh…*milk!* He was asking about the character of Peg's milk secretions.

All business now, every inch the competent, caring professional, he stood there with one hand still resting on the mare's broad back, waiting for her answer.

Good, Jax told herself. That was exactly the way she wanted it to be between them. Professional.

"Her bag started swelling a couple of weeks ago," she told him, resolutely pushing the fantasy aside to concentrate on the business at hand. "I can get her chart if you need the exact date, but it's nothing to worry about. Peg usually bags up weeks before she delivers and doesn't start to show any milk at all until a few days before the big event. It's normal for her. It's also normal for her to carry past the average three hundred and forty days."

"How far past?"

Jax didn't need a chart to give him that information; she carried the delivery stats of this particular mare in her head. She'd been riding Peg O' My Heart when she won her first international Grand Prix championship. "She's never foaled earlier than three hundred and forty-six days, and last time she delivered on day three hundred and fifty-six. We have a pool going if you'd like to place a bet."

"No, thanks." He flashed her a wry glance, knowing that, in this part of Louisiana, what he was about to say amounted to sacrilege. "I never bet on the horses."

"Me, neither," Jax confessed. "It's a sucker's game."

Matt laughed at that, but softly, not wanting to startle

the mare. "She's in perfect health." He smoothed his hand down her neck. "There's nothing we need to do but watch and wait until she's ready," he added, giving the mare a final pat before he stepped away from her.

Anticipating his next move, Jax unlatched the door and backed up, holding it open for him. "I kind of hate to tell you this, since you did such a thorough job examining her and all," she said, closing the door to the stall behind him as he stepped into the center aisle of the barn. "But Peg isn't why I asked you to stop by today."

"She isn't?"

"You said yourself she's in perfect health."

"Why didn't you say something sooner?"

"Well, you'd already started by the time I got here and I was, um, preoccupied at first with, ah…" *Professional,* she reminded herself, feeling the beginnings of another blush. *Let's keep this professional.* "Other things and—"

"Never mind," he said quickly, not wanting to go into that again. The warm color staining her creamy cheeks made him want to reach out and touch her. All over. He leaned down and picked up the shiny red metal toolbox he used as a medical bag from where he had left it just outside Peg's stall. "Which mares am I *supposed* to be looking at?"

"This way," Jax said, leading him down the broom-swept center aisle of the barn to the proper stalls.

He administered the first of a series of prefoaling vaccines to a first-time mother-to-be with Queen of Hearts etched on the brass plaque attached to her stall door. She was high-strung and skittish, objecting to every little thing and making the process more involved than it had to be. Jax entered the stall to assist him, using a halter and a short lead to restrain the mare so Matt could inoculate her.

His other patient, an experienced brood mare incongruously named Gypsy Dancer, placidly nibbled at a small portion of grain Matt had spread over the bottom of her feed pan to distract her while he numbed her vulvar area with local anesthetic. He planned to surgically open the suture line of a previous Caslick's closure in preparation for the impending birth. Jax assisted him again, wrapping the mare's tail to keep it out of the way, fetching the warm soapy water and wads of cotton necessary to wash her genital area before the procedure, picking up a shovel when the food the horse took in at one end made an appearance at the other.

It shouldn't have surprised him—Jax Delacroix had grown up around horses, after all—but it did. It was just that she looked so elegant, like an ad in *Town and Country* magazine in her tan riding breeches, tailored white shirt and well-worn boots, that he couldn't help but be taken aback when she started shoveling manure.

But damned if she didn't look good doing it! The slim-fitting breeches stretched across her backside as she bent over, clearly outlining her curvy little rear end. It was a mouthwatering sight.

"Here, let me do that," Matt said, reaching for the shovel as his Southern-gentleman instincts belatedly kicked in. He was sure it was written somewhere that a gentleman didn't let a lady shovel horse droppings in his presence.

"It's okay. I've got it." Jax hefted the shovel, balancing the malodorous contents so they didn't spill, and backed toward the stall door and the wheelbarrow that always sat in readiness in the center aisle of the barn for just such a purpose. "You're going to have to wash her down again," she said, nodding at the horse. "I'll get some more cotton."

They finished the operation without further incident, Jax handing him his instruments with the nerveless skill of a seasoned surgical nurse.

"We make a good team," he said as he stripped off his

disposable sterile gloves and dropped them into the bucket that held the soiled cotton they'd used to wash the horse.

"Yes, we do," she agreed, and smiled at him.

All of the blood in Matt's brain rushed to another part of his anatomy.

"About what we, ah…discussed earlier," he said.

"Earlier when?" Jax asked as she leaned over to grasp the handle of the bucket.

"At the breeding paddock."

Jax froze for a second, half bent over, the bucket dangling from her fingers. She straightened carefully. "What about it?" she asked, without turning to look at him.

"I was wondering…that is…" God, surely he remembered how to ask a woman for a date! "There's a new restaurant out on Lake Pontchartrain that I've heard is pretty good. I thought maybe this Saturday…we could, ah…"

She turned to look at him, freezing the words in his mouth, turning everything else inside him into an inferno of molten lava.

There was really only one way to do it, he decided, and that was to just open his mouth and take his chances. Asking a woman on a date was the same now as it had been when he was sixteen—terrifying.

"Would you like to have dinner with me Saturday night?"

Jax thought about the reasons she should say no.

Their professional relationship.

His kids.

Not to mention his recently deceased wife.

"Yes," she said.

CHAPTER THREE

"DADDY! DADDY! Look at me!"

Matt heard Amy's high-pitched squeal of excitement as he exited the foaling barn with Jax at his side. He turned his head toward the sound, catching sight of his daughter's bobbing head as she circled the training ring on the back of a small, dark bay gelding with a white blaze and three white stockings. Her blond hair was hidden beneath a child-size, velvet peaked riding helmet with the strap buckled securely under her little round chin. Worn but well-polished riding boots had replaced her pink sneakers. She looked adorable.

Though he was still reeling from the surprise of Jax's soft "yes," Matt determinedly put aside all thoughts of the coming Saturday night and concentrated on being a father.

"I see you, honey," he called, coming up to rest his forearms on the top rail of the fence. "You look great up there."

"She has a good seat." Jax leaned on the fence beside him, being careful not to brush up against his broad, flannel-covered shoulder, and focused her attention on the young rider. "Nice light hands on the reins, too," she commented after a moment. "She doesn't clutch at them for dear life like a lot of novice riders do."

Although Amy was holding the reins, the horse was actually being controlled by Robert Bearclaw, who stood in the center of the ring with the end of a lunge line in his capable hands, slowly turning in place as the horse and rider circled at a walk around him. He wore jeans and boots, his long silver hair hanging loose over the shoulders of his denim jacket, held back from the chisled bones of his face by a beaded headband.

Bear was the head trainer at Delacroix Farms, in charge of anything and everything to do with the Thoroughbreds on the racing side of the operation, answerable only to Jax's brother, Beau, and, through him, to their grandfather Charles Delacroix, patriarch of the clan and owner of Delacroix Farms.

Although he didn't have any direct involvement in the raising and training of her dressage and event horses, Bear was Jax's prime source of guidance and advice whenever a problem came up concerning one of them. He'd taught her to ride in this very ring—as he had all the Delacroix kids—tossing her up on her first horse when she was four years old. She looked upon him as a mentor and a friend.

"How long has Bear been giving her lessons?"

"It's her first time in the saddle," Matt said, his eyes bright with a fond father's pride in his little girl.

"Is it?" Jax glanced at the child again, with more interest this time.

She sat easily atop the horse, her posture erect but relaxed, with absolutely no sign of fear. The fact that Bear already had her on a lunge line, instead of leading her around the ring on a short lead, said volumes about the child's aptitude.

"Looks like she's a natural."

"Makes me feel kind of guilty," Matt admitted.

"Guilty?" Jax turned her head to look at him. "Why?"

He shifted position, lifting one foot to rest it on the lowest rung of the fence, angling his body so that he was facing Jax rather than the ring. Somehow, he managed to close some of the distance between them. Jax didn't move away.

"Amy's been pestering me for months about riding lessons, but I couldn't seem to find the time to do anything about it until now. If I'd known she was going to be this good at it, I might have done something sooner.''

"Well, she's in good hands now. Bear's the best. If you ask him, he'll tell you he taught me everything I know about horses." Her lips turned up in a wry, sweet smile. "He'd be right, too."

"Watch me, Daddy!" Amy hollered imperiously. *"Watch me!"*

Matt lowered his foot to the ground and put both forearms back on the top rung of the fence as he turned to face the ring again. His shoulder was brushing Jax's. "I'm watching, baby."

"Pay attention, Amy," Bear called to his pupil, his voice firm but patient. "Remember what I told you. Back straight. Heels down. Eyes forward."

But Amy was too excited to pay proper heed to his instructions. "Can we go fast now, Mr. Bear? Can we? I want to go fast!"

Without waiting for permission, she tightened her hands on the reins and leaned forward, instinctively squeezing her knees against the gelding's sides. The horse responded immediately, then hesitated, confused when the line attached to his bridle went suddenly taut. He made an abrupt sideways movement, trying to obey all the signals he was getting, unbalancing his rider in the process.

Amy shrieked, making a useless grab for the short pommel on the English saddle, and slid off of the horse.

"Amy!" Matt was over the fence before she hit the ground, with Jax right behind him as he raced across the ring toward his daughter.

But Bear was closer and he got to her first. He was already hunkered down beside her, his hands running lightly over her arms and legs to check for breaks or other serious injury, when Matt reached them.

"She's all right," he said as Matt dropped to his knees in the dirt. "Just an abrasion on her arm, and maybe a bruise or two." His lips tightened in a self-deprecating grimace. "She wouldn't even have that if I'd waited until she had a padded jacket before I put her up on the horse."

"I hurt my arm, Daddy," Amy wailed, holding it up to show him her scraped elbow. Her eyes, beneath a fringe of blond bangs and the short bill of the riding helmet, were filled with tears. "It's bleeding."

Matt's heart twisted in his chest at the sight of his daughter's pain. "Let Daddy see," he crooned, and he reached out, intending to unbuckle her helmet so he could cuddle her against his chest and kiss the hurt away.

He felt a soft hand on his shoulder, stopping him. He half turned, his expression impatient and questioning. Jax shook her head, tilting it toward Bear.

"I knew another little girl who scraped her arm just like that the first time she fell off a horse," Bear was saying to the child. "I washed the dirt off it for her and put on a little Bactine and a Band-Aid, and it was fine. She got right back up on the horse and finished her riding lesson. Now she's one of the best riders I know." Bear glanced up at his star pupil, a small smile curving his strongly chiseled lips. "She's won herself a whole bunch of blue ribbons and fancy medals and such."

Amy sniffed back the incipient tears, the mention of blue ribbons catching her interest. "What little girl?"

"Her," Bear said, pointing over Matt's shoulder at Jax.

Amy tilted her head, her eyes wide as she looked up at the woman standing behind her father.

"Bear taught me to ride when I was a little younger than you," Jax said, feeling as if she had to say something in the face of that wide-eyed gaze. "Right here in this very ring. I fell off lots of times before I learned to ride really well. I still fall off sometimes, even now," she admitted, "if I don't pay attention to what I'm doing. That's the most important part of riding," she added when Amy just continued to stare up at her without saying anything. "Paying attention, I mean," she said, feeling awkward and uncertain at the child's inscrutable silence.

She never knew what to say to children. They were like a separate species—strange and potentially dangerous. You never knew what they were going to say or do.

"I know who you are," Amy said, her tears completely forgotten, the scrape on her arm suddenly unimportant. "I saw you on TV on the horse show. You're the Fabulous Jax, aren't you?"

"Well, ah…yes, I guess I am," Jax admitted.

Fabulous Jax, as in "our next rider is the fabulous Jax Delacroix," was a nickname that had been bestowed on her by the media soon after she'd started international competition. It had been following her around like a bad penny ever since.

"You won the Olympics," Amy said, her voice rising in excitement. "Remember, Daddy?" She turned to her father. "I sat on your lap that time while you an' me an' Mommy an' Jeff watched it on TV. When she stood up on the box an' they gave her the flowers an' played the national anthem, she cried. Remember?"

"I remember," Matt said, amazed that *she* remembered. "That time" had been nearly two years ago; Amy had been five.

"She's the Fabulous Jax, Daddy," Amy said, gazing up at Jax with an expression very much like awe filling her big blue eyes.

Matt grinned.

"She certainly is, baby," he agreed, touched and amused and aroused by the embarrassed blush on Jax's cheeks. "She certainly is."

MATT COULDN'T REMEMBER ever being this nervous about a date. Admittedly, it had been a long time since he'd been on one, so his memory might be faulty, but he honestly couldn't recall ever feeling this much gut-wrenching anticipation before.

He was so nervous he'd scorched the sleeve of his white dress shirt, cut himself while shaving and tried to gargle with aftershave instead of mouthwash. Fortunately, the aftershave didn't do any lasting damage to his taste buds, the cut on his chin stopped bleeding almost immediately after he dabbed it with a styptic pencil, and he decided the suit he'd meant to wear with the white shirt was too formal for the evening he had planned, anyway.

None of the restaurants in Bayou Beltane were what anyone would call dressy, except for the country club out in the new section, which required jackets in the dining room even at lunch. But that didn't really count, because nobody he knew ever went there. Slacks and a knit pullover were usually fancy enough for anyplace in town.

Now, if he'd been planning to take Jax to dinner in New Orleans—to Antoine's or Commander's Palace or Galatoire's—he'd have put on a suit without thinking twice about it. But in Bayou Bel... Hell, he thought, going stock-still in the act of zipping up his khaki slacks. Maybe he *should* be taking her to a restaurant in New Orleans. Maybe someplace like Commander's Palace would suit her better than a little seafood place on Lake Pontchartrain. She was a sophisticated woman, a world traveler used to fine cuisine, elegant surroundings and cultured, cosmopolitan people.

He couldn't offer her those things, not on a regular basis. Bayou Beltane had some mighty fine cuisine, but it was a little short on elegance, and the people, while possessing a unique culture all their own, were mostly Louisiana rednecks or Southern aristocrats.

Hell, Matt was just a good ol' Louisiana country boy himself. The only time he'd ever lived outside of St. Tammany Parish was when he'd gone to Texas A&M to earn his degree in veterinary medicine. The farthest afield he'd been since then was a veterinary conference in Boulder, Colorado, nearly five years ago. Which hardly made him sophisticated. Or cosmopolitan.

He was almost tempted to call her up and cancel the date. Almost.

The memory of those cool gray eyes, that thick, lustrous hair, that smile that turned him inside out, stopped him. That, and the fact that, after ten years abroad, she'd chosen to come back to Bayou Beltane when it was time to settle down, which surely said *something* about her preferences. If she'd wanted sophistication and Continental glamour, she'd have stayed in Europe.

He zipped up his slacks and finished getting dressed, tucking a soft ivory knit shirt into the waist of his pressed khaki slacks, easing his broad shoulders into a casual, sand-colored sport jacket. He slipped his wallet into his back pocket, attached his beeper to his belt and was ready.

"You look nice, Daddy," Amy said, glancing up from the make-believe world she had created on the living room floor. It consisted of a plastic farm she hadn't played with in years, a My Little Pony with a rainbow on its rump and a glittery yellow bow in its long tail, and all three of her Barbie dolls.

"Why don't you put Barbie down for a minute, honey, and come sit on the sofa with me for a little while before Grandma gets here? You, too, Jeff," he said to his nine-year-old son. "Turn off the Nintendo and come here. I want to talk to both of you."

The children settled down on the sofa beside him, one tucked under each arm, their little faces turned up to him expectantly.

He didn't know quite where to begin. "You know I'm going out on a date tonight, don't you?"

Both children nodded.

"With Jax," Amy volunteered.

"That's right," Matt said carefully. The children's psychologist had warned him that they might feel resentment or anger when he finally started dating again. She'd assured him those feelings were completely normal and didn't mean he'd warped their delicate psyches. She'd also assured him that the only way to handle it was to get the kids to talk about their feelings. Dr. Fremont was a great believer in talking.

"How do you kids feel about me dating Ms Delacroix?" He looked into his son's face. The boy was a miniature replica of Matt, except for his hair. It was stick straight, like his mother's had been, and so blond it was nearly white. He wore it in a brush cut that stuck straight up from the top of his head. Combined with the small, wire-rimmed glasses he wore, it made him look like an intellectual punk rocker. "Jeff, what do you think, son?"

Jeff shrugged. "Okay, I guess."

"Does it bother you that I'm going on a date?" Matt prodded, trying to elicit a bit more response than that.

Jeff considered for a moment. "Uh-uh," he said finally. "Mark's dad goes out on dates. David's mom does, too, and his dad just got married to somebody else, so now he has a stepmother and two *more* yucky sisters."

"Sisters aren't yucky," Amy protested. "You're yucky."

"And Rhonda, this new girl in my class," Jeff continued, ignoring his sister, "her dad got a divorce and he goes out on dates—" he rolled his eyes "—*all* the time." The look in his blue eyes grew even more serious than usual. "I wouldn't like it if you went on dates *all* the time," he warned.

"I won't go on dates all the time. I promise. Amy?"
Matt looked down at his daughter. "What do you think
about me going on a date with Ms Delacroix?"

Amy considered the question for a minute. "Will you
ask her if I could see her blue ribbons sometime?"

JAX COULDN'T BELIEVE how nervous she was.

She'd changed outfits four times before finally settling
on a dead-simple black knit T-shirt dress with tiny cap
sleeves and a hem that ended a few inches above her ankles. She'd pinned her hair into a thick chignon at the back
of her neck, then took it down and plaited it into a neat
French braid, then, dissatisfied with both her usual hair-
styles, brushed it out to hang loose on her shoulders. She
fiddled with jewelry, putting half-a-dozen pieces on and
taking them off again before finally settling on a pair of
small silver hoop earrings and a wide silver cuff bracelet.
She still wasn't satisfied, but it was the best she could do,
and he would be here any minute.

When was the last time she'd gone out on a date?

The embassy parties and fund-raisers for the Olympic
equestrian team didn't count. That was business. Public relations. But this was a real, honest-to-goodness *date!*

She wondered if he would try to kiss her...and if she
would let him if he did...and then almost started to hyper-
ventilate at the thought of what might happen after that.

"I think I just heard a car pull up outside," Charly called
from the living room.

Jax put a hand to her breast and took several deep, calming breaths, trying to center herself the way she did before
an especially difficult event. It didn't work. The only thing
to do now was what she did when the breathing technique
failed her during competition. She lifted her head, straightened her back and rode into the ring, anyway, pretending

she had it aced. He was only a man, after all, not a panel of Olympic judges.

"God, you look gorgeous," Charly said, looking up from her seat in the corner of the sofa when Jax entered the living room. "Doesn't she look gorgeous, Shel?"

Shelby Delacroix was the second youngest of Justin Delacroix's five children, the only one who had followed her father into the legal profession. She had the same dark hair as her sisters—though hers was curlier than Jax's sleek do, longer than Charly's—and the same gray eyes. But in Shelby, their mother's patrician features were softened in a way that made them seem almost wholesome. She looked up from the take-out supper she was unloading from a big paper sack onto the hastily cleared coffee table. The rich scents of andouille sausage, barbequed shrimp and Cajun spices filled the air.

"Absolutely gorgeous," Shelby agreed, and grinned at Charly. "Let's stuff her in a closet."

Charly looked as if she were considering the idea. "Naw. She'd only find something even more gorgeous to wear if we did that."

"Do you think it's too much?" Jax touched the long necklace of tiny silver beads she'd added at the last minute. "Too dressy?"

"It's not the dress," Shelby said. "It's you." She set a large, cardboard-topped aluminum container of jambalaya on the table and licked a bit of sauce off of her thumb. "If any of the rest of us wore that dress it would look like what it is, a long T-shirt. On you, it's haute couture."

"I could change into slacks."

"Same difference. It's you, Jax, not the clothes. You'll just have to learn to live with it." Another quick grin lit up her face for a moment. "We have."

Jax returned the grin with a nervous smile and went to

the window to look out. "I thought you said you heard a car pull up?" she said to Charly.

"I thought I did. Isn't he out there?"

Jax shook her head.

"Well, it must have been someone driving by on the way to the stables, or up to the big house or something. Come on over here—" she patted the sofa next to her "—and have a glass of wine with us while you wait. And stop obsessing. He'll be here."

"I'm not obsessing."

"Looks like obsession to me," Charly said, and glanced at Shelby for confirmation. "How 'bout you, Shel? Don't you think she's overreacting to a few minutes' delay?"

Shelby shrugged and took a quick sip of her wine. "At least her date can get here in a few minutes," she muttered into her glass.

Charly's ears perked up. "Do I detect trouble in paradise?"

"Yes. No. Oh, I don't know." Shelby shrugged again and set her wineglass down on the table. "The whole time-and-distance thing is becoming a major issue between Travis and me. It's kind of hard to be spontaneous or romantic with all of Louisiana and half the state of Texas between us." It was a slight exaggeration but it got her point across. "When we decide to go out on a date someone has to get on a plane or drive for three hours."

"There's always phone sex," Charly said helpfully.

"Charlotte Delacroix, what a thing to say!" Jax scolded, before all three women broke into laughter.

A knock on the door interrupted them, sobering Jax instantly. She jumped to her feet, nearly spilling her wine as she reached to put it on the coffee table, and started toward the door. She stopped uncertainly in the middle of the living room when it began to open. Marie Delacroix Henderson stuck her head into the room.

At first glance, she and Shelby looked enough alike to be mistaken for twins. They were nearly the same height, had the same basic build and wore nearly the same hairstyle. But Marie's eyes were a misty blue instead of the gray her three sisters shared, and where Shelby was girl-next-door wholesome, there was something just slightly off-kilter about Marie's delicate features, giving her a faintly exotic, gypsyish look.

"Marie, this is a surprise," Jax said. "What are you doing here?"

"Lucas is on duty tonight—" her husband Lucas was a doctor at Lakeview Community Hospital "—and I didn't feel like spending the evening alone, so I decided to drop by and keep Charly company while you're out on your date. I brought some carnation oil with me. It's very healing. It's good for wounds." She patted the voluminous tapestry bag hanging from the crook of her arm. "I thought you might like me to massage your shoulder," she said to her younger sister.

"How did you know I had a date?" Jax asked.

"Well, I could say I sensed it," Marie said teasingly. Not only was she a successful aromatherapist with an extensive knowledge of healing herbs, she also had an eerie sixth sense that sometimes made the less-open-minded members of her family a little nervous. "But the truth is, Charly mentioned it this morning when I called to see how she was doing."

"Did you bring me the pralines I mentioned, too?" Charly demanded.

Marie patted her tapestry bag again. "Right here," she said.

"Then come on in and sit down," Charly invited. "We could use someone with your powers, anyway."

"My powers?" she said as she closed the door and

joined the group around the coffee table. "Is somebody sick?"

"Poor ol' Charly hasn't been the same since she came out of that coma," Shelby said blandly, sending a sidelong glance at her younger sister as she handed Marie a glass of wine.

Glass in hand, Marie turned to look at the patient sitting on the couch, sporting a Slidell Police Force T-shirt and ratty gray sweatpants. Despite the unusual paleness of her cheeks and the faint air of fragility typical of anyone recovering from a serious injury, she appeared healthy.

"All things considered, Charly's fine," Marie said. "She'll be back in fighting trim in a few weeks. Jax is a bundle of nerves, though. I can see the energy crackling around her. And you—" she turned her mystic, blue-eyed gaze on Shelby "—you're upset and conflicted about something. Your aura's all clouded."

"It's the wine," Shelby said. "I've had just enough to fog my brain."

"Are you and Travis having problems?"

"No. Well…yes. Sort of."

"That's the conflicted part," Charly said helpfully.

Shelby shot her younger sister a sour glance before turning her gaze back to Marie. "Travis has this big fancy shindig he wants me to go to at the end of this month. His father's getting some award at a dinner dance being sponsored by the Quarter Horse Association, or something like that. It's a really big deal. Black tie and everything. The day after the dance, Travis is throwing a big Texas barbecue in his father's honor. He wants me to fly out and spend that whole weekend with him. Friday through Monday, if I can swing it."

"And you don't want to go?" Marie asked, puzzled.

"Oh, I *want* to go. It's just…" She twisted her wineglass around on the table a few times before looking up. "I don't know if I can. Not for all four days, anyway. Maybe not even for two.''

''Why not?'' Jax asked

''With Dad leaving the firm to take the judgeship, and the new offices in New Orleans and all, caseloads have been heavier than normal for everyone. And then I ended up spending all that time on Yvette's case.'' Yvette Avenall was an old high school friend of Shelby's with a nasty custody battle on her hands. She'd recently disappeared, taking her son into hiding to keep him out of his father's hands. ''And who knows how long it will take to resolve that whole ugly mess once she's found? Not to mention the mess with Uncle Philip. He swears up and down that Desiree's deed is a fake because Great-grandfather Hamilton would never have just given away forty acres of Delacroix land, swamp or not, no matter what the circumstances. And even if he had, he would have done it up all right and proper, and registered it at the courthouse instead of giving Desiree a handwritten note.''

''But if he'd done it up 'right and proper,' people would have wondered at the reason,'' Charly said shrewdly. ''And somebody might have guessed. Great-grandfather Hamilton certainly wouldn't have wanted that.''

The ''reason'' was an open secret now, at least in the family. Sweet old Uncle William, the youngest son of Hamilton and Marguerite Delacroix, brother to twins Philip and Charles and elder sister Mary—wasn't. Born to Desiree Boudreaux and an unknown man, he had been unofficially adopted by Hamilton and Marguerite when Marguerite's third pregnancy ended in a life-threatening miscarriage that put an end to any hopes of her having another child. Seeing a chance to give her newborn son a better life than she could provide, the unwed, seventeen-year-old Desiree had relinquished all rights to her baby, giving him into another woman's loving arms. All she'd asked in return was a piece of land to call her own, somewhere close by so she could watch her baby grow up. William had been brought up as a Delacroix, and no one—least of all William himself—had known any different.

Until Philip Delacroix decided to drain the swamp and put in a housing development, thus depriving Desiree and her family of their home and upsetting the fragile ecosystem of the bayou. When it looked as if he couldn't be stopped from going ahead with the project by any other means, Desiree had produced the handwritten deed. Though only a few select members of the two opposing clans had been present when the truth was revealed, the secret, like all such secrets, had quietly spread throughout the family, to everyone but Uncle William and Aunt Mary. Now it was like the elephant in the living room—everybody saw it, everybody knew it was there, but nobody mentioned it. Ever. It was the way the Delacroix handled things.

"Uncle Philip is flooding our office with paperwork," Shelby said. "He's fighting tooth and nail to get the injunction lifted so he can go ahead with his plans to develop the swamp. Granddad has asked me to handle it personally."

"Keeping it in the family," Charly said dryly.

"He doesn't want any more talk about this than there's already been," Shelby said, "for Uncle William's sake as much as much as anyone's. And by assigning it to me, well..." She spread her hands. "It's up to me to try to contain things and keep them running as smoothly as possible until the situation settles down a bit. And I can't do that if I'm flying off to Texas every weekend."

"Why you?" Jax asked.

"Because I'm the only Delacroix at the firm now, full-time. Granddad only comes in a few mornings a week, or to consult on a specific case."

"But what about Toni's husband?" Jax asked, referring

to Brody Wagner, her aunt's new husband. "I've heard nothing but good things about him since I've been back. Grandfather obviously thinks he's more than competent, or he wouldn't have made him a partner. I've even heard Dad singing his praises, and we all know he doesn't hand out compliments lightly."

"Brody spends most of his time in the New Orleans office. And besides, his last name isn't Delacroix," Shelby insisted. "Mine is."

"Well, what about Joanna, then?" Joanna was their uncle Philip's oldest daughter. "Her last name might be Gideon but she was born a Delacroix. That should count for something."

"Joanna has her hands full with Nikki." Nikki was Joanna's rebellious seventeen-year-old daughter, who was currently dating the town bad boy and driving her mother crazy with worry. "I can't ask her to take on more than she already has," Shelby said.

"So you try to take it all on your own shoulders." Marie tsked lightly. "There's such a thing as too much family loyalty, you know. You've got to think about what's best for you and Travis, too."

"I am thinking about what's best for me and Travis. I'm trying to, anyway. But he's got to think about what's best for us, too, instead of just thinking about what he—"

A loud knock sounded on the door, making them all jump. Grateful for the interruption, Shelby shut her eyes for a second, taking a moment to rein in her emotions. When she opened them again, her expression was carefully blank and a determined smile curved her lips.

"You'd better get that, Jax," she said, quirking a brow at her oldest sister, who was sitting on the end of the sofa, frozen in place, staring at the front door the way a rabbit stares at a hungry snake. "I'm pretty sure it's for you."

With her stomach jumping around worse than it ever had

before a competition, Jax rose from the sofa. Her sisters stayed where they were, making no effort to hide their interest.

It seemed to take forever for her to walk across the small room, with her sisters' eyes boring into her back all the way. Another knock sounded on the door just as she reached for the doorknob. She took a quick, bracing breath and opened the door.

"Hello, Matt." She smiled shyly, looking up at him from under her lashes.

"Hello, Jax," he murmured, returning her soft smile with one of his own.

Not knowing what to say after they'd said hello, the two of them simply stood there, on opposite sides of the threshold, gaping at each other like two tongue-tied teenagers on a prom date. Jax couldn't believe that this suave, sophisticated stranger was the same Matt Taggart of the flannel shirts and faded jeans. Matt couldn't believe that this beautiful woman, who looked so elegant in riding breeches and a tailored shirt, could look even more exquisite in a simple black dress.

But he was.

And she did.

Their smiles widened. Warmed. Became almost intimate. Jax's hand was still on the doorknob, Matt's still half raised, as they stood there, staring at each other in helpless fascination.

One of Jax's sisters cleared her throat.

Twice.

Matt glanced away from Jax's face as the sound penetrated his consciousness, his eyes widening at the sight of all three of her sisters ranged around the coffee table in the room behind her, regarding the two of them with blatant, unabashed interest.

Charly grinned at him. "Hey, good-lookin'. How's it goin'?"

He flushed slightly, feeling like a complete fool, and dropped his hand. "I hope I haven't kept you waiting too long," he said to Jax. "Things got a little hectic at the last minute. I probably should have called."

"No, it's all right," she answered politely. "I only just finished getting dressed a few minutes ago."

"Are you ready to go, then?"

"Yes, I—"

"Hey, Jax," Charly said. "Aren't you going to take your purse?"

"You probably ought to take some kind of wrap, too," Marie advised. "It can get chilly out by Lake Pontchartrain at this time of year."

"You might also think about offering Matt a glass of wine before you go," Shelby added. "It would be the polite thing to do."

Jax could have cheerfully throttled all three of her sisters. Instead, she gritted her teeth and smiled. "Excuse me for a moment," she said to Matt. "It'll only take me a minute to get my purse."

She aimed a furious scowl at her sisters as she turned, silently commanding them to behave themselves. They all smiled sweetly back.

"So, Matt," Shelby said, holding the wine bottle over a clean glass. "Say when."

"Nothing for me, thanks." He eyed the three grinning women suspiciously, wondering what they were up to. It wasn't a good sign for a man when a bunch of women looked so smugly pleased with themselves. "I don't like to drink on an empty stomach, especially when I'm driving."

Shelby shrugged. "Wise man," she said, and divided the remaining wine among Charly, Marie and herself. She set the bottle down on the table and picked her glass up by the stem.

Charly and Marie did the same.

"To a very special guy," Shelby said, toasting him with her wine.

Charly and Marie echoed the sentiment.

"A special guy?" Matt's forehead creased in a puzzled frown. "What the hel—heck do you mean by that?"

"You're the only man Jax has agreed to go out with since she came back to Bayou Beltane," Shelby explained. "I'd say that makes you pretty special." She flashed a grin at Jax as she came out of the bedroom with her purse and a light jacket. "Wouldn't you, Jax?"

Jax opened her purse, ostensibly checking for her pager, and pretended she hadn't heard the question—or the outrageous statement that came before it. "I'm ready," she said to Matt, and snapped her purse closed with an audible click.

"Shall we go, then?" He placed his hand at the small of her back, escorting her toward the door.

"There's just one more little thing before you leave," Charly said.

Matt paused, one hand on the doorknob, the other on Jax's back, and looked at her over his shoulder. Jax tensed beside him, refusing to turn around.

What in heaven's name had gotten into her sisters?

"Special or not, you give her a hard time," Charly said, the look in her eyes letting him know she was dead serious, "and you answer to all three of us."

CHAPTER FOUR

"IT WAS A SETUP," Jax said suddenly, staring at Matt across the white-draped, candle-lit table.

Matt looked up from his menu. "Excuse me?"

"The wineglasses." She gestured at the two oversize balloon goblets sitting on the table, one in front of each place setting. "There were five glasses on the coffee table next to the bottle of wine when I came out of the bedroom. Five." She shook her head. "I didn't even notice."

Matt put down his menu to give her his full attention. "So?"

"Don't you see? Shelby didn't just decide to bring Charly dinner from Rick's on the spur of the moment. And Marie didn't just drop by. Charly invited them both. The sneak," she fumed, but she smiled when she said it.

"They're very protective of you," Matt said. "That's nice."

Yes, it was nice, Jax thought. A little odd, since she didn't remember them ever displaying any protective instincts toward her before. She was, after all, the oldest sister, the one who'd looked out for the rest of them when they were children. Obviously, things had changed in the years she'd been away from home. The three teenaged sisters she'd left behind had turned into strong, caring women. Strong, caring, *nosy* women who had nearly managed to embarrass her to death in front of her date.

"I'm surprised she didn't invite Beau over, too. Or my father, to ask about your intentions toward me."

"That would have been a little awkward," Matt said. "Since I don't quite know what my intentions toward you are yet."

Jax didn't know what to say to that, so, wisely, she said nothing. It left a small, taut silence for Matt to fill.

"I know my..." He hesitated, not sure of the right word; he didn't want to get in too deep, too fast. "Feelings," he said, abruptly deciding he was already in over his head so he might as well go for broke. Life had taught him that honesty was usually the best policy. "My feelings for you...well, they surprise me a little. More than a little, if you want to know the truth."

"The truth?" Jax murmured, wondering where all this was leading.

"I'm very attracted to you, Jax." He looked her straight in the eyes. "*Very* attracted. I haven't been this attracted to anyone since my wife died. In fact, I haven't been attracted to anyone at all since Livvy died."

Jax's eyes widened in shock. *No one?* But...but his wife had died a year ago, hadn't she? Did that mean he hadn't been with anyone since then? Not even on a date?

"I haven't even dated," he said, as if she'd asked the question out loud. "So this is new to me, too. You haven't been out on a date since you got back to Bayou Beltane. I haven't been out on a date since..." He lifted his broad shoulders in a shrug. "Well, since the last time I went out with Livvy, way back before we got married. Kind of puts us in the same boat, doesn't it?"

"The same boat how?"

"We're both out of practice with this sort of thing."

"Oh, yes, of course. Out of practice," Jax agreed.

The thought put her at ease in some indefinable way. Knowing she wasn't the only one who hadn't had a date since before time began put them on a more even footing than she'd first thought. Some of her nervousness evaporated, just a bit.

"I guess that means we should take it slow," she said, wondering why the prospect of holding back didn't sound all that appealing.

"One step at a time," he agreed, thankful that she understood.

Once before, a long time ago, he'd gone off half cocked, so to speak—was there ever a more apt expression? he wondered. And it had changed the entire course of two young people's lives. The consequences hadn't been all bad, since Jeff had been the direct result of his impetuosity. And he couldn't imagine his life without Jeff. Or Amy. But Matt didn't intend to let the mindless appendage between his legs make that kind of life decision for him ever again.

"What's the next step, do you think?" Jax murmured. She liked having things spelled out. It was much better for everyone that way. Fewer hurt feelings. Fewer tears and disillusionment.

"The next step? Well..." He reached for his wine and took a sip, giving himself time to think. What had he and Livvy done on dates? No, on second thought, that wasn't a good idea. What he and Livvy had done on dates had gotten him married in his senior year at Texas A&M. Not that he *didn't* want to do with Jax what he had done with Livvy. He wanted to do that very much, but maybe it wasn't such a good idea, right off the bat like that. Maybe this time he should be sensible.

"How 'bout we get to know each other," he suggested. "Take it slow like you said. We go out to dinner again, have lunch, and...oh, I don't know. What else do people do on dates nowadays? Picnics?"

"A picnic sounds nice," Jax said. "I haven't been on a picnic in at least a hundred years." She smiled reminiscently. "When I was a girl, Odelle used to pack up a big lunch...thick peanut butter and jelly sandwiches on home-made bread, some of her bread-and-butter pickles, a couple of big crisp apples and those delicious sugar cookies she makes. We kids would saddle up our horses and ride out in the woods, pretending we were pioneers heading west."

"I was thinking of something just a *little* more romantic," Matt admitted.

"Oh, well..." Jax pressed the tip of her index finger to her chin, thinking. "There was one time Billy Ray Barstow took me on a picnic out to the edge of the bayou over by Belle Terre. It was late spring, I remember, just before summer vacation started. Billy Ray brought wine and candles and a blanket. Is that more like what you had in mind?" She gave him a look from under her lashes. "Before you answer," she cautioned, "you should know that I only managed to drink about two Dixie cups full of that wine—it was Thunderbird, I think, or maybe Ripple—before I threw up all over poor Billy Ray's shoes."

"I'll be sure to bring lemonade," Matt said, imagining himself in Billy Ray Barstow's place. He could see the two of them—himself and Jax—near the water's edge, all alone in the bayou, with the water lapping gently at the shore and the sun shining through the Spanish moss on the cypress trees, dappling her bare creamy skin....

No, he thought, drawing himself back from that little fantasy, *better not.*

"We could go to the movies," he said, his soft Louisiana drawl a bit thickened. "They tore down the drive-in a few years back—" a drive-in wasn't a good idea, anyway, not for a man who intended to take things slow "—but there's a new eight-screen Cineplex over in Slidell now. Or we could drive into New Orleans for dinner or, maybe, check out the action at one of the casinos. Or there's boating on Lake Pontchartrain. Or we could take in an art exhibit in Covington sometime, if you're interested." He reached across the table and covered her hand with his. "Do you like wandering through art galleries, Jax?"

Jax didn't pull her hand away. "Very much," she said, and smiled at him.

"And jazz?" He rubbed his fingertip over her knuckles. "Do you like jazz?"

"I love it," she said, trying to keep her voice light and even. The way he was touching her hand was doing strange things to her breathing. "Good ol' Dixieland jazz was one of the things I missed most while I was living in France. It—" she took a quick little breath "—it just doesn't sound the same played in a Paris café as it does down in the Quarter."

"Jeff loves jazz, too," Matt said, pleased by the discovery. "Especially Dixieland. He's been taking trumpet lessons for a couple of years now. Al Hirt is his hero."

"Jeff?"

"My son. He's nine. Two years older than Amy." Matt circled the small bone on her wrist with the tip of one finger. "You need to know, up front, that my children are the biggest part of my life." His fingertip moved up the back of her wrist and down again, very lightly. "They'd have to be a part of anything between us. I'd like you to get to know them."

Jax's stomach fluttered at the light, hesitant caress of his fingers on her skin, and her whole body felt suddenly warm and liquid and wanting. And then his words penetrated the sensual haze his soft, caressing tone had created in her mind.

My children are the biggest part of my life. They'd have to be a part of anything between us. I'd like you to get to know them.

Alarm bells went off, turning the pleasant fluttering in her stomach to a sensation that more closely resembled butterflies with wings made of razor blades. She pulled her hand out from under his and pressed it to her stomach.

Logically, she agreed that getting to know his kids was the sensible thing to do. If there was ever going to be anything between her and Matt, it was the *only* thing to do. His children were part of him. A big part. And any woman he had a relationship with would have to understand and accept that up front, as he'd said.

She liked Matt Taggart. A lot. And she wanted to have a relationship with him. At some point, maybe, when they could better define what that relationship might be.

But kids scared her. She hadn't been around them much, not since her own sisters had grown up, and she didn't know what to say to them or how to deal with them. Odelle had always taken care of the little ones.

Once, long ago, she'd felt much differently. She'd had a young wife's hopes and dreams. She'd made grand plans for a big, happy family, envisioning herself surrounded by children, raising them with plenty of laughter and hugs, guiding them to adulthood, teaching them to love horses as much as she did. But those grand plans hadn't worked out. Fate had had a different kind of life in store for her, one without the pitter-patter of little feet in it. She'd had to learn the hard lesson that some things just weren't meant to be, no matter how much a person wanted them. For her, children were one of those things. She'd resigned herself to the reality of her situation a long time ago and gone on to make a life out of what fate *had* given her. And it was a good life. Satisfying. Fulfilling. At least, that's what she'd been telling herself for the last ten years.

"Jax, what is it? What's the matter?"

She blinked and forced her thoughts outward, refocusing her attention on her dinner companion. She gave him a charming, empty smile.

"I'm sorry." She patted her stomach lightly. "My stomach's growling like an old bear. I'm surprised you can't hear it.''

"Are you sure you're all right?"

"Just hunger pangs," she assured him. "I haven't eaten since breakfast, and I've been going nonstop all day." She picked up her menu and opened it, scanning the fanciful descriptions of the restaurant's offerings, as if food were the only thing on her mind. "What would you recommend?" she asked.

Matt stared at the top of her bent head for a moment before he answered. He knew something had gone wrong, but he didn't know what. He ran back through their conversation in his mind. She'd seemed easy enough, her manner relaxed, bordering on flirtatious when she told him about the picnic with Billy Ray. Things seemed to be going along just fine, and then she'd stiffened and pulled away, sliding her hand out from under his. Was that it? Had he moved too fast there? Come on too strong?

"I've heard the sole meunière is excellent," he said easily, determined to follow her lead and let her set the pace. It was, after all, a woman's prerogative. He'd made his interest plain. Now it was up to her to decide how they proceeded—*if* they proceeded—from here. "The soufflé potatoes are supposed to be good, too," he added. "And I'd suggest you save room for crème brûlée. It's the specialty of the house."

Jax had made her selections and was handing her menu to the waitress when her gaze was suddenly caught and held by something going on behind Matt's back.

"No, don't look," she said quickly when he made a move to turn in his chair and see what had caught her attention. "If they notice us, we'll have to go over and say hello."

"Who is it?"

Jax wrinkled her nose. "It's Uncle Philip and my cousin Drew."

Philip Delacroix was a Louisiana state senator, a flamboyant Southern statesman from the old school, currently up for reelection in a closely contested race for the legislative seat he'd held for more than twenty years. Technically speaking, he was Jax's *great*-uncle, being her grandfather Charles's twin brother.

Relations between the two branches of the Delacroix family had always been more than a bit strained, even before the current contretemps over the swampland, and friendships between members of the two warring sides had never been encouraged. Were, at times, even actually *discouraged*.

Jax had no idea what had started the long-standing family feud, only that it concerned something that had happened between Charles and Philip before any of the younger Delacroix were born. The cause of the split was never talked about—another example of the family tradition of sweeping scandal under the rug. If there *had* been a scandal.

Jax didn't really know.

Probably only her grandfather and Uncle Philip knew *all* the reasons for the ill feelings between them. And maybe sweet Uncle William, who was a priest and thus kept his own counsel. And certainly Aunt Mary, who—having celebrated her eightieth birthday a few months ago—was the oldest living Delacroix and the much beloved matriarch of the clan.

While everyone on both sides of the family could usually be counted on to remain cordial in public, only at Aunt Mary's behest would they agree to come together in the same room, in private.

Or, at least, the two halves of the family never *used* to get together without Mary's gentle coercion.

Uncle Philip's widowed daughter Joanna, who was a

lawyer, too, had moved back to Bayou Beltane a little over a year ago with her daughter, Nikki, the one who was currently causing everyone so much worry. Joanna had originally gone to work at her father's law firm, as expected. Then, to everyone's complete surprise, she had ended her employment there and started working for Charles instead. Uncle Philip had *not* been pleased. The injunction his daughter's new employer had filed against his land-development company a few months ago hadn't made him any happier.

"They're having dinner with a very striking redheaded woman," Jax said. "At least, Uncle Philip and the woman are eating dinner. Drew appears to be dining on straight bourbon." She shook her head sadly. "Shelby told me she thought he was drinking too much. It looks like she was right." She darted another quick look over Matt's shoulder. "I wonder who she is? She doesn't look like a lobbyist or a lawyer."

"On the slim side?" Matt asked. "Lots of curly dark red hair and kind of a pointed chin?"

"Uh-huh. Do you know her?"

"Just enough to say hello to if I pass her in the street. Her name's Katherine something or other. She's some kind of antiques dealer, I think. From New Orleans."

"What do you suppose she's doing having dinner with Uncle Philip and Drew? If she lives in New Orleans, she isn't one of his constituents. Uncle Philip doesn't usually bother to turn the charm on for anyone who can't vote for him."

"Maybe he wants to buy some antiques. Or sell some. Belle Terre must be chock-full of them."

"Maybe," Jax said doubtfully. "But I don't think Uncle Philip would ever sell any of Belle Terre's antiques. It wouldn't fit in with his genteel Southern statesman image to sell off pieces of his family's history. And Drew wouldn't be scowling like that if they were just discussing furniture. Uh-oh.'' She picked up her wineglass and buried her nose in it, turning her head toward the wall at the same time.

Drew Delacroix stormed past their table without a glance, completely oblivious to them, and to the dozen or so pairs of eyes—mostly female—that watched him wend his single-minded way through the tables in the crowded dining room.

Drew had always attracted approving female glances. Tall, dark and undeniably dashing, tonight he had a dangerous air about him that Jax had never noticed before. She wondered if it was the bourbon or something else that made him look so haunted...and alone.

"He sure has got a mad on," Matt commented as Drew slammed through the front door of the restaurant and out into the parking lot. "And he looked half plowed. I hope he's not planning to drive in that condition."

The subsequent squeal of tires on pavement made that hope a futile one, but there was nothing either of them could do to stop him now.

Jax put her wineglass down and sent another glance over Matt's shoulder. "I wonder what that was all about?"

"Give it a few days," Matt said dryly. "It'll be all over town by then. Even little Becky Lynn Dooley down at the Dairy Queen will know what happened."

Jax laughed at that. He was exaggerating, but not by much. It was one of the things that could make life in a small Southern town like Bayou Beltane a real trial at times. You could hardly swing a cat without hitting someone you were related to, and nearly everyone knew your business almost before you did—and felt perfectly free to discuss it with anyone who wasn't already conversant with all the facts.

The waitress arrived with their salads then, sliding in

front of each of them ice cold plates of tender baby greens sprinkled with crumbled blue cheese and dressed with olive oil and balsamic vinegar. Jax picked up her fork and dug in with ladylike gusto. She hadn't been kidding about being hungry.

"You do know that you and I are going to be a hot topic of conversation down at the D.Q. tomorrow, too, don't you?" Matt said when the waitress had gone away.

Jax paused with her fork halfway to her mouth. Her eyes widened. "You and me? Why?"

But she knew why, even before he told her.

"Because you're a Delacroix," Matt said. "The fabulous Jax Delacroix," he added, imitating his daughter's excited inflection of the phrase. "A world-class equestrian and Olympic medal winner. You've been a topic of conversation in this town for years. Now that you're back for good, the least little thing you do is considered worthy of discussion." He forked up a bite of salad, chewing and swallowing before he continued. "Especially since this is the first time you've been out on a date since you moved back." The look in his eyes, the tone of his voice, made it a question more than a statement. "Everyone will be wondering what it means."

"Ah..." Jax didn't know what it meant, beyond the fact that she found him wildly, even irresistibly, attractive. She hadn't formulated any plans, made any decisions concerning him beyond dinner tonight. Becky Lynn Dooley down at the Dairy Queen knew as much about what it meant as she did. "It means we're having dinner together," she said primly, the look in her gray eyes daring him to deny it.

Matt met her look head-on. "Is that all?"

It wasn't all, of course. If having dinner together was all they were doing, she wouldn't be sitting there with her stomach jumping to beat the band, wondering how to answer him without getting herself in deeper than she already was. All sorts of other things were going on between them on some subliminal man-woman level. Things she wasn't quite ready to acknowledge, let alone put a name to.

"I'd think people would be more interested in why you're having dinner with me, instead of the other way around," Jax said, trying to focus the attention away from herself and her motives. "You said I'm the first woman you've been out with since your wife died. I'd think the actions of a lifelong resident of Bayou Beltane would be of more interest to the gossips than those of somebody who hasn't been around for nearly ten years."

"You'd think so, wouldn't you?" Matt agreed. "But then, I'm not a Delacroix."

"You're kidding, right?"

Matt couldn't help but grin at the incredulity in her tone. "You *were* away for a long time, weren't you?"

"Sometimes it seems like a lifetime," Jax admitted. "Other times..." She shook her head. "When I was a kid, my father was always telling us how important it was to behave ourselves because people in Bayou Beltane expected more of a Delacroix. Heaven forbid we should ever get into trouble or cause a scandal, because people would talk. I took it to heart—more than any of my sisters, I think, and certainly more than Beau ever did. I always tried to avoid doing anything that would cause talk. That one incident with Billy Ray notwithstanding," she added with a smile. "Later, after I'd been living in Paris for a while, where the name Delacroix isn't such a big deal, I guess I kind of forgot how it had been."

"Had been, still is and always will be, forever and ever, amen," Matt said. "Life in a small town rarely changes. Thank God."

"You don't mind the gossip?"

"It's not a matter of minding or not minding it." He leaned back in his chair, allowing the waitress to take away his salad plate and put down his entrée. "It just *is*, like the heat and humidity in the summertime."

"Yes, but doesn't it *bother* you?"

"Not really. But then, my name's not Delacroix." He shrugged. "And I've never given the town tabbies much to gossip about, anyway."

Not since his brand-new bride had delivered a seven-month baby, anyway, but Jax wouldn't know about that. She'd already divorced Greg Martin and left Bayou Beltane by the time Matt had graduated from college and returned home to settle down with his little family. Even then there hadn't been much talk; "premature" first babies weren't all that rare, and the young parents had done the right thing. As far as the people of Bayou Beltane were concerned, that was pretty much all that mattered.

"There was a lot of talk when Livvy was first diagnosed with cancer," Matt continued, almost as if he were thinking out loud, "but that wasn't really gossip, not the way you mean. It was more of a comfort, really, a way for our friends and neighbors to let us know they cared and were concerned for our welfare. In a big city like New Orleans or New York or Paris, people would have minded their own business and we'd have been left to deal with it alone."

"I can see that, I guess," Jax agreed, wondering if knowing other people cared would have comforted her all those years ago. "Still…"

"Still, I'm not a Delacroix," Matt finished for her, "so I'm not subject to the same level of scrutiny you are."

"If we go out to dinner again, you will be. Subject to scrutiny, I mean." Jax lifted a teasing eyebrow. "Think you can handle it?"

"Oh, I think—"

"Good evening, Jacqueline. I hope I'm not interrupting?"

Jax looked up, startled by the voice at her elbow. "Uncle

Philip,'' she said, hiding her grimace of distaste behind a polite smile as she offered her hand. ''No, you're not interrupting anything,'' she lied graciously. ''How are you?''

''Fine, fine.'' He nodded over her hand, holding on to it for a second or two longer than she was comfortable with. ''And you, my dear? How are you doing?''

''Fine, thank you, Uncle Philip.''

Despite his resemblance to her grandfather, which should have predisposed her in his favor, she had never liked her great-uncle. There was something just a bit too practiced about Philip Delacroix's good ol' boy Southern charm. Too slick, as if he could turn it on and off at will. Jax had always had the urge to count her fingers when he let go of her hand.

''You know Matt Taggart, don't you?'' she said, surreptitiously wiping her palm on the napkin in her lap.

''Yes, of course. Known him since he was knee-high to a grasshopper.'' Philip flashed a genial smile. ''How are you, Taggart?''

''Fine, sir.'' Matt rose to shake the senator's hand, then stayed on his feet as Philip Delacroix introduced his dinner companion.

''I'd like you both to meet Katherine Beaufort. Katherine, this is Matt Taggart.''

The two shook hands and murmured the usual pleasantries.

''And this lovely young lady is one of my great-nieces, Jacqueline Delacroix Martin.''

''It's just Delacroix now, Uncle Philip,'' Jax reminded him, smiling through gritted teeth. For some reason, Philip pretended to forget that fact, insisting on addressing her as if she were still married. ''I dropped the Martin ten years ago.'' She stood and offered her hand to the other woman. ''Jax Delacroix,'' she said firmly. ''I'm very pleased to meet you.''

"Katherine is in town to buy antiques," Philip said. "She's been doing her best to try to talk me out of some of my pre-Civil War treasures, but she's just going to have to go home empty-handed this time, I'm afraid." He took one of Katherine's hands in both of his as he spoke and gave it a paternal pat.

Jax thought it was to the other woman's credit that she didn't look as if she appreciated the patronizing little gesture, or the touch of his hands on hers. Jax wondered what a seemingly nice woman like Katherine Beaufort was doing with Philip Delacroix. She wasn't even remotely his type. She had too much class, for one thing, and she looked intelligent.

"I understand you bought some lovely antiques while you were racketing around Europe, Jacqueline. Perhaps Katherine would be interested in seeing them."

Jax shook her head. "They're not for sale," she said, before Katherine Beaufort could say whether she was interested in seeing them or not.

"But surely you can't have room for them in that tiny cabin you're living in over at Riverwood," Philip said, his voice dripping with false concern. "Now, if you were still the chatelaine of that lovely house at Martin Farms, you might have a reason to keep them. As it is..." He sighed and shook his head.

"I have plenty of room for them, Uncle Philip, but thank you for thinking of me. Now, if you don't mind, I really hate to be rude but..." She gestured toward the table, where her and Matt's entrées were rapidly cooling.

"Oh, yes, how thoughtless of me," Philip said smoothly. "Please, sit down. Enjoy your dinner, you two. The sole here is excellent," he added, approving her choice. "And, Jacqueline, do give some thought to showing Katherine those antiques of yours. I'm sure she could give you a good price."

"I'm sure she could, too, Uncle Philip, if they were for sale. A pleasure to meet you, Ms. Beaufort," she added, with a nod at Katherine. "Oh…Uncle Philip," she said, as if she had just remembered something. "Please give my best to Drew, will you? He looked a bit…" She hesitated just long enough to have the three people listening to her wonder if she was going to say what they all knew she really meant. "*Ill* when he rushed out of here earlier," she said sweetly, all cousinly concern and manufactured innocence. "He was in such a hurry, I didn't even get a chance to say hello."

All the warmth drained from Philip Delacroix's eyes. "I'll be sure to tell him you asked after him," he said, and turned away.

"Oh, that was nasty." Matt gave a mock shudder when the senator and his dinner companion were gone. "Remind me never to get between two Delacroix with their claws out."

Jax picked up her fork and stabbed it into a glazed baby carrot. "He started it," she said, refusing to feel guilty for her bad manners.

Except that she did.

Respect for her elders had been drilled into her from the cradle, along with a whole host of other inconvenient virtues. Being a genteel Southern lady was hell sometimes, especially when you had absorbed the lessons too well for your own good. Just once before she died she'd like to let loose and tell someone—*anyone*—exactly what she thought, with no pussyfooting around or polite subterfuge to obscure the truth. But Jax knew it would likely never happen.

As a child, she'd absorbed the unspoken lesson that discretion was the better part of valor, at least in the Delacroix family. Her father had hovered on the edges of her childhood, a distant, if loving authority figure, too involved in his law practice to be emotionally available to his children. Her mother, though more emotionally present, had always seemed to be struggling under the weight of her myriad responsibilities as the wife of an up-and-coming attorney and the mother of five young children.

As a consequence, Jax had learned at a young age to keep her feelings to herself and not burden other people with her problems. The squeaky wheel had not gotten the grease in her family but, rather, a stern lecture on self-restraint and what was due the Delacroix name. Harsh feelings were hidden inside. Harsh words were left unspoken. Be a good girl. Don't cause trouble. Don't call attention to yourself, unless that attention brought glory on the family name.

All of the Delacroix kids had absorbed that lesson to some extent. They were all high achievers, always striving to be the best in their chosen fields. Even Marie, who'd dropped out of premed at Tulane in her sophomore year, had parlayed her interest in herbs and folk medicine into a successful business.

"Shall I ask the waitress to take that back to the kitchen and bring you something else?"

Jax blinked. "Excuse me?"

Matt gestured at her plate with his fork. "You're not eating. I thought there might be something wrong with your fish."

"Oh, no. No. The fish is fine. I was just..." She speared a bite of fish on the tines of her fork and lifted it to her mouth. "Lovely," she said, after she had swallowed. "It has a very delicate flavor. I'm glad you recommended it."

"You were just...what?" Matt asked.

Jax shook her head. "Nothing, really. I let Uncle Philip get to me, is all, and sniped back. I should have just ignored it."

"Instead of sinking to his level, you mean?"

"Something like that."

"Well, don't worry about it," Matt reassured her with a teasing smile. "Your image is safe with me."

"My image?"

"I won't tell anyone that the fabulous Jax has a bitchy side."

Jax smiled. No one had ever called her bitchy before, even indirectly. She kind of enjoyed it. "I knew there was something I liked about you," she said.

They conversed easily through the rest of dinner, keeping it light and impersonal, pretending they didn't feel the little flicker of heat each time their gazes met over the width of the linen-draped table. By the time they'd finished their entrées and the waitress had cleared their plates to make room for the crème brûlée, the brief glances had become lingering looks, rife with a combination of speculation and shyness, anticipation and restraint.

"Would you like coffee?" Matt smiled across the table at Jax as the creamy dessert was set before them. "Maybe an espresso?"

"Yes, espresso would be—"

Jax's beeper went off.

She reached for her purse and opened it, silencing the annoying little beep as she checked the number displayed on the tiny screen. The gesture was unnecessary. She already knew who was calling because she was carrying the beeper for only one reason: she had three mares due to go into labor at any time.

"Excuse me," she said, sliding her chair back and rising to her feet before Matt could move to assist her. "I've got to call the farm."

She hadn't taken more than two steps when Matt's beeper when off behind her. If they were calling the vet, it meant the laboring horse was in trouble. She hurried her pace, almost running to the telephone located in the restaurant's lobby. Matt was standing behind her when she cradled the receiver. She turned to him, her face drained of color.

"It's King Lear," she said, her eyes huge in the sudden paleness of her face. "Bear thinks he was poisoned."

"JUST WHAT THE HELL KIND of performance was that?" Philip Delacroix demanded of his son later that night. He'd found Drew closeted in the den of the big old antebellum house they shared, sitting in front of a fire with the lights out, brooding into a glass of bourbon. Philip snapped on the lamp on the desk. "You were supposed to charm Katherine Beaufort, and instead you end up getting drunk and insulting her."

Drew looked up at his father over the heavy crystal glass of bourbon in his hand. "I'm not drunk. Yet," he added, and took another sip of the fiery liquid. It burned as it went down but didn't quite take the edge off all the roiling emotions inside him. "I haven't insulted her, either. I merely asked her what she's really doing in Bayou Beltane."

"Dammit, Drew, that's as good as calling her a liar. That's a hell of a way to get on a woman's good side, boy."

"Well, isn't that what you think she is? A liar? Isn't that why you asked me to *charm* her? So you could find out what she's really up to?"

"And you're doing a piss-poor job of it, too," Philip spat. "This time you screwed up in front of a whole goddamned restaurant full of people. Jacqueline was there with Matt Taggart. She saw the whole thing, and then had the gall to call me on it."

"Little Jax and Matt Taggart, huh?" Drew raised his glass. "Here's to 'em. They both deserve a little happiness," he said, and drained his glass.

"And what about what I deserve?" Philip said. "You given any thought to that lately?"

Drew nodded ponderously. "I think about it all the time. All the damn time. Damn it to hell!" He rose from the depths of the leather easy chair in one smooth movement, his natural grace obscuring the amount of bourbon in his system. "I need another drink."

"You get yourself another drink," Philip said. "Go right ahead. In the meantime, I'll get Jackson to take over the job, since you haven't got the stomach for it," he said, watching his son for a reaction.

"Fine," Drew said, his voice expressionless, denying his father the response he was looking for. "Let your pet cur try to charm that prickly little Goody Two-shoes." He grinned with evil enjoyment, just thinking of Katherine Beaufort's reaction to Jackson Boudreaux's oily brand of charm. The expression made him look like a fallen angel. "But I warn you right now, she won't give him the time of day. Besides, she's not his type." Drew flung himself back into his chair, sloshing bourbon over the rim of his glass. He tilted his head slightly and licked at the backs of his fingers, catching the errant droplets on his tongue. "Boudreaux only goes for little girls who don't have enough experience to see through his bullshit."

"She's his type if I say she's his type," Philip said. "He'll do whatever it takes to find out why she's here in Bayou Beltane, snooping around and asking questions about some forgotten murder trial and a judge who's been dead for decades, all the while pretending she's only interested in antiques and acting as if butter wouldn't melt in her mouth."

"Why do you care what she knows about an old trial?"

"Because it involves the last case your great-grandfather Hamilton ever tried, that's why. Because it was the only murder trial he ever lost. You mark my words." Philip pointed a bony finger at his son. "That little girl is looking to bring scandal down on this family, one way or another.

I'm not sure yet if she's out for herself, or working for that Johnny-come-lately who's running for my senate seat, but one way or another she means trouble. And I mean to put a stop to it before it happens. This family can't afford another scandal.''

''You mean your campaign can't afford another scandal.''

''One and the same,'' Philip snapped, disgusted that he even had to point that out to his son. ''You see where all this drinking is getting you, boy? It's fogged up your brain so you can't see anything clear anymore.''

That wasn't the real problem, though, Drew thought as he slouched there in the leather chair, staring into the bourbon in his glass long after his father had left. The real problem was that, no matter how much he drank lately—and he was drinking a lot—he was still seeing some things far too clearly.

With a strangled oath, he drew back his arm and heaved the glass into the fireplace, shattering it into a thousand pieces.

It didn't make him feel any better.

CHAPTER FIVE

THE STALLION WAS ON his feet when Jax and Matt arrived at the stables. Barely. He was trembling and sweating, his gait hesitant as Bear slowly walked him around the paddock in an effort to relieve the animal's obvious pain. It almost seemed as if Bear's hand on his lead was the only thing keeping him upright.

Jax gathered up her dress in one hand and slipped between the rungs of the paddock fence without waiting for Matt to open the gate. "What happened?" she demanded, reaching out to touch Lear's damp neck. "How is he?"

The stallion, which normally would have nickered and butted against her in greeting, regarded her with dull, pain-filled eyes.

"He's not as bad as I first thought," Bear said, "but bad enough. He was thrashing around on the floor of his stall when I came down to make my final rounds before hitting the sack. I got him on his feet, and the pain seems to have eased up a little since then."

"You said something about poison?" Matt said.

Bear reached inside his shirt with his free hand, pulling out what looked like a child's toy. "I found this hanging over the stall door," he said, passing it to Matt.

"What the hell?" Matt turned it over in his hands, swiveling his body so that light from the open barn door fell on the object.

It was a small horse, made of straw, with a tail and mane that appeared to be real horse hair. Several pins were stuck in its stomach, driven all the way in so that only the round plastic heads were showing. Around its neck was a garland of green leaves shaped like the horseshoe of roses traditionally draped around the necks of winning racehorses. Matt took a step closer to the light and studied it more closely.

He jerked his head up and looked back at Bear. "Oleander?"

Bear nodded.

Jax gasped and pressed her hand to her mouth.

Oleander was extremely toxic to horses, and there was no known treatment. All you could do was treat the symptoms and hope for the best. If the horse hadn't ingested too much of it, he might recover. And then again, he might not.

"But why would anyone want to poison Lear?" Jax asked.

"I'm not completely sure that anyone has," Bear said.

"But you said..." Jax shook her head in confusion, gesturing at the crude little toy in Matt's hand. "The oleander?"

"I may have jumped to conclusions." Bear stopped the horse in the light from the barn as Matt reached out to press his fingers flat against the animal's jawbone to check his pulse. "Which is probably what whoever hung that thing over the stall wanted me to do," Bear added sourly.

"I don't understand," Jax said.

"His pulse is a little on the high side, but it's regular," Matt said. Lear moaned and pawed the ground, twisting his head around to stare at his belly, as if trying to see the cause of his distress. "Oleander poisoning causes a very fast, irregular heartbeat." He glanced at Bear. "Has there been any diarrhea?"

The trainer shook his head.

"It usually causes severe diarrhea, too," Matt said, handing the straw horse back to Bear and bending to examine the stallion more closely. "And coldness in the extremities."

He ran his palm down the horse's legs, careful to angle himself out of the way of the animal's hind feet, since colicky horses often kicked at their bellies in an effort to relieve the pain. The stallion's legs were wet with sweat but as warm as the rest of the big animal.

"It's too soon to be absolutely sure, but I don't think he's ingested any oleander," Matt said. "Let's get him into a stall so I can take a better look." He glanced at Jax. "Why don't you go change your clothes?" he suggested.

Jax started to object, then realized he was right. She would be more a hindrance than a help the way she was dressed. She gathered the skirt of her dress in both hands and sprinted toward the neat row of cabins at the back of the big house.

Three of them were dark—the two that were unoccupied and Beau's. His Porsche was gone from in front of his cabin, too, making her think he must be out on a date. The porch light was on over her front door, its soft golden glow attracting moths and other suicidal night flyers.

She let herself into the cabin quickly but quietly, tiptoeing into the bedroom to avoid waking her sleeping sister. But Charly was a light sleeper—and she had a cop's instincts. She raised her head from the pillow and peered into the darkness.

"Jax? That you?"

"Yes," Jax whispered. She slipped off the silver cuff bracelet and the beaded necklace, dropping them unceremoniously on top of her dresser, then tugged the black T-shirt dress off over her head. It landed on the floor. "Go back to sleep."

"You're home early."

"Bear paged me." She reached into the closet and

yanked a shirt off its hanger. "One of my horses has colic."

"How bad is it?"

"It's too soon to tell." With the shirt hanging open, Jax pulled out a drawer and grabbed the first pair of jeans that came to hand. "Could be simple indigestion, could be a twisted gut." She yanked the jeans up over her slim hips and zipped them. "Or it could be oleander poisoning."

Charly pushed herself up onto an elbow. "Poison?"

"It's probably colic." Jax grabbed up her boots and sat down on the end of the bed to pull them on. "Matt said the symptoms were wrong for oleander. I hope to God he's right because there's nothing we can do if it *is* oleander except pray and hope Lear didn't eat enough of it to kill him."

"But we don't have any oleander plants on the place, do we?"

"No." Jax got up and then, following an impulse she didn't know she had, bent over and kissed her sister on the forehead. "You lie down now and go back to sleep, baby. I have to get back to the barn. I'll let you know what happened in the morning."

SHE WAS BREATHLESS when she reached the barn, not so much from running as from anxiety over the condition of her horse. Even if he hadn't been poisoned, colic was still the number-one killer of horses. Ten percent of colic cases were fatal.

They'd put King Lear in the stall opposite his usual one, fearing the possibility of oleander leaves in his bedding. He was down again, lying quietly on his side in the straw with Bear at his head. The trainer held a twitch clamped to the horse's upper lip to keep him that way while Matt administered painkillers and sedatives, and did a rectal exam.

"He may not have been poisoned with oleander," Bear

said furiously when Jax came into the stall, "but somebody deliberately caused him to colic." He jerked his head toward the abandoned stall across the aisle. "There're grass clippings mixed with finely ground wheat grain in his feed bucket."

Wheat grain wasn't a part of King Lear's diet. And no grain was ever finely ground, for any horse. Like grass clippings, it tended to compact and clog in a horse's intestines, causing just the sort of problem they were facing now.

"He has an impaction," Matt said, sinking back on his heels, out of the way of Lear's hooves. He stood up, stripping a long, plastic sleeve down his arm as he rose, dropping it inside out into the metal bucket set well back in a corner of the large stall.

"The painkiller and sedative have started to take effect," he said, looking down at the horse. Lear was still breathing a bit heavily, but he'd stopped the restless gyrations that indicated he was in severe pain. "Let's do a peritoneal tap before we get him on his feet. I want to take a look at what might be floating around inside him before I give him a laxative."

Using a long needle inserted into the underside of the belly, Matt extracted some of the fluid surrounding the horse's intestines, placing it into a sterile container to be taken back to his lab and examined later. He did the same with the blood sample he took next. If the animal died, at least they might be able to tell if he'd actually been poisoned or not.

"Okay, let's get him up."

The stallion came to his feet easily, without undue groaning or wincing, indicating that the sedative and painkiller were indeed doing their jobs. With Jax and Bear to assist him, Matt threaded a four-foot-long tube into the horse's nose, waiting until the animal swallowed to ease it into his esophagus and down into his stomach. After extracting some clear, watery fluid in his stomach—also to be checked at the lab—he administered a gallon of mineral oil. He checked the horse's vital signs again after he removed the tube.

"Everything looks as good as can be expected," Matt said. "His temperature is normal. The pulse is a little fast but not dangerously so." He peeled back one of Lear's eyelids, checking the color of the membrane, then did the same for his lips. "Color's good. No signs of cyanosis." Cyanosis, or blueness, would indicate a lack of oxygen in the blood, pointing to possible poisoning rather than colic. Matt pressed a thumb to the horse's gums for a moment, producing a small white spot, then drew it away, watching to see how fast the color returned. "Capillary refill time is well within normal limits." He ran his hand down the horse's long, sleek neck in a caressing gesture. "All we can do now is walk him around to get the gut moving and hope nature takes its course."

An hour later, nature did.

Within fifteen minutes after that, Lear was almost his old self, head up, ears cocked, looking at the people around him with interest and attention. They put him in a spanking clean stall, freshly swept, with new straw bedding, and a small flake of hay in the rack for added roughage in case he felt like eating. He looked as if he had come through the experience without any lasting ill effects, but he would be watched closely, his diet even more carefully monitored than usual for at least forty-eight hours to make sure his delicate digestive system was back on track.

"Leave that alone for now," Matt said, stopping Jax when she picked up a pitchfork and headed for King Lear's regular stall to muck it out.

"It's all right," Jax said, thinking he was objecting because of the lateness of the hour. "It needs to be done sooner or later, and I'm too keyed up to turn in yet."

"That's not what I meant." He plucked the pitchfork out of her hand and set it against the wall. "The police are going to want to look at the stall the way it is."

"The police?"

"Lear was deliberately given food that would colic him. He may or may not have been given oleander—I won't know for sure until I can do some tests. But I do know that a crime was committed. Whether it comes under the heading of cruelty to animals or destruction of property or simple vandalism, I don't know. That'll be up to Sheriff Trahan to decide. Bear's gone to call him."

THEY HEARD JAKE TRAHAN arrive twenty minutes later, his boot heels clicking against the hard-packed earth floor as he made his way down the center aisle of the big barn and up the short flight of wooden stairs to the office, tucked into the farthest corner of the building.

"Coffee, Sheriff?" Matt asked, his hand already on the handle of the coffeepot when Jake rapped lightly on the open door to announce himself.

"Don't mind if I do," Jake said pleasantly, his voice low and unhurried, as he stepped into the office. Everything about Jake Trahan was unhurried. "And it's Chief now, remember?"

Matt handed him the coffee, black. "I'll try to remember that." One corner of his mouth lifted in a grin. "Sheriff."

Jake sighed. He'd been the sheriff of St. Tammany Parish for three years and the chief of police in Bayou Beltane for only a few months. It was taking a while for those he served and protected to get used to the change.

"Ms Delacroix." He lifted his forefinger to the brim of his hat in a brief salute. "I don't believe we've actually met, ma'am. I'm Jake Trahan. *Chief* Jake Trahan."

"I remember you from high school. You were a couple of years ahead of me," she said, smiling at him from her seat on the cracked leather sofa that stretched along one wall of the office. "And call me Jax, please—" she paused "—Sheriff," she added, with the exact tone and inflection Matt had used.

Jake Trahan grinned at her over the rim of his coffee mug, then took a slow sip, savoring the brew. He hitched a hip up onto the corner of the big wooden desk opposite her. "What's this Bear tells me about someone trying to poison one of your horses?"

"We aren't sure he was actually poisoned." Matt sat down on the arm of the sagging sofa next to Jax, coffee mug in hand. "We won't know that until I've had a chance to run some toxicity tests on the fluid samples I took. But somebody sure as hell tried to kill him. There were grass clippings in his feed bucket."

"How can grass clippings hurt a horse?" Jake asked. "That's what they eat out in the pasture, isn't it? Grass?"

"Grazing is a whole different thing, and even that has to be approached carefully if a horse has been strictly hay and grain fed. Especially if the horse is a pampered Thoroughbred," Matt said, and explained briefly about a horse's delicate digestive system and how easily it could be upset or compromised.

"Where does the poison come into this?" Jake asked when Matt had finished his explanation. "Was it mixed in with the grass clippings?"

"Somebody tried to hex him." Bear reached inside his shirt, pulling out the straw horse, and handed it to Jake. "That's oleander hanging around its neck. Highly toxic to horses. People, too."

Jake put his coffee down next to his hip on the desk and took the object from Bear.

"Hexed?" Jax said, looking back and forth between the two men.

"It's a voodoo fetish. A gris-gris," Jake said, turning it over in his hands as he examined it. "That's a kind of charm to focus the hex," he explained to Jax. "This thing is supposed to represent the horse that was poisoned. Makes the hex stronger."

"I know what voodoo is, Chief," Jax said. She had, after all, grown up in southern Louisiana. "What I don't know is why someone would want to use it against one of our horses."

"Do you know a woman named Flora Boudreaux?"

"I know *of* her. She's the mother of the boy my youngest cousin is dating. Not a very nice woman, from what I understand. She's reputed to be some kind of—" Jax's voice trailed off as she realized the significance of what she was about to say "—voodoo priestess," she finished, falling silent again as her mind jumped from one supposition to another. "Are you saying you think Flora Boudreaux had something to do with that?" She pointed at the object in his hand.

"No. I'm just saying that, in these parts, when a situation involves voodoo it usually involves Flora Boudreaux, too, in one way or another. Maybe only to the extent that she made this for someone without knowing what it was for." He put the gris-gris down on the desk and picked up his coffee. "Unless you can think of something you might have done to make her mad?"

"No." Jax shook her head. "As I said, I don't really know her."

"How about the rest of her family? Any bad blood there?"

Good question, thought Jax, wondering how to answer it. There was certainly no bad blood as far as she was concerned, but since the whole business about Uncle William and the deed and everything had come up, there might very well be some ill will coming from *somewhere*. Although why anyone would take their feelings out on her horse was another question entirely.

"No," Jax said, automatically shielding the family. "No bad blood. I barely know the Boudreaux family, really. Desiree, of course, but everyone in town knows Desiree. I've run into her a few times here and there since I've been back, and I've used a couple of her herbal poultices on my horses, but that's pretty much the extent of our acquaintance. Jackson Boudreaux, Flora Boudreaux's eldest son, works for my Uncle Philip, but again, I couldn't really say that I *know* him. I doubt I've exchanged more than a few words with him in my entire life. As for her second son..." Jax shrugged. "All I know about him is that he's got a bad reputation and Joanna's worried sick because Nikki is dating him. But I doubt I'd recognize him if I passed him on the street."

"You probably want to keep it that way," Jake advised, and sipped at his coffee, regarding her thoughtfully over the rim of the mug. "Have you got any enemies?"

"Not that I know of."

"Fired anybody lately?"

"Bear would know more about that than I do. He and Beau do most of the hiring and firing."

"What about ex-boyfriends? Is there someone hanging around who might still be carrying a torch?"

"No," she said firmly.

The only ex she had in Bayou Beltane was her ex-husband, Greg Martin, and he'd hardly be carrying a torch for her. He was the one who had ended the marriage. She hadn't seen or spoken to him or anyone in his family in nearly ten years.

"What about somebody who'd rather not have to compete against your horse at the racetrack?"

"King Lear isn't a racehorse," Jax said. "He's an event horse. Dressage, open jumping and cross country," she added at Jake's questioning look.

"Do event horses get trophies like this when they win?" He reached down and tapped the horseshoe-shaped garland of oleander leaves with the tip of one finger.

"No, not usually. They get trophies like those."

She gestured at the wall behind her. Mixed in with the racing trophies and framed photographs of Delacroix Farm's prize winners—human as well as equine—were dozens of ribbons, mostly blue, and two shiny Olympic medals mounted in a locked, glass-fronted display case.

"I guess there's a lot of money involved?"

"If you mean winnings, no, not really. Not like in racing. Eventing competitions are more about prestige and points than money. Over the long haul, the purses usually don't even add up to enough to cover expenses. There can be big money in breeding, though, if you have a champion. Bloodlines count as much in event horses as they do in racehorses."

"And this King Lear is a champion?"

She gestured at the shadow box on the wall again. "I was riding him when I won those."

"I expect you carry a lot of insurance on him?"

"Of course. He's a very valuable animal."

Matt put his hand on Jax's shoulder. Startled, she shifted her gaze to his face to see what he wanted, but he wasn't even looking at her. His gaze was fastened on the police chief, his expression intent, full of a subtle warning that somehow made her feel both protected and desired at the same time.

"What are you suggesting, Jake?" His low voice held the same subtle note of warning.

"I'm not suggesting anything." Jake's gaze shifted from

Matt to Jax and back again. "I'm just trying to get a feel for things."

"Well, that particular feeling is dead wrong."

"I don't doubt it," Jake agreed easily. He tipped his head back, swallowing the last of his coffee, and picked up the voodoo fetish. "I guess I'd better go take a look at where you found this."

"I'll show him," Bear said when Jax moved to get up off of the sofa. "You finish your coffee, girl, then get yourself into bed. You look beat."

"I love you, too, Bear," she said easily, and put her hand to her mouth to stifle a yawn. She hadn't realized how tired she was until he mentioned it. The roller coaster emotions of the evening, from nervous excitement to anxiety to near panic to relief, had apparently taken a toll on her without her noticing. "Thanks."

"I'll need written statements from all three of you," Jake said, pausing in the doorway Bear had just gone through. "You can drop by the station one day early next week, whenever it's convenient. I'll want the results of those toxicity tests, too, Matt."

"Sure thing." Matt rose from his seat on the arm of the sofa as he spoke. "I'll get them to you as soon as they're written up." He extended his hand to the police chief. "Thanks for coming out so late."

"All part of the job. Jax." He nodded politely from the open doorway. "It was a real pleasure to finally meet you."

"Likewise, Chief," she said, sketching a brief nod in return.

"One more thing... I don't know what kind of security measures you're used to taking around here, but I'd advise you to think seriously about increasing them. This might not be an isolated incident."

Jax nodded again. "I'll talk to Beau about it first thing tomorrow."

"You do that." Jake touched two fingers to the brim of his hat and turned to follow Bear down the stairs.

Jax sat for a moment, thinking about what Jake had said, listening to the rhythmic sound of the men's footsteps on the wooden stairs. Bear's tread was softer, more measured, followed by the sharp, authoritative click of Jake's boot heels. She could hear the faint murmur of their voices, growing fainter, then fading altogether as they made their way toward King Lear's stall at the other end of the barn. Crickets chirped. A dove cooed from the rafters. A horse nickered softly, blowing a sleepy greeting through its nose. Wood and hinges creaked as Lear's stall door was opened.

The familiar, peaceful sounds should have been comforting. Instead, they made Jax think of how vulnerable they all were. As far as she knew, they'd never had a problem with crime at Delacroix Farms before, not even petty theft. As a result, the only thing they had that even resembled a security system was the closed-circuit camera setup in the foaling barn, which had been installed to help monitor the mares that were near term. Up to now, barn doors had been closed only to keep out the weather. Latches and locks were used to keep horses in, not keep intruders out.

In the space of an evening, all that had changed. Bear, she knew, would sleep in the barn tonight to guard against a repeat of what had happened to King Lear. Tomorrow, he and Beau would take whatever steps were necessary to keep something like this from happening again.

Jax sighed and rose to her feet, intending to collect the empty coffee mugs from around the office and rinse them out in preparation for the next day before she went to bed.

But Matt had beat her to it. "Sit," he said, waving her back down with one hand.

"You didn't have to do that," Jax protested, but she sat.

"It's done." Matt tossed the paper towel he'd been using to wipe the mugs with into the trash can next to the desk.

"You look about done, too. Bear was right." He reclaimed his seat on the arm of the sofa and looked down at her. "You look beat."

She gave him a wry little smile. "Thanks."

"On you, beat looks good," he assured her. "Kind of frail and vulnerable."

"Little old ladies are frail," she informed him dryly.

"Did I say frail? I meant fragile." He tilted his head as if to study her from another angle. Her skin was as pale and creamy as magnolia petals, so delicate it seemed as if he might bruise her with the merest brush of his fingertips. "Definitely fragile. You look like some exotic hothouse flower just beginning to droop on its stem."

"Droop?"

He grinned at her dour tone. "It's very becoming," he assured her. Very—" he reached out to tuck a strand of hair behind her ear. It was as silky as he'd imagined it would be. As soft. His grin faded. "Sexy," he murmured as his fingertips drifted down the side of her neck.

Her own smile fading, Jax went stock-still, mesmerized by the sudden look of rapt fascination on his face.

His eyes were focused on his hand, following the motion of his fingers like a man totally enthralled by what he was touching. There was such gentleness in his expression. Such tenderness. Such naked desire. All mixed up with a look of dazzled wonder that made her insides quiver and melt.

"Matt," she murmured, not knowing if she spoke his name in acceptance or denial of what she saw in his eyes.

"I know," he whispered. "I know. I said we'd take our time getting to know each other, didn't I?" He traced the center line of her throat with his thumb...down...then up...slowly. "I said we'd take it step-by-step." He sketched the line of her jaw with a whisper-soft caress, skimmed the curve of her lush bottom lip. "I said we'd take it slow until we knew where it was going.'' His fingers were at her nape now, under the heavy curtain of her hair. "And I am taking it slow. I *will* take it slow. I just..."

He moved his hand up into her hair, his palm curving to conform to the shape of her skull, and lifted his other hand, the one with the horseshoe-shaped scar on the back of it, to the other side of her head to hold her still. He didn't seem to realize that she hadn't moved a muscle, except to say his name.

"One kiss," he murmured as he lowered his head. "Just one—" he gently pressed the pads of his thumbs against the underside of her chin, tilting it up "—kiss."

Jax closed her eyes, letting her head fall back into the cradle of his palms as his mouth touched hers.

His lips were warm and soft. They tasted her with subtle delicacy, not taking more than she was willing to give. His hands in her hair were as careful as if she were made of spun glass. He held his body away from hers, not pressing, not encroaching, not invading her space with the demands she knew he wanted to make. He was trembling.

Such exquisite gentleness.

Such fierce tenderness.

Such blatant, unabashed, flagrant desire, held oh-so-carefully in check.

The combination of passion and restraint was irresistible. Unaware of her own movements, responding only to the intensity of his need and the feelings it aroused in her, Jax lifted her hands to his thighs to steady herself and leaned into him, opening her mouth beneath his.

With her unspoken acquiescence, the nature of the kiss changed, became deeper, wetter, hotter. His mouth opened over hers, all searing heat and intemperate, tempestuous passion. His tongue slid between her open lips. His hands tightened in her hair and then moved down, gliding over her slender back, pulling her close.

Half rising from the sofa, her small, firm breasts pressed against his unyielding chest, her fingers biting into the hard muscles of his thighs, she strained upward, kissing him as passionately, as ardently as he was kissing her.

It seemed to go on forever, this erotic mating of their mouths. They stroked and explored with their tongues, tasting each other, savoring each other in an act nearly as intimate as sex. His breathing was slow and deep, each breath dragged up from the depths of his laboring lungs. She could feel his heart thudding in his chest, pounding out the rhythm of passion against her breasts. Her own heart was fluttering like a bird's, flinging itself against her rib cage like a wild thing. Her breath was caught somewhere in her throat.

And still the kiss went on.

He slid down from his perch on the arm of the sofa, one knee between her and the cushioned back of the sofa, his other leg stretched out and braced against the floor. Her hands slid up his thighs as he moved toward her, gliding over his hips to his waist and around his back, gripping the fabric of his soft knit shirt in her fists as he gathered her closer. His hands slid lower, cupping her bottom, lifting her into the rock-hard erection straining against the fly of his pressed khaki slacks.

She felt encompassed by him. Surrounded by his big, hard body, sheltered in the trembling strength of his arms, she was overwhelmed by the sheer intensity of his hunger for her. She'd never been wanted the way he wanted her. She'd never made a man tremble with the force of his desire. And no man had made her tremble, either, except in fear and shame.

The urge to surrender, to succumb to the rampaging desire in his kiss, was strong. So strong she didn't even think—couldn't think—of resisting it. Time didn't matter. Place didn't matter. Nothing mattered except this feeling surging between them. Not his kids. Not her own insecurities and inadequacies. Nothing. Without breaking the kiss, she leaned backward, silently urging him to press her down onto the sofa and do with her what he would.

Matt nearly lost his head. For one brief, delicious, delirious moment, he almost believed it would happen. Almost believed he could throw caution to the winds and *let* it happen. God knew, he *wanted* it to happen. With every fiber of his being, he wanted it. Wanted her. He was tied up in knots, wanting her.

He slid his hands up to her back, halting her downward movement, and lifted his mouth from hers.

Jax tightened her arms around him and pressed a soft, openmouthed kiss to his throat. "Matt," she murmured, her voice low and husky. "Oh, Matt."

Every muscle in his body tightened at the sensual invitation in her voice. It was the most seductive sound he had ever heard. *She* was the most seductive woman he'd ever held in his arms. Soft and warm and more than willing. And he wanted her more than he wanted his next breath.

"That was some kiss," he said gruffly, in a voice that sounded as if it came from somebody else.

"Mmm," she agreed, and nuzzled his cheek, trying to recapture his mouth with hers. "More."

He shifted his hands to her shoulders and held her a little away from him, waiting until she opened her eyes to look at him before he tried to explain.

"Matt?" she said, blinking in confusion.

"I don't have anything with me. Protection," he said when she continued to stare up at him with a bewildered look in her eyes. "I didn't intend for things to go this far, this fast, and I—" he rubbed his hands up and down her biceps in a gesture meant to comfort them both "—don't have anything."

It took her a second or two to absorb his meaning. "Oh."

He was talking about birth control. "Oh, that's all—" She'd started to say it was all right, that he didn't need anything for birth control, and then clamped her lips shut. If she told him, he might think less of her. Her ex-husband had; he'd ended their marriage because of it.

"I'm sorry," Matt said, misinterpreting her expression. "I shouldn't have let it go this far. I shouldn't have even started it, I guess. It's just..." His one-sided smile was wry and self-mocking. "I've been wanting to kiss you for weeks."

"Weeks?"

"Months, really," he admitted. "I've been wanting to kiss you for months. Ever since you came back to Bayou Beltane, in fact."

Jax was charmed. And flattered. The little sting of rejection niggling at the back of her mind died before it had a chance to form into anything more than vague disappointment that their kisses wouldn't lead to more. "You never even gave me a hint."

"Because I didn't want you to know. I thought the feeling would go away and—" He broke off, shaking his head. "No, that's not true. I didn't say anything because I knew it would happen just this way. I knew if I kissed you, I'd go crazy. I just didn't know how crazy." He touched his forehead to hers. "You pack quite a punch, Ms Delacroix," he drawled, deliberately exaggerating his Louisiana accent to lighten the mood.

"I do?" she said, delighted. No one had ever said anything like that to her before. "Really?"

"You do," he affirmed, wondering why she seemed so surprised.

"So do you," Jax whispered. "Pack quite a punch, I mean," she added, and offered her lips.

He groaned and took them.

The kiss was hot and sweet and lasted long enough to have both of them breathing hard again when it was over.

"No more," he said, dragging his mouth from hers. "Please. I'll go stark-raving insane if we do that again."

"It's not my fertile time of the month," Jax said. It wasn't a lie. No time of the month was fertile for her. "We could—"

"No." He put her firmly away from him this time. "I won't take that chance. Not again."

"Again?"

He hesitated for a moment, debating with himself. "Livvy was pregnant when we got married," he said, deciding Jax had a right to know. After all, he'd just led her down the garden path, so to speak, and then stopped before they'd gone through the gate. "Don't get me wrong. I loved my wife." He'd learned to love her, after he'd gotten over feeling trapped. They'd had a pretty good marriage. Not a great one, but a good one. He'd have stayed married to her if she'd lived—for the children's sake, if nothing else.

"She was a wonderful woman and a really terrific mother. I can't even begin to imagine my life without Jeff and Amy, but being—" he hesitated, looking for the right word, one that wouldn't dishonor Livvy's memory; she had been no more to blame for what happened than he had "—being obliged to get married isn't the best way to start a relationship."

"No, I don't guess it would be."

"It wasn't something either of us had planned on, but we were careless and we got caught. I don't want to get caught like that again." He reached out and touched her cheek, disturbed by the look on her face. Her expression was strangely distraught. "It's for both our sakes, sweetheart. I hope you realize that."

"Yes, of course," Jax said, wondering if she should just go ahead and tell him he didn't have to worry about getting caught with her. But what did it matter, really? They weren't going to have sex. At least, not tonight. And when they did—*if* they did—he would be using protection. She'd never have to admit to her defects. He'd never have to know she was less than a complete woman. "The last thing I'd want is an unplanned pregnancy," she said firmly.

"I knew you'd understand," he said, relieved. He stroked his finger down her cheek. She might be as pale as magnolia blossoms, but the skin under his fingertip was so warm and alive, he could have sworn he could feel the blood coursing just below the alabaster surface. "Next time I'll be prepared. And, Jax—" he put his finger under her chin, turning her face up to his "—there *will* be a next time."

"You think so?" she said archly, trying to pretend a coolness she didn't feel.

"I know so. I haven't come this far to be scared off now." He pressed a soft kiss on her lips, then let her go and stood. "Come on," he said, holding out his hand. "I'll walk you to your door—" he sent her a sideways glance, rife with anticipation and undisguised desire "—and you can kiss me good-night and I'll try to cop a feel."

CHAPTER SIX

"Is that Amy up there on Rocky?"

Matt turned his head to look at the man who'd suddenly appeared beside him at the rail of the training ring. Beau Delacroix had his twin sister's gray eyes and thick dark hair, and there was something similar about the slant of their cheekbones, but that's where the resemblance ended. Jax Delacroix was all female, from the top of her glossy head to the toes of her well-polished boots; her brother was six feet plus of muscled male animal.

The two men had known each other nearly all their lives. They'd become fast friends in grade school, despite the year's difference in their ages, enduring the same scoldings from the stern-faced Sister Agnes for the same boyish misdeeds. They'd played on the same football team in high school, dated many of the same cheerleaders. Both of them lettered in track in the off season. College had separated them, and Matt's marriage to Livvy and subsequent early fatherhood had further divided their paths. On the surface, it didn't seem as if they had much in common anymore, and they didn't interact on a regular basis except where it concerned the health of the Thoroughbreds at Delacroix Farms, but the two men still considered themselves good friends.

"That's my little girl," Matt said with a pardonable touch of pride in his voice.

"Bear said she was a natural. As good as Jax was when she first started riding." Beau slanted a censuring look at the vet. "How come you waited so long to put her up on a horse?"

"Stupidity," Matt admitted easily. "I didn't think she was old enough to start riding until now."

"Jax started when she was four," Beau informed him. "She was winning first-place ribbons by the time she was Amy's age."

"Well, for heaven's sake, don't tell Amy that or I'll never hear the end of it."

"She won't hear it from me," Beau promised. He glanced out over the ring, for all the world as if his entire attention was on the child on horseback. "You get the results of those toxicity reports on King Lear yet?" he asked.

Matt nodded. "I delivered the official report to Jake on my way over here. I didn't find any traces of oleander poisoning."

"Then the gris-gris was just for show."

"That'd be my take on it," Matt agreed. "Somebody was trying to deliver a message, and the oleander was just to let you know what kind of damage they could have done if they'd really meant to kill that horse." He glanced at the other man. "Have you considered the possibility the message wasn't for Jax?"

"The gris-gris was decked out like a derby winner," Beau said, understanding instantly. "And Jax hasn't got an enemy in the world, unless you count her ex-husband's old battle-ax of a mother." His teeth flashed in a humorless grin. "And I don't think poison would be Cecilia Martin's weapon of choice. She'd rather flay you to death with nasty innuendo." He shook his head. "I, on the other hand, have more enemies than I can count, starting with most of the Martin clan *and* good ol' Uncle Philip. They've all had horses running against Delacroix Farms at one time or another. And the winners are mostly on our side," he added, a note of satisfaction in his voice. "That tends to make some people feel downright inhospitable."

"What has Jax's ex-mother-in-law got against her?" Matt asked.

Beau lifted an eyebrow at that, in an expression very much like one his sister habitually displayed. "That's something you'll have to discuss with Jax." He grinned again, this time with real humor in his eyes. "If you dare."

"I take it she doesn't like to talk about her marriage."

"Far as I can tell, she doesn't even like to think about it. That period in her life is pretty much a closed book."

"Do you know what happened?"

"Like I said, you'll have to ask Jax about that."

"Ask me what?" Jax said as she came up behind the two men.

As they turned toward her, Jax was struck by how similar they were. Although Beau's hair was the same dark color as hers and Matt was as blond as some Nordic god, they were nearly the same height, both lean and well-muscled, with the same sort of easy masculine grace that told the world they were at home in their skins. During their years as high school football stars, the two of them had cut a pretty wide swath through the female student body. According to local rumor, Beau was still breaking more than his share of hearts.

"What are you two up to?" she asked, tilting her head to study them. "And don't tell me nothing. The pair of you look as guilty as a couple of foxes on the way out of a henhouse."

Beau leaned back against the fence, his elbows propped up on the top rail behind him. "I was just warning the doc here about taking advantage of my sister."

Matt shot a startled look at his ol' buddy.

Jax's eyebrow rose. "Excuse me?"

"I was sitting out on my porch last night, enjoying a

glass of Dad's best brandy before I turned in, when you two came strolling up from the barn,'' he said blandly. ''Next time you probably ought to turn out the porch light before you start necking like a couple of teenagers.''

''Before we start...'' Jax's face went beet red. ''We weren't...that is...'' She pulled herself up to her full height and stuck out her chin. ''Matt merely kissed me good-night,'' she said with as much dignity as she could muster.

''Uh-huh. Looked like more than a good-night kiss from where I was sitting. I distinctly saw him put his hand on your backside.''

Jax planted her hands on her hips. ''And just what do you think you were doing, hiding in the dark, spying on people?'' she said, trying to turn the tables on him. ''You should be ashamed.''

''I don't know why I should be ashamed.'' Beau's gray eyes were gleaming with amusement. ''I wasn't the one standing on the front porch, letting some guy grope me on the first date.''

''Grope me! I—Charles Beauregard Delacroix, you take that back right now!'' she demanded, regressing to her six-teen-year-old self in the face of her twin's deliberate prov-ocation.

Beau laughed and reached out to snag his sister around the neck, dragging her against his broad chest. ''Isn't she just cuter than a two-day-old filly when she gets all huffy and aristocratic?'' he said to Matt.

Matt nodded, at a loss for words. Despite Beau's teasing laughter, Matt was more than halfway sure he was serious about his warning. Matt *had* been doing a bit more on that porch than just kissing Beau's sister good-night. And Southern men tended to take any attempts on their sisters' virtue seriously.

''You sound just like Odelle when you call me by all

three of my names like that,'' Beau chortled, knuckling the top of Jax's head the way he'd done when they were kids.

Jax made a strangled protest and punched him in the ribs.

''Temper, temper.'' Beau caught her fist in his hand. ''Calm down, now.'' He gave her a minute, tightening his hold until she quit struggling. ''You calm yet?''

A string of unintelligible words erupted against his chest.

''Such language,'' he observed mildly, although he hadn't actually been able to make out what she said. He eased up his stranglehold around her neck. ''If Odelle heard you talk like that she'd wash your mouth out with soap.''

''*Merde!*'' Jax said distinctly, cursing at him in French. Beau laughed and let her go.

Jax stepped back, eyes downcast to avoid looking at either of the two men, hands busily brushing the front of her tailored white shirt as if Beau had actually ruffled it up. The red in her cheeks gave her pale skin a rosy glow. ''You don't deserve I should tell you this, since you're such a—''

''Language,'' Beau reminded her, making no effort to hide his amusement.

''Jerk,'' Jax said, ignoring his comment, ''but Bobbi asked me to tell you they're getting ready to take Hot Shot out on the track. She said she thought you'd probably want to be there.''

Beau was suddenly all business. ''Damn right I want to be there. Hot Shot is turning in some incredible times.'' He flashed a look at Matt. ''I'm thinking of entering her in the Bayou Stakes against Uncle Philip's horse.'' He turned toward the training ring before Matt could comment and raised his hand. ''Bear!'' he hollered, making a motion with his thumb as if he had a stopwatch in his hand. ''Hot Shot.''

Bear looked up, saw the group at the fence, then nodded and signaled to the young rider and the horse on the end of the lunge lead to slow down.

"Is the lesson over already?" Amy complained, although she instantly complied with her instructor's signals. "We haven't cantered yet."

"You've got to learn to keep your balance at a trot before you can canter," Bear informed her. "You're still bouncing all over the saddle."

"But—"

Bear just looked at her.

"Okay," she said meekly, and swung her right leg out behind her and over the back of the horse to dismount.

Bear coiled the lunge line, tying it securely with a thin length of rawhide, and hooked it over Amy's arm, showing her how to lead the horse from the training ring.

"The lesson isn't really over yet," he said as he opened the gate for her and stood back so she could lead the horse through. "Learning how to take care of your horse after you ride is as important as learning how to stay in the saddle." He looked at his former star pupil. "Jax could probably be persuaded to show you how to do that, if you asked her real nice."

Jax looked at the trainer, startled. "Me? But I—"

"*Jax* could..." Amy paused, glancing up at her father. "I mean, Ms Delacroix," she amended, her voice rising in delight. "Ms Delacroix could show me?" She gazed up at Jax with open admiration, her big blue eyes sparkling as if she'd just discovered Christmas was going to come twice a year from now on. "Oh, Ms Delacroix, *will* you? Will you show me how to take care of Rocky? Please?"

Jax didn't know what to say. She didn't know how to deal with children. How to talk to them. She'd never had a child as a student, either. But she didn't have the heart to say no, not with Amy staring up at her as if she were Cinderella's fairy godmother and the Easter Bunny rolled into one.

"Yes, of course," she said, flashing a quick, how-could-you-do-this-to-me look at the trainer.

Bear just smiled serenely and turned away, heading toward the track with Beau.

Jax looked back down at Amy. "I'd be happy to show you how to take care of Rocky."

"Oh, thank you!" Amy reached out, grasping one of Jax's hands in both of hers, dropping the lead in the process.

The horse tossed his head as the coil of rope hit the ground, and took a quick, dancing step to one side.

Amy didn't even notice. "Ms Delacroix is going to help me, Daddy," she announced, beaming up at her father.

"The first lesson you have to learn is not to let go of your horse." Jax reached for the lead, capturing it with her free hand before the animal had taken more than a single step. "If he gets loose, either he, you or someone else could get hurt." She handed the lead back to the child. "He trusts you to take care of him and keep him safe," she said, unconsciously repeating the advice Bear had given her when she was first learning to ride.

Amy took the coil of rope in one hand, sliding it to the crook of her elbow the way Bear had shown her, without letting go of Jax. Unless she wanted to yank her hand out of Amy's, there was no way Jax was going to get free.

She cast a half-panicked glance at Amy's father.

He smiled at her and shook his head, silently declining to intercede on her behalf. She was going to have to deal with Amy on her own.

"What do we do first, Ms Delacroix?" Amy asked impatiently, almost bouncing up and down in her excitement. "Huh? What do we do first?"

Not knowing what else to do, Jax turned in a wide circle to accommodate the horse and headed toward the barn, her hand still firmly in the little girl's grasp.

Matt followed a few paces behind them, close enough to hear what was being said but not close enough to be easily included in the conversation. He wanted them to relate to each other without his help, but he was ready to intervene if things started going downhill.

Amy was fairly dancing as she walked along beside her new hero, her face upturned, peppering Jax with nonstop questions.

"Do I get to brush him? Can I comb his tail? Does he get his hay now? How come you named him Rocky? How many ribbons do you have? What does an Olympic medal look like? How many other horses do you have? Can I ride them sometime?"

Jax's responses were cordial but reserved. Despite the small hand clutching hers, she held herself aloof, obviously uncomfortable under the onslaught of Amy's undivided attention and wide-eyed adoration. Well, Matt thought, trying to give Jax the benefit of the doubt, she wasn't used to kids—the rarefied world of international equestrian competition was hardly overrun with children, after all—and his daughter's enthusiasm and high spirits had been known to be a bit daunting even to people used to dealing with children on a regular basis.

Jax would have to get used to it, though. As he'd told her at dinner last night, if there was ever going to be anything between them, his kids would have to be part of it. The three of them were a package deal.

They stopped outside the barn near the tack room, in an area specifically designed for saddling and unsaddling the horses. There was a wide, broom-swept cement apron underfoot to keep things from getting muddy, and several iron rings fastened to the wall of the barn at fairly wide intervals for securing the horses. A wooden cabinet held grooming supplies—brushes, currycombs, shoe picks, sponges, shampoos, hoof oil and the like. Metal buckets were stacked neatly against the side of the barn, one inside the other, and a coiled hose was attached to a water spigot, meant for bathing the pampered four-legged athletes.

As Jax showed Amy the proper way to exchange Rocky's bridle for a halter before securing him to one of the iron rings, Matt ambled over to the wooden bench positioned under the overhang of the barn's slanted roof and sat down.

"Here, hold these, Daddy," Amy said imperiously, running over to hand him her little velvet-covered riding helmet and the bright pink parka she'd been wearing.

He took them, setting them down on the bench beside him. Then, with his legs stretched out and crossed at the ankles, his hands loosely clasped over his stomach, the back of his head lolling against the side of the barn, he prepared to enjoy the sight of Jax and his daughter getting to know each other.

Amy was a quick study, especially when the subject at hand interested her. She paid close attention to everything Jax did, asking question after eager question, one following upon the other in surprisingly logical progression for a child of her tender years. Jax patiently answered each rapid query, adding a practical demonstration where necessary. Her stiffness slowly melted away, bit by bit, as she forgot Amy's age and began to respond to her as an individual. Soon they were just two horsewomen, the expert and the neophyte, sharing their mutual love of the big, beautiful animal they were grooming.

They were using the rubber currycomb when Jax reached over Amy's shoulder, placing her hand on the child's to show her the proper motion and pressure to use for maximum effect. For a few moments they moved as one, hands together on the currycomb, making the circular patterns meant to loosen dirt and massage the horse's glossy hide.

Amy looked up over her shoulder, asking Jax a question Matt couldn't hear.

His daughter giggled at the answer.

Jax smiled, lifting her free hand to touch Amy's hair.

Matt smiled, too, relieved to see that they were getting along so well. Not that he'd really had any doubts about it. Amy hadn't stopped talking about Jax since the day of her first lesson, when she'd found out Ms Delacroix was the "fabulous Jax." And Jax, for all her hesitancy, seemed to have a natural affinity for children.

"Jax said I could see her ribbons," Amy announced a short while later, after they had finished grooming the horse and returned the currycombs and brushes to the wooden cabinet. "She said I could call her Jax," she added, before her father could object to the familiarity.

"I said you could call me Jax if it's all right with your father," Jax amended.

"Can I, Daddy?" She leaned against her father's knee, smiling up at him from under the silky fringe of her bangs. One of her pink, poodle-shaped barrettes had come loose from its moorings and was dangling from a few strands of hair over her right cheek. She brushed it back with an impatient gesture. "Ms Delacroix *is* kind of a mouthful," she said, obviously parroting Jax.

Matt bit down on the inside of his cheek to keep from laughing and reached up to reposition the dangling barrette. "If Jax doesn't mind, neither do I," he said, smiling over his daughter's head at the woman standing behind her.

Jax felt as if she'd just been given another blue ribbon.

"Well," she said, flustered by the look in Matt's eyes, and her reaction to it. "Let's put Rocky in his stall and give him some hay for being such a good boy, then we can go look at those ribbons before you go." She slanted a quick look at Matt. "I'm sure your father has better things to do than sit around all day watching us work."

"There's no big hurry," Matt said lazily. "Jeff's spending the day with my father. They won't be home for another hour or so."

"Grandpa an' Jeff went fishing right after church," Amy said, looking up at Jax from her position at her father's knee. "Jeff said they're gonna bring home a mess of crawfish, but I hope they don't." She wrinkled her nose. "I don't like crawfish unless Daddy peels them for me," she announced, with a sidelong look at her father. "They have yucky feet."

"Yucky feet or not—" Matt tweaked his daughter's nose, letting her know he was on to her tricks "—you're big enough to peel your own crawfish if you want them. Meanwhile, Rocky looks like he's getting impatient over there." He put his hands on his daughter's shoulders, moving her aside as he stood.

The horse stamped his foot as if to emphasize what Matt had said.

"See there? He wants his hay." Matt bent down, picking up the riding helmet and parka Amy had given him to hold, and handed them to his daughter. "You take these," he said, "and go on up to the office with Jax to look at those ribbons. I'll put Rocky in his stall and give him some hay."

"Don't you want to see the ribbons, too, Daddy?"

"I've already seen them."

"But don't you want to see them *again*?"

"I'll be along as soon as I've put Rocky in his stall." He wanted to check on King Lear, too, while he was at it. "You go on with Jax."

"Okay," Amy agreed. She turned, offering her hand to Jax as if it were the most natural thing in the world.

This time Jax knew what was expected of her. She reached down and took the child's hand, enfolding it in hers. And nearly gasped at the surge of warmth she felt.

It wasn't as if she were the maternal type.

She wasn't the kind of woman who hankered after babies, the way her aunt Toni had recently started doing. Jax had never even held a child's hand in hers before, not that she could remember. None of her siblings had children; there were no nieces or nephews clamoring for her attention. Although there were two teenagers on the other branch of the Delacroix family tree—Joanna's Nikki and Annabelle's Cade—Jax hadn't been around them when they were small. Joanna had returned to Bayou Beltane with her daughter only a year ago, and Annabelle and her family lived in Florida.

Nothing in her life had prepared Jax for what she felt now, standing in the stable yard with Amy Taggart's hand in hers. It shook her to realize she felt anything at all. She hardly knew the child, and yet it felt...nice to be walking through the barn with Amy's hand in hers, listening to her bright, nonstop chatter as they made their way up the stairs to the corner office. It felt *right*.

Maybe kids weren't a completely separate species, after all. Some of them, the ones who loved horses the way Jax did, might actually be kind of pleasant to have around once in a while.

"Oh, there are so many of them!" Amy said as they stepped into the office. She turned her gaze from the wall of ribbons to look up at Jax with something like awe in her face. "Are they all yours?"

"Not all of them." Jax was somehow loathe to admit it, afraid her stock would somehow be lowered in Amy's eyes. "Some of them are racing trophies. Those big silver cups there were won by my brother Beau's horses."

"But which ones are *yours?*" Amy presented.

"Most of the ones on this side of the wall. I won that one—" she pointed to a frayed, faded blue ribbon "—when I was just about your age."

"When you were *my* age?"

"Uh-huh. And those right there are the medals King Lear and I won at the Olympics. Would you like me to take them out of the case so you can see them close up?"

"Oh, *could* I? Really?"

Fifteen minutes later, Matt entered the office to find them sitting side by side on the sagging leather sofa. Amy had both medals draped around her neck, her little face glowing as she listened to Jax recount how she had won them. Neither of them noticed him. He leaned against the doorjamb and listened, as enthralled as his daughter.

"Sounds pretty exciting," he said when Jax had finished recounting how it had felt to stand on the podium and receive her medals in front of a cheering hometown crowd.

"Oh, Daddy, look!" Amy jumped up from the sofa and ran to him. "She let me try on her Olympic medals. Look. This one's silver—see?—for the three-day event." She said it as if she actually knew what a three-day event was. "And this one's *gold*—" her voice dropped to a reverent whisper as she said the word "—for the dress…dress…"

"Dressage," Jax supplied.

"For the dressage. And all those ribbons—" she waved her hand at the wall "—are hers, too. She won them all herself. Well…" Amy cast a quick look over her shoulder. "Not *all* by herself. The horse is half the team," she explained, obviously quoting her newfound authority on the subject. "Someday me and Rocky are going to win an Olympic medal, Daddy, just like Jax and King Lear."

"That's a wonderful ambition, baby." He crouched down so they were eye-to-eye. "But it's going to take lots of hard work. You know that, don't you?" he warned, afraid she'd expect too much, too soon, and be disappointed. "You won't get as good as Jax overnight."

"I know. Jax said it took years an' years for her to get good, an' she started riding horses when she was *four*,"

Amy said accusingly. "But I'll work really, really hard, Daddy, an' do everything Mr. Bear tells me. I promise."

"I'm real proud of you, sweetheart." He hugged her hard and stood. "I guess we'd better get going," he said to Jax. "My parents are coming over tonight for Sunday supper, and we need to make sure the house is reasonably clean or my mother will spend the whole evening scrubbing the stove." One corner of his mouth lifted in a wry smile. "She'll probably scrub the stove, anyway, so I don't know why I bother but..." He shrugged.

"We don't want Grandma to think we live like slobs," Amy reminded him, "even though we do."

Jax laughed.

Matt shook his head. "Never say anything in her hearing you don't want repeated to the whole world," he advised Jax. He nudged his daughter's shoulder. "Give Jax back her medals so we can get going."

Amy carefully lifted the medals over her head, handed them to Jax, then sat down on the sofa and began tugging at her riding boots.

"Why don't you keep those," Jax suggested. "There aren't any little girls around here who can use them."

"But these are *your* boots. Mr. Bear said so."

Jax stuck out her foot. "I don't think they'll fit me anymore, do you?"

Amy shook her head.

"Here, why don't you take this with you, too." She handed Amy the peaked riding helmet. "I don't think it will fit me anymore, either. And you'll need it for your lessons."

Wide-eyed, speechless, Amy stood up and took the helmet.

"What do you say?" Matt prompted when his daughter just stood there, staring up at her hero.

"For always?" Amy asked breathlessly. "To keep for my very own?"

"Yes, of course, to keep for your own."

"Oh, thank you!" Amy threw her arms around Jax's waist, whacking her in the small of the back with the brim of the riding helmet. She hugged her hard, pressing her head against Jax's belly and squeezing for all she was worth. "This is the best present I ever had."

Jax didn't quite know what to do. Her hands fluttered in the air for a moment, hovering around Amy's head before dropping, finally, to the child's shoulders. "You're welcome," she said, forcing the words past the sudden lump in her throat.

"You're the best person in the whole world except for my daddy," Amy declared passionately, giving Jax another hard squeeze before she stepped back. She jammed the riding helmet on her head. "I want to say goodbye to Rocky before we go, Daddy. Okay?"

"Okay." He nodded his permission, stepping aside as she dashed past him. "Walk," he ordered automatically as she headed down the stairs. "And don't go in his stall," he added, in case it occurred to her to do so.

The two adults were left standing alone in the office, staring at each other without the buffer of the child between them. The air was heavy with emotion.

Matt's feelings were a combination of paternal pride, gratitude that his child's specialness had been noted and approved, and tenderness for the woman who recognized that specialness and had made his little girl so happy.

Jax felt a confused yearning, a sudden need to hold a small warm body in her arms, nascent feelings of long-buried, furiously denied maternal instincts bubbling to the surface.

They both felt the heat—a warm, gently pulsating flow

of emotion that had nothing to do with the child…and yet everything to do with her.

"That was a sweet thing to do," Matt said.

Jax shrugged. "They were just going to waste, lying around here. There hasn't been anyone to wear them for years."

"Maybe," Matt agreed. "But it was still a sweet thing to do. You couldn't have given her anything she'd treasure more."

Jax shrugged again, unsure of what to say because she was unsure of how she felt. All kinds of strange, frightening emotions were swirling around inside her.

"I'd like you to come to dinner tonight," Matt said.

"Dinner?"

"At the house. You've met my daughter. Now I'd like you to meet my son."

"But your parents…" She shook her head. "I couldn't intrude on a family dinner."

"You wouldn't be intruding. My parents would be thrilled to meet you."

"I couldn't. Really. I—"

"Please?"

A searing look passed between them, fraught with longing and uncertainty. Neither of them knew where this was going. Both of them were half afraid to find out, more than half afraid not to.

"All right," Jax said. "What time do you want me there?"

All the time, he thought. *Every day. Every night. Forever.*

"Six-thirty," he said.

"TELEPHONE FOR YOU, CHIEF!"

Jake Trahan's secretary hollered the words through the open door of his office. They had a perfectly good intercom system, but Ms Luella claimed she could never remember which button was which. It was a claim Jake tended to believe, because whenever she tried to put callers on hold, she usually ended up cutting them off. She refused to use the computer because, she said, the screen gave off radiation. She made Jake change the paper on the fax machine and put the toner in the copier because, she said, the chemicals used in both products gave her a rash.

But she made the best coffee he'd ever tasted, she never misplaced or forgot a message, and she could type out a report on the battered old manual Royal she used faster than most people could turn one out on a laser printer. Without errors. And what the hell, hollering worked just fine. Jake never missed a call. Besides, she was the only one who ever remembered to call him Chief.

Jake picked up the receiver. "Chief Trahan," he said into the mouthpiece.

"Beau Delacroix here," said the voice on the other end.

"Beau." Jake threw his pen down on top of the report he'd been working on. "I had a hunch I'd hear from you today." He got up from behind his desk as he spoke and closed the office door. "You can hang up the phone now, Ms Luella," he said into the receiver as he settled back down into his chair. "I've got it."

There was an audible click as Ms Luella hung up.

"What can I do for you?" Jake asked.

Beau got right to it. "You have any ideas about who was behind what happened out here last night?"

"Lots of ideas," said Jake. "No solid evidence."

"We both know Flora Boudreaux made that gris-gris."

"Do we?" Jake said carefully.

"She's the only one hereabouts who does that sort of thing."

"What about Desiree Boudreaux?"

Beau dismissed that idea with an impatient snort. "Desiree is a harmless old woman. A folk healer. She uses her so-called voodoo powers for good. She wouldn't purposely do anything to harm anyone, animal or human.''

"Well, then, answer me this. If Flora Boudreaux did make that gris-gris—and I'm not saying she did, I'm only saying *if*—but if she did, why? What's she got against your sister?''

"That gris-gris wasn't aimed at Jax. I'm sure of that. It was meant for one of the race horses. For me. Targeting King Lear was a mistake on somebody's part."

"All right, then." Jake didn't disagree about the gris-gris not being aimed at Jax. That was pretty much his conclusion, too. "What's Flora Boudreaux got against you?''

"Against me personally, nothing, as far as I know," Beau admitted. "I've been racking my brain, trying to come up with something, but no dice. There's that business with Philip over draining the swamp. If he manages to get the injunction lifted and goes ahead with the project, Flora loses her home—so that doesn't make any sense, either.''

"She'd have planted her hex at Belle Terre rather than Riverwood if that was her motivation.''

"Exactly."

"So maybe it wasn't Flora, after all," Jake suggested.

"No, dammit, I *know* she's involved in this somehow, even if it's only to the extent that she made the gris-gris and sold it to somebody else.''

"Who?''

"I haven't got a clue," Beau said.

CHAPTER SEVEN

MATT PEELED HIS daughter's crawfish for her. He buttered her corn bread, made sure she ate more steamed green beans and fresh corn than fried okra, and caught her glass of milk before it tipped—twice—all the while eating his own dinner and keeping track of the conversation as talk and laughter bounced back and forth across the kitchen table.

Obviously, neither Matt nor his parents believed in the old dictum that children should be seen and not heard. Both Jeff and Amy were encouraged to talk about their day, and neither child appeared to feel any compunction about offering opinions about anything that came up during the course of the conversation.

In contrast, dinner conversation in the dining room at Riverwood—at those times when children under twelve were actually allowed in the dining room—was quiet and circumspect. When permitted to share a meal with the adults on some special family occasion, the Delacroix children had been expected to keep their opinions to themselves. Comments of a personal nature—by anyone—were discouraged, and giggling was frowned upon.

As a child, Jax had often envisioned a family dinner just such as this one at the Taggarts'. As a bride, she'd dreamed of presiding over her own dinner table, asking her own children how their day had gone, sharing a smile with her husband as one of their brood recounted some exciting adventure.

The reality had been far different.

After her grand society wedding, she'd moved into her husband's family home in the northeast corner of St. Tammany Parish, just a stone's throw from Riverwood. Her dining room table had been presided over by her mother-in-law. There had been no shared smiles with her husband. There had been no children.

At the time, Jax had been devastated. Now she recognized it for the blessing it was. Any children she and Greg might have had would have locked her into a lifelong struggle with Cecilia Martin, who would have tried to raise her grandchildren the same cold-blooded way she had raised her son.

Six months into her marriage, when her body had once again provided proof that she had not yet conceived, Jax was made painfully aware of her real status in the Martin household. She had been selected to serve as a brood mare—a vessel with the proper bloodlines and pedigree. It was her duty, Cecilia said, to provide her husband with an heir. By the time Jax's marriage was over for good, it was a duty she was wholeheartedly thankful she had failed to fulfill. In the years since then, she'd almost managed to convince herself she'd never really wanted a family, anyway.

Almost.

But now, sitting at Matt Taggart's table, surrounded by his noisy, loving family, she began to wonder if those youthful dreams of a family of her own had died, after all.

Amy was the kind of little girl Jax had always dreamed of having, back when she'd allowed herself to dream of children. The child was bright, happy, well-adjusted, full of laughter and self-confidence, as crazy about horses as Jax had been at her age. Jeff…well, Jeff was still an unknown quantity. He hadn't said anything beyond a polite hello when Matt introduced them, and Jax hadn't gathered up her courage to say anything more than hello back. Matt's parents were the salt of the earth, with enough gift of gab to fill any conversational lull caused by their taciturn young grandson, or a tongue-tied guest.

Henry Taggart had retired from the commercial fishing industry several years ago, but still kept his hand in, taking the occasional tourist out on Lake Pontchartrain in his flat-bottomed bass boat, teaching fishing lore and techniques to his nine-year-old grandson. He worried about the rampant misuse of the state's wetlands, decrying the Louisiana legislature's lack of leadership on the issue and lamenting proposed plans to drain part of the local swamp to make way for a housing development.

Halfway through his tirade, he seemed to remember that the man behind the drive to drain the swamp was Louisiana State Senator Philip Delacroix, and he broke off with a stuttering apology, worried about having offended his son's elegant guest.

"Please, don't give it another thought, Mr. Taggart," Jax said graciously. "Most of the rest of the family don't agree with what Uncle Philip is trying to do with that swampland, either."

Matt's mother worked part-time at the Lakeview Community Hospital in the admissions department, which made her privy to all the latest gossip about some of the most intimate details of the lives of Bayou Beltane's residents.

"The things I could tell you," Amelia Taggart said. "My oh my, you just wouldn't believe. Why, the commotion that went on when that young Dr. Henderson was appointed deputy coroner. Such a nice young man, and so good-looking. All the nurses were in *such* a tizzy over him, trying to catch his eye, don't you know. And then he up and got married, right out of the blue like—" She broke off, suddenly recalling that the woman the newly appointed deputy coroner had so precipitously married was Jax's sister Marie.

"Yes, that was a seven-day wonder, wasn't it?" Jax said, deftly smoothing over the other woman's faux pas. Jax hadn't spent all those years attending embassy parties and fund-raisers for nothing. "The entire family was as surprised as everyone else in town when we found out Marie had gotten married. But Marie said he just swept her right off her feet and she couldn't help herself." The tiny white lie slipped out as easily as if it had been the exact truth. "Personally—" Jax leaned forward slightly, her lips turned up in a conspiratorial smile "—I don't blame her one bit. Lucas is a real charmer."

"Oh my, yes. And such a handsome devil, too." Amelia sighed. "And how is your sister doing now—the, uh…" She colored, stumbling over another Delacroix scandal. "The one who got shot, I mean—young Charlotte…not the one who married Dr. Henderson."

Marie, the sister who'd so recently married the charming Lucas Henderson, had also had her aromatherapy shop in New Orleans machine-gunned *and* been cleared of the suspicion of murder.

Charly's condition fortunately, was less fraught with conversational stumbling blocks; she'd been shot in the line of duty. The incident had been—and apparently still was—grist for the Bayou Beltane gossip mill. Calamity was almost as good as scandal in keeping people talking.

"Everyone at Lakeview was very worried about her, what with that nasty head wound and the surgery on her shoulder and all," Amelia said. "And, of course, everyone wondered why your mother didn't come to see…"

And yet another Delacroix family scandal reared its head. Madeline Delacroix hadn't set foot in Bayou Beltane or

Louisiana since she'd divorced Jax's father more than ten years ago.

"Charly is doing fine, Mrs. Taggart. She's very anxious to get through her recuperation period and go back to work."

"What's recuperation?" Amy asked.

Henry and Amelia both gladly took on the task of explaining the word to their granddaughter.

Matt smiled at Jax down the length of the table before once again rescuing his daughter's glass of milk and setting it safely out of reach.

Feeling suddenly shy, as if all her renewed dreams and hopes might be reflected on her face, Jax turned her attention to Matt's son, who sat on her right.

By far the quietest member of the family, Jeff Taggart was a thin young boy with a shock of nearly white hair that seemed to stand straight up on its own, like the bristles of a brush. His eyes, framed by a pair of small, wire-rimmed glasses, were the same clear blue as his father's. His wrists and hands, the curve of his neck as he bent his head over his dinner and the thin shoulders underneath his Saints T-shirt still had the touching fragility of childhood, but the bones of his face, strong and pronounced like his father's, already showed hints of the young man he would become.

Jeff Taggart was going to be a gangly, awkward preteen, but once he got past that stage he would be a heartbreaker, the kind of boy who made girls wonder what was going on behind those quiet, steady eyes of his. Just like his father.

Right now, though, he seemed to be concerned with getting as much food into his skinny little frame as possible. Unlike his sister, he had no qualms about peeling his own crawfish. He grasped them with easy expertise, one after the other, breaking off the heads and sucking out the succulent flesh with noisy gusto.

Jax searched her mind for a gambit to open a conversation, finally coming up with one just as he lifted his glass of iced tea to his lips. "What grade are you in at school?" she asked him, remembering what people had always seemed to ask her when she was a child.

Jeff put his glass down, swallowing a mouthful of tea before he answered. "Fourth," he said, and reached for another crawfish.

Jax tried again. "Do you like school?"

"It's okay, I guess." He shrugged, his eyes on the shellfish in his hands as he broke it in half. "I like it more now that I have a special tutor from Slidell high school twice a week," he added as he lifted the crawfish to his mouth.

"Oh?" Jax murmured sympathetically. In her experience, tutors always meant you were having trouble in school. "What subject are you being tutored in?"

With the back of his hand he swiped at the barbecue sauce that had trickled down his chin. "Differential equations."

"Differential...?" Jax blinked.

"Our Jeff is a certified mathematical genius," Amelia said proudly. "He's taking all sorts of special classes from the teachers at the high school—in computers and calculus and things like that." She beamed at him from across the table. "We're all so proud of him we could just bust our buttons."

Jeff rolled his eyes. "Oh, Gran'ma," he complained, sounding like any normal nine-year-old boy.

"Don't talk with your mouth full," Amelia said, sounding like any normal grandmother. "And use your napkin."

Jax couldn't help but smile at the normalcy of it all.

"I'D SAY THAT WENT pretty well," Matt said as he came back into the living room after settling his children into bed. His parents had left shortly after dinner. He went to the old rosewood sideboard that served as a bar.

"Really?" Jax leaned forward and put her coffee cup down on the low table in front of her. "How can you tell? I was sure I stuck my foot in it at least a dozen times."

"*Au contraire.* You very graciously kept my mother from choking on *her* foot at least a dozen times." He lifted a crystal decanter by the neck, silently offering to pour Jax a drink along with the one he was pouring for himself.

She shook her head.

"And Jeff just informed me that you're not so bad." Matt's lips curved up in a teasing smile as he brought his brandy to the sofa and sat down beside her. "For a girl, that is. He says you didn't ask too many dumb questions, and he likes the way you smell."

"The way I smell?"

"You aren't wearing—and I'm quoting verbatim here—'any of that smelly girly stuff that makes my nose itch.'" Which surprised Matt a little because, if he'd thought about it, he'd have expected Jax to be wearing some expensive French perfume. "He said you smell like flowers when the sun shines on them."

"Flowers?" Jax smiled with delight. "Really? He said I smell like flowers?"

"With the sun shining on them." Matt leaned sideways and sniffed at her neck. "He's right. You smell like a sun-warmed meadow full of wildflowers."

Jax tried to ignore the little spark of heat that sizzled down her spine. "I'll tell Marie you said so."

"What's Marie got to do with the way you smell?"

"I'm wearing a herbal body oil she blended especially for me."

"Body oil, hmm?"

Jax picked a bit of nonexistent lint off of her pleated linen slacks and pretended she hadn't heard that sexy rumble beneath his Louisiana drawl. "I wouldn't have thought little boys noticed things like the scent a woman wears," she said, just for something to say.

"Jeff's a pretty observant kid. Very aware of nuances. The last few months before Livvy died, he was always bringing her flowers from his grandmother's garden to cover up the medicinal smell of her room. He hated it. And yet Amy..." Matt shook his head and looked down, swirling the brandy in his glass. "She never even seemed to notice there was a smell. She was more concerned that her mother couldn't get out of bed and play with her anymore."

"It must have been very hard on the children, losing their mother like that, in such a—" Jax hesitated, searching for a word "—lingering way." She flashed him a shy look from under her lashes, wanting to know, yet not wanting to ask. "It must have been hard on you, too."

"Yes, it was." Matt sighed and took a sip of his brandy. "We're all coping with it 'beautifully,' though, according the psychologist."

"Psychologist?"

"The kids have had regular sessions with a child psychologist over in Covington since shortly after Livvy became bedridden. Dr. Fremont has helped them a lot. She's helped us all a lot."

"Do you see her, too?" Jax asked, unable to completely squelch the little spurt of jealousy she felt at the warmth in his voice when he mentioned the other woman, even though she knew it was unwarranted and petty. He *should* feel warmly about the woman who was counseling his children. "On a professional basis, I mean?"

"We've had a couple of sessions together as a family, mostly to keep me up to date on how the kids are doing and to make sure I'm handling things the right way."

"I can't imagine you'd handle anything in any but the right way."

Matt slanted her a speculative, sideways glance. "Anything?" he asked, the low, sexy rumble back in his voice.

"Ah...your children, I mean." Jax's gaze flickered to his and then dropped, coming to rest on his hand where it rested against his thigh, cradling the snifter of brandy in the curve of his palm. "I can't imagine you handling your *children* in any but the right way."

Matt leaned forward and set his brandy on the table next to her cooling cup of coffee. Then he stretched, lifting his arms into the air with an exaggerated gesture. When he leaned back and settled down, his arm was resting along the back of the sofa behind her head.

Jax sent him another skittering glance. "The children—" she began nervously.

"Forget the children for now." Matt ran his fingertips up and down her arm, caressing her through the thin sleeve of her silk blouse. "The children are asleep."

"But—"

He stretched his arm out across the back of the sofa and switched off the lamp that sat on the end table, plunging the room into soft, seductive darkness.

Jax caught her breath and went very still, waiting for what would happen next.

She felt his fingers on her arm again, lightly caressing, raising ripples of goose flesh in their wake. His breath tickled the sensitive skin beneath her ear. His chest pressed against her shoulder. He lifted his other hand, trailing one fingertip along the line of her jaw, turning her face toward his.

"Wanna neck?" he whispered.

Jax's stomach muscles fluttered in anticipation.

Growing up at Riverwood, she'd never had much opportunity for even the most innocent sexual experimentation; there were always too many people around, too many eyes monitoring her behavior. As a Delacroix, she'd had an image to live up to.

After she'd become Greg Martin's wife...well, Greg hadn't seen the point in wasting time wooing the woman who was already his. Sex with Greg had been the fulfillment of a duty...for both of them.

In the years since, she had known men whose idea of romance was a straightforward, no-strings-attached request to hit the sheets. Others conducted their flirtations like a sophisticated game, without any involvement of heart or soul.

But no one had ever invited her to sit with him on the sofa in a darkened living room, with Patsy Cline crooning softly in the background and two children sleeping in another part of the house, and just...neck.

Jax peered up at him, trying to read his eyes in the dim, shadowed light shining in from the hallway. What she saw set her heart to beating just a little bit faster. "Kiss me," she said, surprising herself with her own audacity.

He kissed her cheek first, and then the tip her nose and the delicate arch of her eyebrow...the corner of her eye...and down the other side of her face. Slowly. Softly. Telling her without words that it was *she* he wanted and not just some warm, available body.

Jax sighed and let her head fall back against his arm.

He kissed her lips then...almost...planting small, nibbling, tasting kisses at the corners of her mouth, licking at her lips with the tip of his tongue, waiting—as he had waited last night—for her to show him she was ready to move on to the next step.

She opened her mouth under his in unmistakable invitation, lifting her hand to the back of his head to urge him to take what they both wanted.

He sealed his lips to hers and slid his tongue into her mouth, exploring, tasting...savoring her as if she were a rare and exotic dish he wanted to make last as long as possible. Delicious minutes passed as they feasted on each other with lips and tongue and teeth.

The air grew heavy, heady with the scent of passion.

Their bodies grew damp.

Softening.

Swelling.

Patsy Cline crooned softly in the background, singing of helpless, hopeless desire. *Crazy.* Oh, God, yes. Crazy!

They were both crazy with desire.

Jax could hear Matt's breath, feel it sloughing in and out of his lungs, and knew her own was just as ragged. She could feel her heart beating, thundering a counterpoint to his, sending the blood careening through her veins like heated brandy.

His hand slid down her arm to her waist, and then lower, to the curve of her hip, kneading her flesh through the material of her slacks, the way he had last night when they stood together in the glare of the porch light, kissing goodnight like two desperate, lovesick teenagers.

Only they weren't teenagers.

And they weren't standing on the porch.

Jax shifted on the sofa, turning more fully toward him, wrapping both of her arms around him as she sank back into the plump cushions. The feel of him in her arms, the width of his broad shoulders, the long, sloping muscles of his back, the strength of his hands, the sheer weight of his hard male body above hers—so different from her own—thrilled her to her feminine core, filling her with unspeakable delight, flooding her entire being with unbearable longing. She arched her back, pressing her breasts into his chest to relieve the ache.

He tore his mouth away from hers and peeled back the collar of her chic silk blouse, burying his face in the curve of her neck. "Are you as hot as I am?"

"Hotter," she breathed, compelled by something inside herself to be absolutely honest with him. "I've never been this hot before."

He moaned and shifted his hand from her hip, reaching up to cover one small, firm breast. He could feel her nipple, hard against his palm beneath the silk of her blouse and bra, and gave in to temptation, strumming it with his thumb.

Jax bit back a ragged moan and reached up, pressing his hand more closely to her breast, halting the teasing torment of his stroking thumb, trying to ease the ache with a firmer pressure. "Please," she murmured.

"Yes, please," he said into her neck. "Please. I want you, Jax.... Good God in heaven, how I want you!"

He lifted himself away from her, propping himself up on one elbow as he moved his hand to the line of tiny mother-of-pearl buttons between her breasts. He flicked the first one open.

"I want to please you," he murmured.

The second button gave way, then the third.

"I want you to please me."

He pushed the edges of her blouse aside, revealing her bra. It was made of sheer, nearly transparent silk, almost the same color as her creamy skin. Even in the dim light, he could see her nipples through the fabric. The aureole surrounding each tight little nub was the size of a quarter.

"I just want you. Period."

She covered his hand with hers, stopping him when he would have flicked open the front clasp of her bra. "Are you sure?"

"Sure?"

"You said you wanted to be sure of your feelings," she reminded him. "To be sure where this was going before you went any further. So I'm asking. Are you sure?"

"The only thing I'm sure of is that I want you so much, I'm shaking with it."

"Is that enough?"

"It is for me." He lifted his gaze from her breasts to her face. "Is it enough for you? Are you willing to just trust to luck, without any guarantees or promises, and see where this goes?"

Jax didn't even have to think about it. She'd made her decision before she'd pulled him down on top of her. She wanted, just once in her life before she died, to have sex with a man who really, truly wanted *her*. Not her family connections, not her fame, only her, with no strings attached. "Yes," she said, and flicked open the clasp of her bra herself.

With a ragged, grateful, deeply heartfelt sigh, Matt lowered his head to her breast and took her nipple into his mouth.

The sensation was exquisite—for both of them.

Jax felt a rich, liquid warmth, a tugging that went straight to her womb, sending sparks of need shooting into every fiber of her being.

Matt felt her nipple pearl against his tongue, felt her breast swell against his lips, offering sustenance to his soul, nourishment for that part of his masculine psyche that had gone hungry for far too long.

Several long minutes slipped by as he feasted, moving slowly back and forth from one breast to the other, using his fingers to further tease and torment. She was arched beneath him, naked to the waist, writhing and moaning under the onslaught of his single-minded concentration on her breasts before he was finally able to divide his attentions enough to reach for the zipper on the back of her slacks.

"Mom." The cry was high and wavering. "Mom."

The two people on the sofa went stock-still.

Her back was still arched, her hands clenched in his hair to hold him to her.

His face was still pressed against her breasts, the hand

he'd slipped beneath her back already halfway down her panties, cupping the firm curve of her buttock.

"*Mom!*" There was an edge of panic in the word.

Matt withdrew his hand from inside Jax's silk panties. "I have to go to him," he said. "He's having a bad dream."

"I know." Jax uncurled her fingers from his hair and put her hands on his shoulders, pushing him up and away from her. "Go. I'll be all right," she reassured him when he hesitated. "Go on. Your son needs you."

JAX WAS COMPLETELY dressed and on her feet when Matt came back into the living room. "Is he all right?"

"He's fine. I gave him a few sips of water and sprayed some Nightmare Destroyer under the bed. Scented room deodorizer with a homemade label," he explained at Jax's blank look. "He said he was too big for that kind of baby stuff anymore—" Matt smiled slightly, remembering the look on his young son's face when he'd sprayed the deodorizer around the bedroom "—but he didn't object when I used it. Before he could finish telling me what the dream was about, he was asleep again."

"Does he have nightmares often?"

"Not so often as he did right after Livvy died, but still too often for my peace of mind. The psychologist said he'd have fewer and fewer over time. So far, she's been right on the money, so I have no reason to doubt she's right but... It's been a good five months since the last one. I was kind of hoping we'd seen the last of them."

"He called for his mother."

"The dreams are about her. She's lost and he can't find her. Or he's lost and crying for her but she doesn't come."

Jax felt something twist painfully in the region of her heart. "Poor little boy."

"Jeff's a tough cookie," Matt said. "He'll be fine." He

took a step closer and reached out, taking Jax's hands in his. "The question is, will you?"

"I'm a tough cookie, too," Jax assured him. Her lips quirked up in a little half smile. "Besides, nobody ever died of frustration."

"Are you sure?"

Jax managed a wavering little laugh. "No."

Matt tugged her into his arms and hugged her tight. "I'm sorry about tonight, sweetheart," he said into the silky hair at her ear. "Maybe this wasn't such a good idea, after all."

Jax went very still in his arms. "What wasn't a good idea?" she asked, instantly thinking he'd changed his mind about her, about what they'd been about to do.

"Necking with you on the living room sofa with my kids sleeping down the hall. Five minutes more and I might not have heard Jeff cry out. I shudder to think what would have happened if he'd gotten up to find me. Especially if we'd been five minutes further along."

"Oh, my God," Jax said, picturing the scene in her mind.

"Exactly."

She drew back to look up at him. "We could have scarred him for life."

"I think the possibility of that's a bit remote. Thank heavens. But I'd have been faced with a lot of questions I'm not ready to answer yet."

"What are we going to do?" Jax swallowed. "Do you want to forget the whole thing?"

"Forget the whole thing? You mean us?" He gestured toward the sofa where they'd almost gotten carried away. "That?"

Jax nodded.

"Hell, no. Not in a million years. Do you?" he asked carefully, half afraid of the answer.

Jax shook her head. "No," she said fervently. "No, I don't want to forget it."

"Well, then, we'll just have to put our heads together and think of something else. Some*place* else."

"We can't use my place. At least, not right now. Charly's there."

"I'd rather not use your place ever," Matt admitted. "Whether your sister's there or not, Beau's right next door," he reminded her. "And half of the rest of your family lives within shouting distance."

"A motel?" she suggested hesitantly. She didn't like the idea of checking into a motel for sex, but if it was the only way she could be with him, she'd do it.

"And have everybody in town know about it ten minutes after we checked in?" Matt shook his head. "I don't think so."

Besides, a motel wasn't what he wanted for her. She deserved better.

"Then what?"

"I'll think of something."

"When?" she demanded, amazed at her own temerity.

Matt grinned. "Are you that hot for my body?" he teased.

Jax didn't even crack a smile. "Yes."

Matt's grin faded as all his blood suddenly rushed to his groin. "Tomorrow night," he promised. "I'll think of someplace we can go and I'll pick you up tomorrow night at seven. Unless I die of frustration before then."

CHAPTER EIGHT

"GRANDMA HAS BRIDGE CLUB tonight so Courtney will be baby-sitting," Matt said as he stood with his back to the kitchen table, loading the dinner dishes his children brought him from the table. "I want you to mind her and not give her a hard time, okay? She already knows what your bedtimes are and what programs you can watch after your homework's done, so don't even try to talk her into letting you stay up and watch 'The X-Files.'" He glanced over his shoulder at his son. "Understand"

"Mark's dad lets him watch 'The X-Files' all the time, and 'Sliders,' too." Jeff handed his father a food-smeared dinner plate. "I don't see why I can't."

"Because I said so, that's why," Matt said lightly as he fitted the plate into the dishwasher. "And I'm the father. It's not a program for little kids." He flashed a quick, significant look at Amy, who was busy gathering the used silverware off of the table. "It scares your sister."

"She could go into her bedroom while it's on," Jeff argued.

"I don't want to go into my bedroom," Amy declared. "It's my TV, too."

"You never watch what's on TV, anyway," Jeff countered. "You're always playing on the floor with your Magic Pony and your dumb Barbies. You could do that in your bedroom."

"Do to watch TV." She dropped a handful of silverware

into the sink, managing to bodycheck her brother with her hip at the same time. "And my Barbies aren't dumb."

Jeff pushed her back. "Are to."

"Are—"

"That's enough, you two," Matt said mildly. "Jeff, hand me that bowl, there." He nodded at the large glass salad bowl sitting on one end of the kitchen table. "Amy, you put the butter back in the fridge and the bread in the bread box, then go take your bath. I want both of you in your pj's and robes and ready for bed when Courtney gets here."

"I don't know why we have to have a dumb old baby-sitter, anyway," Jeff groused.

"Because, as smart as you are, you're still not old enough to stay by yourself, that's why. And don't call Courtney dumb. It's not polite."

"If you took me an' Jeff with you on your date, we wouldn't have to stay by ourselves an' then we wouldn't have to have a baby-sitter," Amy suggested slyly.

"Nice try, kiddo—" Matt grinned at his daughter "—but no cigar. Jeff, the bowl, please."

"I don't see why you have to go out on another date, anyway." Jeff stood at the table, fingering the edge of the bowl, and gave his father a mutinous look through the lenses of his little round glasses. "You said you wouldn't go out all the time."

Matt reached for a pot sitting on the stove. "Two dates hardly constitutes all the time," he said as he began to scrub it with a scouring pad.

"Three dates," Jeff corrected him. "You went out to dinner the first time, then she was over here last night and now you're going out again. That's three times in a row already, and tonight isn't even the weekend. You're only supposed to go out on dates on the weekend."

"Sometimes, when two people are just getting to know each other, they go out more often," Matt explained as he scrubbed. ''Like when David first moved in down the block last summer—'' he glanced over his shoulder ''—remember? You guys spent nearly every waking moment doing things together for the first month or so.''

''But Sunday dinner is supposed to be just the family,'' Jeff insisted. ''That's what you always said before you met *her*.''

''I liked it last night when Jax came over for dinner,'' Amy said. ''I wish she'd have dinner with us all the time.''

''That's because you're just a dumb little kid and you don't know any better,'' Jeff said.

''I am not dumb,'' Amy flashed back. ''You're just a nerd egghead geek four-eyes.''

''And you're—''

''I said that's enough, you two,'' Matt interrupted, biting back his irritation. He didn't have time for this right now. He was supposed to pick Jax up in less than an hour, and he still had to finish cleaning up the kitchen, get the kids through their baths and get himself dressed before the baby-sitter came. ''Amy, go take your bath,'' he ordered in a voice that brooked no argument. ''Jeff, hand me that bowl, please. Now.''

Jeff picked the bowl up and handed it to his father, who reached out with a wet hand to get it. It slipped. They both grabbed for it and missed. It hit the tiled floor with a loud crash, shattering into several dozen pieces that went ricocheting in as many directions.

Jeff looked up at his father, his blue eyes wide behind his glasses. ''I didn't do it on purpose,'' he said fervently.

Too fervently.

''I know you didn't, son,'' Matt said carefully, wondering if that was the absolute truth. Not that he thought Jeff had deliberately, *consciously* let the bowl slip. But subconsciously, maybe? The child psychologist had warned him the kids might act out when he started dating again. Was this what she'd meant?

And how was he supposed to handle it?

"Accidents happen, Jeff. It's all—"

"I heard a loud crash!" Amy declared, rushing in from the direction of the bathroom in her underwear. "What happened? What was that noise?"

"Don't come—" Matt began, but it was too late.

Amy had stepped on the glass.

Before her eyes even had time to well up, Matt had swooped down on her, snatching his barefoot daughter up in his arms. He set her down on the edge of the kitchen table.

"Let Daddy see," he cajoled, lifting her tiny foot in his hand and turning it to the light.

Two small shards of glass protruded from the ball of her foot. Holding her still with a hand around her ankle, Matt pinched his thumb and forefinger together and pulled each one out with a quick tug. Amy screwed her face up and howled loudly enough to be heard in the next parish.

"I'm sorry, Dad," Jeff said, his own eyes glistening. "I'm sorry. I didn't mean to break the bowl. Honest."

"I know you didn't mean it, Jeff." Matt consoled him as he lifted Amy off of the table and cuddled her. *Not consciously, anyway.* "It was an accident. Accidents happen and they're nobody's fault."

"I'll clean it up," Jeff said.

"*No!* No, don't touch it," he added, moderating his tone as the glitter in Jeff's eyes welled up into incipient tears. "I don't want you to get cut, too. Come on." He held out his free hand. "You come on into the bathroom with me while I put some antiseptic on your sister's foot. Careful where you step," he admonished as Jeff made his way across the kitchen to his father's side. "You don't want to get any glass on the bottom of your shoes, or it'll be all over the house before we know it." Matt put his hand on Jeff's shoulder and gave it a reassuring squeeze. "We'll clean this up together after I get Amy into the tub," he said as he steered his son out of the kitchen.

They would also have a little heart-to-heart conversation while they swept up the glass, which meant he was going to be late for his date with Jax.

She'd just have to understand.

"I UNDERSTAND. REALLY," Jax said. "Things happen. Last time it was one of my horses, this time it was your kids." She reached over and touched his hand lightly. "And this is much better than a movie, anyway." Her smile was sweet and just a little shy. "I've never done this before."

"Done what? Parked out on the bayou?"

"Parked *anywhere*. Ever."

"Ever?" Matt demanded incredulously. "Not even once?"

"Not even once." Jax flashed him a quick sideways look, suddenly feeling as sassy and confident and flirtatious as a head cheerleader at a high school football game. She'd never felt that way before. She tossed her hair back over her shoulder. "I'm not like all those trashy girls you used to date in high school."

"You're not, huh?"

"No, I'm not."

"Then what are you doing here with me now?"

"Saving your life?"

"Saving my life?"

She shot him another teasing look out of the corner of her eye. "I wouldn't want you to die of frustration."

"Well, then…" he drawled, his voice low and warm and sweet, as inviting as sin on a hot summer night, "what are you doing way over there?"

Jax giggled, the sound bursting from her throat like champagne bubbles escaping from the bottle, and scooted over next to him. As she melted against his chest, he wrapped his arms around her, carefully lowering her onto the open sleeping bag he'd spread over the floor of his van.

He pressed a soft, fervent kiss to her forehead. "I wish it could be better than this," he said against her skin. "I wish we were lying on satin sheets, on a real bed. You deserve a real bed, in a real room, with flowers in a crystal vase on the dresser and champagne cooling in a silver ice bucket and a Do Not Disturb sign on the door. And all night long for me to make love to you."

"No." She lifted her hand to brush at his hair, skimming her fingertips behind his ear, cupping the curve of his jaw to lift his head and make him look at her. "No, this is perfect. I've got flowers."

A nosegay of delicate magnolia blossoms and feathery green ferns sat atop the console between the front seats of the van in a crumpled paper cup filled with water from the bayou.

"And wine."

Two glasses and an untouched bottle of chardonnay were nestled in an acrylic ice bucket on the floor.

"And music."

Willie Nelson serenaded them with sultry forties torch songs from the CD player.

"I've got the moon shining on the water. And the night all around us. And you, wanting me," she whispered, unbearably thrilled by that simple fact. "All I need now is for you to make love to me...." She lifted her head slightly, pressing a soft kiss to the corner of his mouth. "*With* me..." she murmured, her voice thick with need, then nipped his bottom lip.

He groaned deep in his chest and covered her mouth with his. He could have hurried her then, and she would have accepted him. He could have unbuttoned the long row of buttons down the front of her soft cotton dress and stripped her out of her panties and taken her, right then, and she would have received him into her with a glad cry of welcome.

But he gave her everything he had the night before. The deep, soft, lingering kisses that went on and on. The slow disrobing. The tender, single-minded, mind-blowing attention to her breasts. And when he had her to the point where they'd been interrupted the night before—when she was writhing against the sleeping bag, naked and damp, gasping and arching her back for him; when the air inside the van was moist and heavy enough to fog the windows and their hearts were pounding like voodoo drums—he took her one step further.

With one arm pillowing her head and his mouth tugging at her breast, he slipped his hand down between her legs and gently, very gently and delicately, stroked the heated core of her.

She was slick and wet and swollen, and the first soft touch of his fingers sent her careering toward the edge. She didn't want to go over it alone.

"Matt," she breathed, her voice rasping and jagged. "Matt, wait. Wait."

He hesitated, lifting his head to see what was wrong, his hand stilling.

"I want you inside me when I come."

Something inside him snapped.

He rolled away from her, onto his back, dragging his polo shirt off over his head, ripping at the front of his slacks in a blind frenzy to be rid of them. Jax's soft, strong hands hampered and enhanced the process, her slender fingers grasping the tab of his zipper before he could find it himself, her knuckles brushing against his erection as she pulled the zipper down. When she reached inside his open fly and curled her fingers around him, he nearly exploded.

He was on fire, full to bursting with the need to be inside her, wild to give in to the maddening urge to pump his life force into her welcoming body. He was reduced to basics, a primal male animal with the scent of his mate in his nostrils and his blood beating a savage rhythm in his veins.

But he didn't forget the condom.

He tore at the small foil packet with his teeth, ripping it in half in the process.

He stared at it, dumbfounded, nearly panic-stricken, until his brain cleared just enough for him to remember he'd brought more than one with him. Grabbing his discarded slacks by the waistband, he stuck his hand into the pocket and groped for another one.

"You don't need that," Jax said.

"What?" he muttered, intent on not tearing the second condom as he opened it. "Don't need what?"

"This." She reached up and pinched one corner of the foil packet between her fingers. "You don't need it."

He resisted the tug of her fingers, holding on to the condom.

"I swear to you," she said. "You don't need it."

"Are you on the Pill?"

She couldn't quite bring herself to admit to the truth, even now. What if it made him change his mind about her? About this? What if it made a difference in the way he felt? And it would make a difference, she knew. She couldn't bear the thought.

"I won't get pregnant." She tugged the packet from his hold, tossing it aside with one hand, reaching up with her other to cup the back of his head and draw him down to her. "I promise," she whispered against his mouth. "Come inside me. I want you inside me, Matt."

He sealed his mouth to hers and slipped into her, as

smooth and easy as if he had done it a hundred...a thousand...a million times before. Some of the frantic need left him now that he was where he wanted to be. Inside her. Snug and warm. Skin to skin, with no barriers between them. He hadn't realized until just this moment that he'd wanted it that way, that it needed to be that way, that it was the *only* way it could be between them.

The first loving was a slow discovery of feeling and hot, delicious sensation that seemed to go on forever. They paused often for kisses, taking time to nuzzle and nibble, to murmur and sigh, to pet and caress and fondle, without ever losing that primary, elemental connection of man to woman. He wanted to be inside her more than he wanted life itself. She wanted to be filled with him more than she wanted her next breath.

The climax, when it finally came, was deep and slow and forceful, like a huge tsunami rolling slowly toward the shore, gathering strength and power before it finally, inevitably crashed onto the beach.

Jax arched into her lover's body as her orgasm slammed into her. She clenched her fists, trying to hold on to sanity and self. Her back bowed, the muscles in her stomach stretched and quivering. Her strong, slender horsewoman's thighs clamped around his hips, holding him deep inside her as all the tiny, delicate muscles of her woman's body convulsed.

Matt locked his arms, his hands flat against the sleeping bag on either side of her head, instinctively bracing himself to meet the stunning force that rose up to greet him. He squeezed his eyes shut and pressed his hips down hard, surging into her, every muscle in his body tensed and shaking from the unexpected power of his climax.

When it was over—when they could breathe without feeling the breath rasping in their lungs; when the blood wasn't thundering in their ears—they opened their eyes and smiled at each other.

And began it all over again.

The second time was faster, and more frantic, with more flash and fireworks. He kissed her all over, exploring each little nook and cranny of her body, from her ears to her toes, and every place in between, bringing her to climax with his hands and his mouth before joining his body to hers.

The third time, she used her mouth on him, driving him to the point of insanity before straddling his hips to ride him to mutual oblivion and release. His frenzied response set the van to rocking on its wheels, sending the paper cup full of flowers splashing over the front seat.

THEY SPENT THE NEXT WEEK alternating between acting like two mature, responsible adults trying to determine if they had anything in common besides an uncommonly strong physical attraction, and groping each other in a swelter of sexual heat, like two lovesick teenagers who thought they'd just invented sex.

The mature, responsible part of each of them agreed that they should slow things down and take it one step at a time, the way they'd originally agreed.

Their newly discovered, passionate side found every opportunity to be alone.

"Here?" Jax said, wide-eyed with excitement, when Matt locked the door of the tack room, stripped her riding breeches down to her boot tops and bent her over a saddle for a few mad, delicious minutes during one of Amy's riding lessons.

"Someone might come in," he cautioned, wary but unable to resist when she lured him up to her office on the pretext of going over the medical records of a promising yearling she was thinking of buying. Instead they spent fifteen sweaty, breathless, glorious minutes making love on the old leather sofa.

"We're going to get caught," they murmured to each other as they pressed their yearning bodies together against the back wall in a corner of Peg O' My Heart's roomy stall.

They almost were.

"Jax? You in here?"

They both froze, Matt with his mouth pressed against her bared nipple, Jax with her hand down the back of his unbuttoned jeans.

"Oh, my God! It's Beau."

They broke apart like two guilty teenagers caught necking on the living room sofa and started yanking at their clothes, fumbling at bra clasps and buttons, brushing at bits of straw in an effort to make themselves presentable.

"Jax?"

She stuck her head over the stall door. "Over—" She swallowed and tried again. "Over here, Beau," she called brightly. Behind the stall door, she was furiously tucking her shirt into the waistband of her form-fitting riding pants. "Just checking on Peg," she offered by way of explanation as her brother came down the aisle of the barn toward the stall.

"How's she doing?" He leaned an elbow on the wooden door and peered inside. "Has she gone into labor?"

Matt straightened up, looking at Beau over the top of the mare's back. "Nothing yet," he said as if he had just been examining her.

"Hey, Matt." Beau greeted the vet with a smile. "Didn't know you were still here."

"Ah, yeah…just checking on Peg before I—" Matt began.

"I asked him to check on Peg before he—" Jax chimed in.

"Left," they said together.

They both flushed and looked anywhere but at each other.

"So..." Beau glanced back and forth between the two of them, his expression rife with speculation. "How is she?"

"Fine," Matt said.

"She's fine," Jax agreed.

"Are you all right?" Beau asked, looking at his sister. "You look a little flushed."

"I'm fine, too," she said inanely. "Why? Did you want me to ride another horse for a potential buyer?"

"No. Brad Wilson is here with that mare King Lear is supposed to cover. I wanted to know where you want to put her." He tilted his head, regarding his sister from under a raised eyebrow. "Are you sure you're all right?"

"Of course I'm all right. Why wouldn't I be?" She opened the door to the stall and stepped outside, linking her arm with her twin, turning him away from the stall. "Let's go get Mr. Wilson's mare settled in," she said. "I'll see you in a couple of days," she said to Matt, tossing the words over her shoulder as she went off with her brother.

Matt dropped his forehead to the mare's back and vowed to restrict his lovemaking to less public locations from then on.

"I DON'T KNOW HOW TO TALK to kids," Jax warned her lover as they followed the two excited children across a Slidell parking lot toward a popular pizza parlor that catered to young kids.

"You talked to Amy just fine."

"About horses. I can talk to anyone about horses." Jax slanted him a hopeful look out of the corner of her eye. "Is Jeff interested in horses, too?"

"If he is, he's never mentioned it."

"What *is* he interested in, then? Besides differential

equations?'' Lord, she didn't even know what a differential equation was!

"Don't let his brainpower scare you," Matt advised. "He's into the same kinds of things most other nine-year-old boys are."

"As if that helps," Jax said dryly. "I haven't got the faintest idea what most nine-year-old boys are into."

"He likes fishing with his grandfather. And reading about dinosaurs and fossils. And spiders. He has a tarantula in his room. You'd probably make big points if you asked him to show it to you."

"A tarantula? A *live* tarantula? In his room?"

"It's in a glass terrarium on his desk. It's perfectly safe."

Jax shuddered.

"How about football, then? He's a big Saints fan."

"I was still in high school the last time I went to a football game. And I only went then because Beau was playing."

Matt shook his head in mock distress. "And you call yourself a Southerner," he chided gently, grinning at her.

Jax narrowed her eyes at him. "You're not helping."

"And you're worrying too much. You'll be fine. Besides—" he reached around her to open the door of the pizza parlor "—you're not going to have to do much talking this time, anyway." The last few words were spoken close to her ear as a wave of noise blasted through the door and hit them square in the face.

Loud, booming music with bouncy singsong lyrics mixed with the high-decibel sounds of dozens of electronic video games and the high-pitched squeals of excited children. The rich smells of pepperoni, cheese and tomato sauce competed with the scents of popcorn, soda pop and cotton candy. There were clowns and balloons and bright flashing lights throwing rainbows of color on the tent-draped walls.

And there were children.

Everywhere.

They sat at the long tables eating pizza and drinking pop, wearing colorful paper hats shaped like circus animals. They stood three and four deep around the video games, jostling for a turn, cheering or jeering as each laser blast of noise and light signaled the death of another evil alien. They swarmed over a massive indoor jungle gym made of colorful rope ladders, and child-size crawling tubes and chutes, shrieking with laughter as they slid into a pool of what appeared to be large multicolored sponge balls at the bottom of the play area.

Jax took a step backward and came smack up against Matt's chest.

He put his hand on the small of her back. "Oh, no, you don't," he said, and pushed her forward.

Amy grabbed one of Jax's hands in both of hers. "Come an' watch me on the jungle gym," she said, bouncing up and down in excitement. "Come an' watch me."

Jax hung back for a moment, looking to Matt for direction.

And protection.

He threw her to the wolves.

"You go on," Matt said, raising his voice to be heard over the noise. "I'll go order the pizza and find us a table."

"But—"

"Pepperoni okay with you?" Matt asked.

"Yes, but…"

"Good. That's settled then. Jeff—" he touched his son's shoulder, giving him a little nudge "—why don't you go with Jax and your sister and play on the jungle gym while I wait in line."

Jeff hung back. "I want to go with you, Dad," he said. "You're going to need me to help carry the pizza and the sodas and stuff. Besides—" he cast a disparaging glance at his sister, managing at the same time to look through Jax as if she wasn't there ''—the jungle gym is for babies and little kids.''

Matt sighed and let it go. The child pyschologist had warned him not to push. Jeff would warm up to Jax in his own good time.

"Okay, come on, then." Matt cupped his hand over Jeff's shoulder. "We'll meet you in the table area in ten minutes," he said to Jax before father and son headed for the counter to place their order.

"Come on," Amy said, tugging on Jax's hand.

She had no choice but to follow the child.

It wasn't so bad, actually, she realized after a moment. Away from the blaring jukebox and the electronic video games, the noise was considerably less, which was a blessing in itself. And all she had to do was stand outside the red cargo net that enclosed the play space and watch while Amy scampered up the rope ladders and through the colorful tubes. It was no hardship at all, really.

Amy was by far the cutest, most athletic child in the play area, Jax decided as she stood there, watching the seven-year-old climb over the apparatus. She looked adorable in her denim jeans and *101 Dalmations* T-shirt, with her purple, kitten-shaped barrettes already hanging at odd angles in her silky blond hair. She was as agile as a monkey, displaying the same keen sense of balance on the swaying ropes as she did on the back of a horse.

"Watch me now, Jax!" Amy shouted as she gained the top of one of the ladders. She inched her way out onto a horizontal section on her hands and knees. "Watch me!"

"I'm watching," Jax assured her, smiling and waving from her position outside the net.

Amy let go of the ropes and stood, one tiny, sneakered foot balanced on either side of the rope bridge. "Watch—"

Another child climbed out on the rope ladder just behind Amy, causing the rope to sway. Amy shrieked, losing her balance, and the two children tumbled off, disappearing into the mass of colorful balls at the bottom of the enclosure.

"Amy!" Jax's shriek of alarm was nearly as loud as Amy's had been.

She started forward as if she meant to tear her way through the net, then realized that not one of the other adults standing outside the enclosure had so much as batted an eyelash.

Jax tensed, her hands on the net, waiting.

A small head popped up through the soft, spongy balls. The child was laughing, obviously unhurt.

It wasn't Amy.

Jax waited another second, then two, but Amy didn't surface.

Jax started around the edge of the enclosure. "Oh my God, oh my God, oh my God," she muttered under her breath, her hands sliding along the net, faster and faster as she hurried toward the opening at the end, where a wide set of stairs provided a way out of—or into—the play area.

Matt had left his child in her care for one minute, one *minute,* and this was what happened. Poor Amy was probably lying beneath all those balls, suffocating. Or worse. Jax should have told her not to climb so high, or warned her about standing up, or something.

Fighting panic, she stumbled up the wide, child-size stairs and all but fell into the sea of multicolored balls. They puffed up around her with a whooshing sound, soft as feathers. She pushed herself up to her knees and batted them out of the way, trying to keep her balance on the soft, spongy surface beneath them. It was like trying to balance on a half-filled water bed.

"Amy!"

The child popped up, directly in front of her. "Boo!"

she shrieked, and fell over backward, arms outspread, giggling as she sank into the balls.

Without thinking, Jax reached out and grabbed her by the arms, hauling her upright, ready to shake her for playing such a thoughtless trick. *"Amy Taggart, don't you ever—"* she began to say furiously, and then stopped and closed her eyes, willing herself to calm down.

When she opened them again after a count of five, Amy was standing before her, her childish laughter stilled, her big blue eyes beginning to fill, her full lower lip quivering.

Jax felt like a heartless beast. A monster. Snow White's wicked stepmother, Cruella de Ville and the witch from Hansel and Gretel all rolled into one. Amy was just a child. She'd been playing, that was all—showing off—and Jax had reacted as if she'd deliberately misbehaved.

Now what?

"I'm sorry," Jax said. "I didn't mean to yell at you. But you scared me." She ran her hands lightly up and down the child's arms. "I thought you'd hurt yourself when you didn't stand up right away, and I got scared."

Amy's eyes overflowed.

Oh, good Lord, Jax thought. Jeff already hated her. Now Amy would hate her, too. Wonderful! Now what should she do?

"Oh, don't cry, Amy. I'm sorry. Don't cry."

With a muffled sob, Amy threw herself forward, wrapping her arms around Jax's neck. "I'm sorry, too. I didn't mean to scare you, Jax. Honest, I didn't! I just wanted to surprise you."

Jax's arms went around her automatically, catching her, keeping them both from falling backward into the sea of balls. "It's okay." Not knowing what else to do, she patted the child's back. "Don't cry," she crooned, feeling awkward and inadequate. "It's okay. Don't cry."

She'd never held a child in her arms before.

Never soothed a child's tears.

Never *caused* a child's tears.

Oh, Lord, she was making a mess of it!

Where the hell was Matt?

"Jax? Amy? What's going on here? What happened? Is everybody all right?"

Oh, thank God! Reinforcements!

"Amy's fine," Jax hastened to assure Matt, knowing that would be his first concern. "She isn't hurt. She fell and I—"

Amy lifted her head from Jax's neck. "I'm sorry, Daddy," she wailed before Jax could finish her explanation of what had happened. "I didn't mean it."

Matt looked back and forth between the two distraught faces staring at him through the red netting. Jax wore a bewildered expression, caught somewhere between distress and embarrassment. Amy looked guilty.

"Come on out of there, both of you," he said, going around to the opening while they made their way through the sea of spongy balls.

Jax stayed on her knees until she got to the steps, finding it easier to balance that way, then rose, accepting the hand Matt held out to her as she exited the play enclosure. Amy scrambled out on her own and took up a position beside Jax. She looked up at her father from under her lashes and smiled tentatively, without quite meeting his eyes. Knowledge of some wrongdoing was written all over her face.

Matt bit the inside of his cheek. "All right, let's hear it."

"Amy was climbing up the ladder and she—"

"Not you, Jax," Matt said, motioning her to silence as he stared down at his daughter. "What have you got to say for yourself, young lady?"

"I didn't mean to do it, Daddy."

"Uh-huh. What didn't you mean to do?"

Amy ducked her head. "I stood up on the ropes," she mumbled.

"I see." He studied the top of his daughter's bowed head, knowing there was more. She was showing too much penitence for there not to be. "What else?"

"An' I fell off."

"I guessed that much. What else?"

Amy twisted her hands together in the hem of her T-shirt, pulling it out of shape, and hunched her shoulders. "I played a trick on Jax."

"What kind of trick?"

Jax couldn't stand it any longer. The poor child looked miserable. "It's all right, Matt, really," she said, reaching out to put her arm around Amy's shoulders. "She was only play—"

Matt silenced her with a look. "Amy?" he said quietly, demanding an explanation from his daughter.

Amy took advantage of the support offered and leaned into Jax's hip. "I stayed down in the balls an' pretended I got hurt," she said in a small voice, "an' I scared Jax when she came to find me."

"And do you think that was a nice thing to do?"

"No." Amy's voice was almost inaudible now. A tear welled up and slid down her plump little cheek.

Her contrition wrung Jax's heart. She cupped Amy's shoulder in her palm and hugged her closer, offering silent comfort, wishing she hadn't overreacted and made such a big deal out of what was really nothing. The child had only been playing, after all. She had no way of knowing her actions would scare Jax spitless. "She said she was sorry," Jax offered, trying to smooth things over.

"I'm happy to hear that," Matt said, "but that doesn't mean she isn't going to be punished."

Jax clutched Amy a little closer. "Punished?" she said, aghast. "But she apologized for scaring me."

"Scaring you isn't the main issue at the moment. Is it, Amy?"

Amy bit her lip and looked up at Jax. "I'm not suppose to stand up on the ropes," she admitted reluctantly. "We have a rule about that."

"And what do you think your punishment should be for breaking that rule?" Matt asked.

Amy scrunched up her forehead and pressed her lips together, scowling at the floor as she thought about it.

And thought about it.

And thought about it.

Matt crossed his arms over his chest, shaking his head at Jax when she opened her mouth as if to offer a suggestion.

"We're waiting," he reminded his daughter, when she'd drawn things out to about the limit of his patience.

Amy sniffed and wiped at her tear-stained cheek with the heel of her hand.

Jax's heart tightened in her chest and she lifted her gaze to Matt's face, an expression of pleading on her own.

Matt's own expression didn't change by so much as a flicker of an eyelash.

Amy sighed. "No video games while we're here?" she said at last.

"Do you think that will teach you a lesson?" Matt asked.

Amy nodded. "Yes, sir."

"All right. No video games," he agreed. "And no more playing on the jungle gym this trip, either," he added. He waved an arm toward the eating area. "Your brother's waiting over there at a table with the pizza. See him under the polka-dot clown on the wall? You go sit with him while Jax and I get the drinks."

Amy nodded obediently and turned away, dragging her feet as she threaded her way through the tables toward the one where her brother sat.

Jax turned her head to look at Matt. "You must have a heart of stone," she said accusingly.

Matt just grinned. "And yours is obviously made of marshmallow fluff."

"How can you smile?" she demanded. "Your daughter was heartbroken about what happened."

"My daughter was playing you like a violin." He put his hands on Jax's shoulders and turned her around. "Does she look heartbroken to you now?"

Amy had reached the table where her brother sat and had boosted herself up onto her knees in a chair, reaching for a crayon to color the place mat in front of her, talking a mile a minute to the clown who was tying a balloon to the back of her chair. If she was dejected or unhappy, she was certainly hiding it well.

Jax sighed. "I told you I didn't know anything about kids."

"You were so sweet," Matt said later that night, holding Jax in his arms as they lay, naked and sated from their recent lovemaking, on the sleeping bags in the back of his van. "You were more upset than Amy was."

"I saw her fall off of that thing and I just..." She shrugged against his shoulder, embarrassed by her reaction. "My heart nearly stopped in my chest when she didn't pop up right away like that other little kid."

"She fell twice as far when she tumbled off of Rocky," he reminded her. "Onto the hard ground of the training ring. I didn't see you get all panicky then."

"I could see she wasn't hurt when she fell off of Rocky. And she was wearing a helmet. And you were there to take charge." Jax pushed herself up onto her elbow to look down at him. "*I* wasn't responsible for her." That was the crux of it, as far as she was concerned. "I've never been responsible for a child before, even for a few minutes."

"Well, you did just fine." Matt smoothed his hand down the curve of her bare back, soothing her. "Amy wasn't hurt."

"But I *yelled* at her."

"She's been yelled at before."

"Maybe, but I—"

"Jax, sweetheart..." He ran his hand down her back again, coming to rest on the warm curve of her bottom. "Do you really want to talk about Amy?" He stroked the cleft between her buttocks lightly, with the tip of one finger. "Now?"

Jax sucked in her breath. "Well..."

His fingers wandered farther afield, delicately probing between her thighs.

Her eyes clouded with the desire he seemed able to call from her with his slightest touch. "I guess not," she murmured, and bent her head to kiss him.

"IT'S MY TURN TO PICK the video." Jeff opened the cabinet beneath the television in the Taggarts' cozy family room. "But since you're the guest—" he looked up at Jax over his shoulder "—you can pick," he said grudgingly.

Jax knelt down beside him on the carpet and peered into the video cabinet. There was a whole row of animated Disney movies, as well as another shelf of something called *Fairy Tale Theater*, which seemed to be live-action remakes of all the children's classics. Below that were two more shelves of family-oriented entertainment, plus a whole host of educational videos aimed at kids.

Jax reached out and ran the tip of her finger along the titles, watching Jeff out of the corner of her eye as she did so. He liked dinosaurs, his father had said.

"I know you've probably already seen it a hundred times, but would it bore you to see *Jurassic Park* again?" she asked. "I haven't seen it yet."

Jeff looked at her as if he couldn't believe such a thing was possible. "You haven't seen *Jurassic Park*?"

Knowing it probably doomed her to the realm of the totally uncool in the world of nine-year-old boys, Jax shook her head. "No. I've heard it's good, though."

"I guess," Jeff said noncommittally, as if it weren't his favorite movie in the whole world.

"What's it about?" Jax asked, watching him as he pulled the movie out of its plastic case and slid it into the video machine. "Besides dinosaurs, I mean."

"It's about this guy who gets dinosaur DNA from about a million-year-old mosquito trapped in this chunk of amber so he can build an amusement park, like Disney World, only better," Jeff said, his enthusiasm for the movie getting the better of him for a moment. "He hires these scientists to make dinosaurs in a lab, even a raptor, and then—"

"Why don't you wait and let her see it for herself," Matt suggested as he came into the living room with the big bowl of popcorn he and Amy had made. He flashed Jax a quick, approving look that warmed her to her toes as he scooped up individual bowls of popcorn for everyone. "It'll be more interesting for her that way."

Jeff shrugged. "Yeah, sure."

They settled down on the sofa, the adults at either end, the children between them. Amy curled up in the curve of her father's arm, leaving the space next to Jax for her brother. Jeff slouched down on the sofa, his bowl of popcorn in his lap, and stared at the television screen with absorbed fascination, as if it were the first time he'd seen the movie, ignoring Jax as if she wasn't there.

Jax tried to watch the flickering images on the screen without flinching. She made it through the opening scenes and the Tyrannosaurus Rex's escape from its enclosure and even managed to watch as the huge dinosaur started terrorizing the children, knowing they were going to survive the attack unharmed. She gave in and covered her eyes with one hand when it ate the lawyer, though.

Jeff snorted into a handful of popcorn. "It's only a movie," he said scornfully. "The T-Rex didn't really eat him. It's just special effects. Even Amy knows that."

After that, he seemed to take ghoulish delight in warning Jax as each scary segment was about to be shown, embellishing the action a bit. "The dinosaur inside the Jeep is eating that guy's guts out while he's still alive," he told her as they sat watching the vehicle rock back and forth on the screen. "That's why he's screaming."

Jax smiled weakly.

"That bloody arm is all that's left after the raptor got through with the computer guy," he said with boyish enthusiasm for all things gory as a bloody stump fell over the lady scientist's shoulder.

Jax felt like she'd been through the wringer by the time the movie was over. Amy was asleep in her father's arms. Jeff jumped up from the sofa and punched the rewind button on the VCR.

"I could watch it again right now," he said to no one in particular.

"Not tonight," Matt said. "It's time for bed."

"Already?" Jeff protested automatically.

"You have school tomorrow," his father reminded him. "Help Jax gather up the popcorn bowls and soda glasses and take them into the kitchen while I get Amy into bed."

Jeff did as he was told without any argument, following Jax into the kitchen and showing her how to place the bowls in the dishwater.

"I can see why *Jurassic Park* is your favorite movie," Jax said, trying to make conversation. *Don't let his brainpower scare you*, Matt had said. "It was pretty scary, but it was good. I liked it. Do you think scientists could really make dinosaurs like that?"

"Naw." Jeff shrugged. "It's just a story," he said, sounding surprisingly mature for a nine-year-old.

"But it would be nice to think they could, don't you agree? Just the non-meat-eating ones, I mean. The veggie-saursus," she added, using a word one of the characters had used in the movie.

Jeff looked up at her out of the corners of his eyes, his gaze serious and speculative, as if he were wondering just how far she was willing to go to get into his good graces. "I have a pet tarantula in my room. He's kind of a veggie-saursus. His name's Oscar. Like Oscar the Grouch—you know, the Muppet." Jeff gave her a sweet smile. "Would you like to see him?"

"I DON'T KNOW HOW YOU CAN let him keep that big, hairy thing in his room." Jax shuddered. "Just *looking* at it gave me the willies. When he took it out of the terrarium and asked me if I'd like to hold it...ugh," she said, and snuggled into Matt's embrace.

"I thought you liked big, hairy things," Matt teased.

"Not ones with eight legs, I don't," she said vehemently.

"Just the four-legged variety, huh?"

Jax snuggled deeper into his embrace, wrapping her arms around his lean waist as they stood in the shadowy kitchen and lingered over their good-nights. "I was thinking more of the two-legged variety myself," she murmured, and rubbed her nose into the wedge of golden hair visible in the open V of his flannel shirt.

Matt smiled against her temple. "I'm sorry Jeff scared you."

"It's all right. I overreacted."

She could say that now. At the time, all she could do was let out a shriek of pure primal fear and turn tail, fleeing the room when Jeff tried to transfer the tarantula from his hand to her arm.

"Jeff knows he's not supposed to take Oscar out the terrarium. He could get hurt."

"Who? Oscar or Jeff?"

"Oscar. He almost got stepped on when you went running out of the room."

"My heart bleeds for him."

Matt chuckled and cuddled her closer, loving the feel of her in his arms, so soft and warm and alive. "Who?" he teased. "Oscar or Jeff?"

Jax sighed. "Jeff." She leaned back, tilting her head to look up into her lover's face. "Did you really have to ground him for a whole week? He's going to hate me for sure, now."

"He doesn't hate you," Matt countered. "In fact, according to Dr. Fremont, it's probably the other way around. Jeff likes you. And he feels guilty about liking you because you're not his mother. That makes him feel disloyal, and he's conflicted about it, so he acts out. He'll come around. Eventually. He just needs time to get used to the whole idea."

"And what 'idea' is that?" Jax asked carefully. Since their first date, they hadn't really discussed their relationship and where it might be going.

"The whole idea of me and you together," Matt said, just as carefully. "Dating each other on a regular basis."

"Just dating?" Jax asked.

"For now," Matt hedged. That's all it could be, for now. "It's only been two weeks," he reminded her.

Two weeks. It seemed longer. It seemed as if they had been lovers forever. And yet surely only seconds had passed since the first time they'd looked at each other with desire in their eyes.

Jax sighed. "I guess I'd better be getting home," she said, and started to slip out of Matt's arms.

They tightened around her. "One more kiss good-night," he murmured, loath to let her go.

Jax tilted her head back and offered her lips.

The kiss started out slow and sweet, a gentle declaration of the feeling growing, unacknowledged, between them. It ended with Jax pressed up against the kitchen counter, Matt's arms tight around her, his hard thigh between hers, his tongue thrusting between her lips in imitation of the way he wanted to be thrusting into her body. Finally, Jax tore her mouth away.

"We can't do this here," she reminded him, her breathing as ragged as his. "The children."

"I know. God, I know." Matt put his hands on her shoulders and held her away from him for a moment, trying to regain some control. "I want to spend the night with you, Jax," he said softly, his voice still thick with passion. "The whole night. In a real honest-to-goodness bed. I want to wake up in the morning with you in my arms. I want to be able to make love to you without worrying about getting caught, or having to put my clothes on to go home as soon as it's over."

"I want that, too," Jax whispered.

She didn't see how it could happen, though. Not with Charly still sleeping at her cabin. And Matt's kids just down the hall from his bedroom.

It was one thing for children to see the evidence of a loving relationship between two committed adults, quite another to make them a party to the sexual escapades of two people who weren't quite sure where they were headed. Especially when one of those people was their father—and one of the children wasn't any too happy about the fact that his father was dating at all, let alone kissing a woman who wasn't his mother.

"Let's go out of town for the weekend," Matt suggested. "Next Saturday is Valentine's Day. Let's go to New Orleans. I'll get my folks to take care of Jeff and Amy and we'll get away for the weekend, just the two of us. We'll stay at some swanky hotel in the French Quarter. Have dinner at Galatoire's on Saturday, maybe stop by your aunt Toni's club and listen to some jazz. Then, on Sunday, we can have chicory coffee and beignets at the Café du Monde and do the whole tourist thing. We could take a cruise on the *Delta Queen* or a carriage ride, whatever you'd like. How does that sound?"

"It sounds wonderful."

He brushed her hair back with his palm, tucking it behind her ear. "So why do I hear a *but* there?"

"Not a *but*," Jax said. "A *maybe*. Peg is due to deliver any day. Any hour, really. If she went into labor while I was in New Orleans, I probably couldn't get back in time for the birth."

"Bear's more than qualified to handle it."

"I know that. And I'd be more than happy to let him handle it, if it were any other horse." Two other horses were nearly as close to term and she was more than willing to let Bear handle either or both of them when the time came. She was willing to have Bear handle Peg's delivery, too, but she wanted to be there for it. "Peg's special."

"All right. Let's do it this way, then. If Peg delivers by Friday afternoon, we go to New Orleans this weekend. If she doesn't, we'll go the weekend after that. And if she hasn't delivered in two weeks, I'll induce labor, and we'll go the weekend after that. Deal?"

"Deal," Jax said, and pressed her lips to his, sealing the bargain with a kiss.

CHAPTER NINE

EARLY FRIDAY AFTERNOON, Jax met her sisters at Rick's Café for lunch. Their monthly get-togethers had become something of a tradition. There was nothing structured or formal about them. If you could attend, you did; if something else came up, you could cancel with no hard feelings. If you wanted to bring a friend, that was fine, too, although by tacit agreement males of the species were frowned upon. The monthly luncheons were the Delacroix sisters' equivalent of a girls' night out.

They always talked about trying someplace other than Rick's—it had turned into a bit of a teenage hangout over the years—but so far they hadn't. The lunchtime crowd was still mostly businesspeople from the local establishments, and Rick's was close, convenient and familiar. They'd been eating at the restaurant since they were teenagers themselves. Besides, Rick made the best chocolate pecan pie in St. Tammany Parish.

Today, the day before Valentine's Day, was Charly's first outing since what everyone in the family referred to as her "accident."

"How are you feeling?" Jax asked as, without letting go of her sister's elbow, she reached for the handle on the front door of the café and pulled it open. "Everything still okay? Any faintness or dizziness?"

"I'm fine," Charly said irritably. "I'm not feeling faint. I'm not *going* to feel faint. I've never felt faint in my entire life. If I'm suffering from any dizziness it's because all the fluttering you're doing is making my head spin." She tried, unsuccessfully, to yank her elbow out of her sister's grasp, becoming even more irascible when she couldn't accomplish even that small task. "Stop hovering, will you? You're driving me crazy."

"Dr. Greenbaum specifically told me to hover. He said if you were going to be stubborn enough to go walking around town on your own, then I had to be stubborn enough to shadow your every move so I could catch you when you passed out. He didn't seem to think it would do your head any good if you whacked it again too soon."

"Dr. Greenbaum's an old woman. And I'm not walking around town, dammit. I'm walking from the car into Rick's. And I'm not going to pass out, either, so back off," Charly growled, infuriated that she was, in fact, feeling just a little bit light-headed. "I can't breathe with you standing so close. You're using up all my oxygen."

"I'll back off when you're sitting down," Jax said evenly, inured to her younger sister's crabbiness after the last few weeks of enforced intimacy. Charly's bark was worse than her bite. Usually.

"Well, if it isn't the wounded hero." Shelby pulled a chair out as her two sisters approached the table, unobtrusively angling it so Charly could sit down without having to waste energy trying to squeeze between it and the table. "Who let you out of bed?"

"Stuff it," Charly said as she sat, hiding behind a bad-tempered scowl the fact that the room was beginning to spin. She put her elbow on the table and rested her chin on her hand, hoping that would steady things before she fulfilled Dr. Greenbaum's prediction and keeled over, face first, onto the Formica tabletop. "What does a person have to do to get a drink in this joint?" she grumbled. "I'm dying for a glass of iced tea."

Shelby grinned at her sister's show of bravado—Charly

was nearly as white as the paper napkins on the table—and looked around for the teenage waitress. "Two more iced teas, please, Lucy," she said. "And bring us a couple of menus, will you?"

"Is Marie coming?" Jax asked as she pulled out her own chair and sat down. "Or is this all of us today?"

Besides Jax, Shelby and Charly, "all of us" included Joanna Delacroix Gideon. Jax still found it a little startling to look across a table and see a member of the "other" branch of the Delacroix family sitting there. And smiling, no less.

Ten years ago, before Jax had left Bayou Beltane with her tail between her legs, such a thing would have been considered highly improbable, if not downright impossible. The two branches of the family simply didn't mix if they could avoid it. And now here was Philip's oldest daughter, working at Charles's law firm and having lunch with his granddaughters, in public, without Aunt Mary around to make sure they all behaved themselves.

It was enough to boggle the mind.

"I feel the same way sometimes," Joanna said, correctly interpreting the expression on Jax's face.

"Sorry." Jax leaned back a bit as the waitress placed a sweating glass of iced tea in front of her. "I didn't know I was so easy to read."

"Oh, Joanna's good at that," Shelby said. "Reading people's faces, I mean. It's one of the things that makes her such a top-notch litigator."

"Not everybody's face, unfortunately," Joanna said with a sigh.

Jax remembered all the things she'd been hearing lately about the trouble Joanna was having with her daughter, Nikki, and wondered if that was the source of the shadow that suddenly dimmed the sparkle in her relative's lovely blue eyes.

"You ladies ready to order yet?" the waitress asked, obviously hoping they were.

"No, we've got one more com—" Shelby broke off as the front door of Rick's opened. "Over here, Marie," she called, lifting her arm to draw her sister's attention.

Marie turned her head, smiled and began wending her way through the crowded tables toward them. "Sorry I'm late, everybody," she apologized, settling into her chair in a flurry of swirling, feminine skirts. The delicate fragrance of something faintly herbal clung to her clothes. Colorful strands of crystal beads swung from her ears, playing peek-a-boo with her dusky curls.

Next to Joanna and Shelby in their chic lawyer suits and heels, Charly in her tattered jeans and Slidell Police Force sweatshirt, and Jax in her elegant riding breeches and boots, Marie looked like an exotic gypsy. She dressed that way partly, she said, because it was good for business and partly because that was just who she was. Marie wouldn't be Marie in gabardine and pearls.

"The contractor who's repairing the damage to the shop was late, and then Aunt Mary called and said she's almost out of the rosemary oil I mix up for her and would I send her some, so I made up another batch to bring with me before I... Thanks, Lucy," she said, smiling up as the waitress placed a glass of iced tea and a menu in front of her. Marie handed the menu back without looking at it. "I'll just have a bowl of Rick's okra gumbo and—" she glanced around the table "—does anyone want to split an order of garlic bread with me?"

"I'll split it with you," Charly said, and then gave her order to the waitress.

The rest of them followed suit.

"So," Marie said, after the waitress was gone. "How's everybody doing?"

"Well, let's see," Shelby said. "Where to start? Lyle

Masson's attorney came down on me like a ton of bricks this morning. They still haven't found any trace of Yvette, and Lyle's got it into his head that I must know where she and the boy are hiding."

"Do you?" Charly asked.

"Haven't got a clue, Officer. I wish to God I did, though. Poor Yvette is in more trouble than she knows. Lyle's threatening to file kidnapping charges against her for taking Dante."

Marie shook her head. "That's not why your aura is still clouded," she said. "It's something much more personal."

"Yeah, well..." Shelby shrugged. "I'm going to have to call Travis sometime today and tell him I won't be able to fly down for his dad's big shindig at the end of the month. Not for all four days, anyway. He's not going to be pleased."

"There's no way you can swing it?" Marie asked.

"Don't you start on me, too," Shelby said. "I'm going to get enough of that from Travis."

"Sorry, I didn't mean to criticize. It's just that you look so..."

"I know. My aura is clouded, and you're concerned."

Joanna leaned forward in her seat. "What's all this about a 'clouded aura'?" she asked, her gaze going back and forth between Marie and Shelby.

"Didn't you know?" Shelby managed a teasing grin that almost hid the unhappiness in her eyes. "Marie's a witch. She's psychic."

"I've heard, ah...rumors," Joanna said diplomatically. "But I assumed it was some kind of clever advertising gimmick for the shop."

"I'm not a witch," Marie protested. "And I'm not psychic. Psychics can tell the future. I just...sense things."

"What kind of things?" Joanna queried.

"Moods and emotions, usually. Sometimes thoughts, but

that's rare. And sometimes I can tell what's wrong with someone physically, but not always.''

"Can you read my aura?" Joanna asked, faintly intrigued by the possibility.

"Well..."

"Go ahead, Marie," Shelby said. "Tell her what you see when you look at us."

"Yes, go ahead, Marie," Joanna urged when she hesitated. "It might be interesting."

"If you're sure...? Okay, then... Your aura is even more clouded than Shelby's," she said to Joanna. "You're deeply worried. Most of it concerns Nikki, of course—we all know that, so it's not as if I'm telling secrets. But there's something...some*one* else in your family who's worrying you. It's not as big a worry, but it's there, niggling at the edge of your consciousness.''

"There's always something niggling at the edge of my consciousness," Joanna said, clearly unimpressed—and just a little disappointed—with Marie's so-called powers. Joanna had based her life on the principles of common sense and practicality. And common sense told her that anyone who knew her family knew there was always plenty to worry about; it didn't take any special powers to figure that out.

"Dad's always raising Cain over something," she reminded them lightly. "Drew's drinking too much. And Annabelle's getting a divorce.''

"A divorce?" Shelby said. "Annabelle? When did this happen?"

"I'm not sure when, or even why, exactly," Joanna said. "I only heard about it recently. She's moving back to Bayou Beltane and bringing Cade with her. And that's all I know." She glanced at Marie with a look that was half teasing and half challenging. "Unless you're picking up something in my 'aura' that I'm not even aware of.''

"No, I don't think so," Marie said. "You're a very self-aware woman. Very controlled. You do have some fairly intense pain building up on the left side of your head, though, mostly around your eye. A tension headache or the beginnings of a sinus infection, I'm not sure which. I'd recommend a mixture of bergamot, mint and lavender to relieve the pain."

Marie shifted her gaze to her younger sister's face as Joanna self-consciously lifted her hand to the left side of her head, pressing her fingertips to the throbbing ache just beside her eye.

"Charly's tired and feeling the strain of being up and around for the first time since her accident, and she doesn't want anyone to know. And Jax is..." Marie tilted her head to consider Jax more closely. "I can't quite put my finger on the reason for it but..." She frowned, obviously puzzled by what she saw. "Jax is glowing like a candle, from the inside out."

"Getting laid regularly will do that for a woman," Charly quipped, seeing a chance to get a little payback in exchange for all the hovering and fussing she'd had to endure over the past few weeks.

Jax's face turned red, the hot color rising up from the collar of her tailored white shirt. Everybody else laughed, except Marie.

"No, it's more than that. Her aura is more pronounced than usual. Wider, with a stronger glow. It's not just the effects of good sex, it's—" her eyes widened for just a second as she stared into Jax's flushed face "—something else."

"Maybe Matt Taggart knows some neat little trick all the rest of the boys in Bayou Beltane don't," Shelby suggested. She cocked her head at her sister. "How 'bout it, Jax? Has Matt got some secret talent that put that extra glow in your aura?"

Jax threw her a fulminating glare and refused to answer. She picked up her glass of iced tea instead and buried her nose in it, half hoping she could cool her cheeks from the inside out. Did everybody in town know she and Matt were…seeing each other? Or was the knowledge limited to family?

"I guess that means she's not going to share," Shelby said mournfully.

"Darn." Charly snapped her fingers. "And here I was hoping I might learn something useful."

Jax put her glass down with a snap and gave them a haughty glare. "I don't know what happened to you over the last ten years," she scolded her sisters. "You used to be a lot more respectful of your elders."

"We used to be kids who worshiped at the altar of Saint Jacqueline," Charly said matter-of-factly. "But now we know you're one of us and—"

A loud crash rent the air, glasses and crockery shattering, silverware clanging and clattering as it hit the floor and bounced in a dozen different directions. Everyone in the little café turned toward the sound.

A petite young woman, barely more than five feet tall, stood in the middle of the explosion, an overturned wooden crate at her sneakered feet, the broken crockery and spilled silverware mixed with what appeared to a large quantity of fresh shrimp. There was a smear of blood on her thigh just below the hem of her denim cutoffs, where she'd apparently been cut by flying glass.

Jax recognized the woman as Claudia Landry, one of her uncle Remy's employees. She ran the bait shop for him, rented out boats and fishing gear and booked swamp tours.

"Oh dear, oh dear, oh dear," Claudia said, her voice full of distress and embarrassment as she looked up at the young man towering over her.

He wore a white T-shirt with a pack of cigarettes rolled

up in one sleeve, tight blue jeans faded to white at the stress points, and a food-spattered white apron tied around his lean waist and hanging down past his knees. His hair was long and dark, confined at his nape with a strip of black leather. His face was narrow, with high, sculpted cheekbones. He looked like a rock star in some kind of surreal music video about angry youth, right down to the sneer that curled his lips.

"I'm sorry, Steve," Claudia said. "I didn't see you. I—"

"Stupid cow! Look at the mess you made. Why can't you look where you're going?"

"I said I was sorry."

"Sorry doesn't get it," he snarled, railing at her in English tinged with a Cajun accent. "You ruined a bran' new pair of Nikes." He reached out and grabbed her arm. "Who's gonna pay for 'em, huh?"

Before anyone could react to the threat of violence, Rick Roswell, the owner of the café, came out of the kitchen to take charge of the situation. He was a round, bearded man of medium height. A born mediator, he always carefully trod the middle ground, which was part of the reason his café had been a favorite local hangout for so many years.

"Good Lord," he exclaimed as he bustled into the dining room. "What's all the fuss about out here?" He slipped between the two combatants, skillfully forcing Steve to drop Claudia's arm without making a big deal about it. "I could hear the commotion all the way back in the freezer."

"The clumsy bitch dumped her stinkin' shrimp all over me," Steve snarled.

"Oh, dear! Well. What are you doing out here in the first place, so she could spill shrimp on you? You're supposed to be in the kitchen."

"I was givin' Lucy a hand," he retorted. "The *'tite*

chatte was tryin' to lift a tray that was too heavy for her,'' he added, smiling caressingly at the young waitress.

Lucy beamed and smiled back at him, thrilled at being called a little cat.

"Oh, well, very commendable, I'm sure," Rick said, "but Lucy knows better than to overload her trays." He gestured at the waitress. "Run on out to the back and get a broom and a bus pan. This mess needs to be cleaned up before somebody gets hurt."

"She made the mess." Steve gestured at Claudia. "Let her clean it up."

"Cleaning up messes is part of what Lucy gets paid for. Go on, Lucy." Rick waved at the girl, shooing her away. "Do what I told you." He held his hand out to Claudia to assist her to step out of the scattered heap of shrimp and broken crockery at her feet. "Let's get some disinfectant on that cut, shall we? No sense taking a chance on its getting infected."

Steve blocked their way. "I say she oughta clean this mess up herself."

"I believe you've got a couple of orders on the wheel," Rick said, staring the young man down. "We have customers waiting," he added, reminding him of their audience.

Steve hesitated for a split second, long enough to make everyone in the café wonder what he would do, then lifted one shoulder in a negligent shrug. "You owe me ninety bucks for these shoes, Landry," he said to Claudia. "They smell like one of your father's stinkin' shrimp boats."

With that he turned and sauntered into the kitchen.

"I'm sorry, Rick," Claudia said, looking up at the café owner in confusion. "I don't know what happened. I just..." Her hands fluttered in front of her. "I'm such a klutz."

"Don't worry about it. It's just some broken glass and a few shrimp."

"But Steve... He was so mad."

"Don't worry about Boudreaux, either," Rick said as he led her to one of the back booths and handed her a paper napkin to daub at the blood on her leg. "He'll cool off."

The show was over, the crisis averted. The diners returned their attention to what was in front of them.

"Poor Claudia." Shelby shook her head. "I swear, I don't know how she keeps from tripping over her own feet. I keep expecting to hear that she fell off one of Uncle Remy's tour boats and got eaten by a gator."

"Will he try to hurt her, do you think?" Jax asked.

Shelby didn't need to ask who she meant by *he*. "Not unless he wants Uncle Remy to wipe the floor with his sorry butt," she said with some satisfaction. "And if Remy doesn't put the fear of God into him, she's got four great big older brothers who I'm sure would be happy to pound him to a bloody pulp before they drop him into the swamp."

"Oh, I wish they would," Joanna said. "God forgive me, I wish they would! Then he might leave Nikki alone, too."

Jax turned to look at the elegant woman sitting across the table from her. Two spots of furious color stained Joanna's chiseled cheekbones. Her beautifully manicured hands were clenched together on the table.

Jax abruptly put it all together.

That snarling, angry young man was Steve Boudreaux. Steve was the English translation of Etienne. And Etienne Boudreaux was the boy Joanna's seventeen-year-old daughter was dating.

He was at least nineteen, maybe older, but far too old for Nikki, in any case. In experience, if not in actual years. He had the kind of reputation that took more than just a bad attitude to sustain, and the kind of looks that would appeal to a lot of young girls—dark, wild and just a little bit dangerous. Jax had no doubt that he was all three of those things.

No wonder Joanna was worried.

"Can't you ground Nikki or something?" Jax said, horrified at the thought of her young cousin dating someone like Steve Boudreaux. "Forbid her to see him?"

"I tried that," Joanna admitted. "I've tried everything I can think of, short of nailing the windows to her room shut. And believe me, if I thought that would work, I'd try that, too. But everything I do just seems to make it worse."

Marie laid her hand over Joanna's. "Maybe he'll break it off with her himself," she said. "Or she'll break it off with him. There were some pretty strong vibes there just now between him and Lucy. Either they've got something going or they will have shortly. Surely Nikki wouldn't put up with that?"

"I don't know what Nikki would or wouldn't put up with," Joanna admitted. "She doesn't talk to me about her feelings anymore. She doesn't talk to me about any..." Joanna closed her eyes and pressed her lips together, obviously fighting for control. In a surprisingly short time, she had it.

Jax suddenly believed everything she'd ever heard about Joanna's skill as a litigator. The woman's command of her emotions was truly awesome. No one looking at her now would know she had just been on the verge of tears.

Unless that someone was Marie.

"Would you like to leave, Joanna?" she asked gently. "We don't have to eat here. There's a little tea shop that just opened up a couple of streets over. We could go there. Or the Woolworth on Cypress. They still have a sandwich counter."

Joanna shook her head. "We've already ordered."

"That doesn't mean we have to stay and eat," Charly said. "I vote we blow this joint."

Joanna's eyes almost filled again. "Thank you," she said, her gaze touching each one of them in turn. "I appreciate what you're trying to do, but it isn't necessary. Really. I'm not going to break down, and I'm not about to let some low-rent, imitation James Dean dictate my actions. I came in here to have lunch with you all, and that's what I'm going to do."

"Hear, hear," Shelby said, and raised her glass of iced tea.

The five women clicked glasses, each softly echoing the cheer, but their good spirits had deserted them. They ate their lunch with acid-inducing haste, each of them declining dessert when it was offered despite the outstanding quality of Rick's chocolate pecan pie.

"I hate to be the one to break this up," Jax said, waving away the waitress's offer of more iced tea, "but I think it's about time Charly and I headed back to Riverwood. I think she's been up long enough for her first outing."

It was a measure of just how tired Charly was that she didn't object to being told she was tired.

Joanna laid a few bills on the table to cover her share of the cost of lunch. "I should get going, too. I have a deposition this afternoon." She rose gracefully from her chair. "Shelby? You ready?"

"I'm going to run out to Aunt Mary's before I head back to the office. I've got a little Valentine's gift to deliver." She glanced at Marie as she got to her feet. "If you're in a hurry to get back to the shop, I'll be happy to take that rose oil to her for you."

"Rosemary," Marie corrected her automatically. "And, thanks. It'll really save me some time." She dug into her voluminous tapestry shoulder bag and pulled out a pale green glass vial. "Give her this, too," she added, drawing a plump sachet out of her bag.

Shelby lifted it to her nose. "Smells good. What is it?"

"Mostly eucalyptus with a little sage and cinnamon and just a pinch of saffron. It promotes healing."

"Will Aunt Mary know what she's supposed to do with it?"

"Tell her to put it under her pillow at night."

Shelby nodded and put both items into her own purse.

Five minutes later, after the flurry of goodbyes and last-minute comments and conversation common to five women taking their leave of one another, Jax stood on the sidewalk in front of Rick's Café, holding open the passenger door of her Mercedes for Charly. While her sister gingerly lowered herself into the seat, she felt a light touch on her shoulder and turned to find Marie standing beside her.

"Can I talk to you a minute before you head back to the farm?" Marie said. *"Privately?"*

"Yes, of course." Jax shut the car door, then leaned down, smiling at her youngest sister through the open window. "Give me a minute, will you, Charly? I'll be right there."

"Yeah, sure." Eyes closed, head back against the headrest, Charly waved her hand. "Take your time."

Jax turned, following Marie to the rear bumper of the classy little sports car. "What is it?" she said anxiously. "What do you see? Is there something wrong with Charly's aura?"

"It's not about Charly." Marie bit her lip. "It's about you."

"Me? What about me?"

"Well, I know this is going to sound preposterous. And it's a terrible invasion of privacy but...well..." She shrugged. "I see what I see."

"Just spit it out, Marie. What is it?"

"You're pregnant."

"I'm *what?*"

"Pregnant. With child," she added when Jax just stood

there staring at her. "In an interesting condition. Jax, honey." Marie grabbed her sister by the arms and shook her lightly, trying to get a response. "You've got a bun in the oven."

"That's impossible."

"Nothing's impossible."

"But—but..." Jax's mouth opened and closed a couple of times, like a fish gasping for air. "Greg and I...we tried to... For almost four years, we tried. I had all those tests and the fertility shots and... They said the odds were so stacked against my ever getting pregnant that we should consider it impossible and adopt. Greg and his mother refused to consider that, of course, and I wasn't—" She clamped her lips shut, realizing she was babbling. "I can't be pregnant, Marie. Matt and I...we've only been, ah—" she flushed slightly "—intimate for a week or so."

Marie flashed her a wry look. "It only takes once, with the right man."

"No." Jax shook her head, refusing to let herself believe it. "It's completely, absolutely impossible."

"It's not impossible. I can see it, clear as day, when I look at you. You've got two distinct auras."

"Auras! You're basing this on *auras?*"

"I see what I see," Marie repeated stubbornly. "You weren't so quick to dismiss it when you thought I saw something in Charly's."

"Yes, but that was... I'm sorry, you're right. It isn't fair of me to use a double standard like that. If I was willing to believe you could detect things about Charly, I guess I have to believe you can about me, too. But Marie...my God, Marie, couldn't you be wrong?"

"I could be," Marie conceded. "I've never actually seen a baby in anybody's aura before, so there's room for doubt, I guess," she said, but it was obvious she didn't feel any.

"It must have something to do with you being my sister. I'll have to ask Desiree."

"No!" Jax put her hand over her heart, instinctively trying to calm herself. "No, don't ask anyone. Don't tell anyone. Don't say *anything* about this. Not until I know for sure."

"All right," Marie agreed. "I won't say a word to anyone. Not even Lucas." She opened her voluminous shoulder bag, digging through it as she spoke. "You go take your pregnancy tests and visit a couple of high-priced New Orleans obstetricians. Do whatever you need to do to convince yourself of the truth. In the meantime, start making your breakfast tea with this." She put a small plastic bag in Jax's hand. It was filled with tiny bits and pieces of leaves. "I mixed this up and put this in my purse this morning before I left the shop. I didn't know why. Now I do."

Jax lifted it to her nose. "What is it?"

"It's peppermint. For nausea. You're going to need it."

SHELBY FOUND HER Aunt Mary outside in the garden of the house she shared with Uncle William, kneeling in the soft, warm dirt of her flower garden.

"Shelby, what a surprise," she said, looking up at her great-niece from under the wide brim of a straw hat that had seen better days. She wore her gardening clothes, a long-sleeved cotton shirt and wide-legged slacks. Flowered cotton gardening gloves covered her hands. Her gorgeous snowy white hair, usually worn in a soft bun on top of her head, hung halfway down her back in a thick, loosely plaited braid.

"Should you be out here working in this heat?"

"I was just doing a little weeding." Mary drew off her gardening gloves, dropping them into the basket by her side, and held her hands up, allowing Shelby to assist her to her feet. "Nothing strenuous, I promise. It relaxes me."

Shelby bent her knees a little, peering at her great-aunt's face under her wide-brimmed hat. "You do look more rested than you have in a long time."

"Thank you, my dear. I'll take that as a compliment." She tucked her hand into the crook of Shelby's arm. "Let's go up onto the veranda and have a nice cool glass of lemonade while you tell me what brings you to visit your old aunt in the middle of the day. Nothing's wrong, I hope?"

"No, nothing's wrong." Shelby walked slowly, matching her aunt's steps as they made their way across the backyard and up the steps to the wide, sheltered porch. "I just wanted to stop by and bring you a little Valentine's Day gift."

She handed her aunt into one of the graceful cushioned wicker chairs scattered over the veranda, then set her briefcase on the glass-topped table and unsnapped the latches.

"Chocolate truffles," she said, handing her aunt a small oblong box wrapped in gold foil. "I stopped by that little French bakery on Cypress on my way into work this morning to get some pastries to take to the office. I saw these and remembered they're your favorites. Happy Valentine's Day, Aunt Mary."

"Oh, how thoughtful." Mary was clearly delighted with the gift. "I'll have to hide them from William or he'll have them all eaten up before dinner." The two women shared a smile. "I think sweets are his only vice."

"Marie asked me to give you this." Shelby set the small bottle of oil on the table. "She said you'd know what to do with it. And this." She handed her aunt the sachet. "She said you're supposed to put it under your pillow at night. Everyone else—Jax and Charly and Joanna—said be sure to tell you hello. Charly said she'd have Jax bring her over sometime next week, when she's allowed out again."

Mary spent a few minutes discussing Charly's recuperation. She frowned over Joanna and the disturbing situation with Nikki. And then, inveterate matchmaker that she was, she asked about Jax.

"I've heard rumors that young Matt Taggart and Jacqueline have been seeing a lot of each other lately." Her dark eyes glittered at the possibility of romance. "Is it serious, do you think?"

"I have no idea," Shelby said truthfully. "You know Jax. She always plays it pretty close to the vest. So far as anyone knows, they're just dating."

They were doing a good bit more than that, of course, but Shelby wasn't about to mention it. Mary Delacroix was a genteel Southern spinster, with all that label implied. She didn't need to know that one of her great-nieces was rumored to have been spending her evenings of late in the back of a white Chevy van parked down by the bayou, with a man not her husband—or even her intended, as far as anyone knew.

Mary had already had one heart attack.

"And how is your romance going, dear? Have you and Travis set a date yet?"

Shelby shook her head. "Not yet."

"Well, don't wait too long. If you put it off, sometimes things..." the old woman's voice trailed off and her eyes grew misty for a moment, as if she had suddenly gone far away. "Things happen when you wait too long to act on your true feelings for a person," she said, as if speaking to herself. "Things...change," she murmured.

Shelby reached out and laid a gentle hand on her aunt's shoulder. "Aunt Mary? Are you all right?"

Mary shuddered delicately and put a frail, veined hand to her heart.

"Should I call someone?" Shelby asked. "Do you need your medicine?" Shelby shook her aunt's shoulder. "Aunt Mary?"

Mary dropped her hand. "What?" She blinked like someone coming out of a trance. "Yes? What is it?"

"Do you need your medicine?"

"Medicine? Oh, no, dear, thank you." Mary looked up at her niece and smiled reassuringly. "A goose must have walked over my grave, is all. I felt a little shivery for a moment."

"Should I go get you a sweater?"

"Land sakes, no, child! I'm quite comfortable as I am." She reached out and grasped Shelby by the wrist. "You haven't broken your promise to me, have you?"

"My promise?"

"About your great-grandfather Hamilton's papers. You haven't read them, have you? You destroyed them, didn't you?"

"I didn't read them, Aunt Mary. Honest. I promised you I wouldn't."

"Good." Mary patted Shelby's hand before she released it. "You're a good girl, Shelby." She rose from the wicker chair. "Let's go inside now and see about that lemonade, shall we?"

Shelby followed her great-aunt into the house, feeling like a heel, wondering if keeping half a promise counted in the scheme of things. She hadn't read Hamilton Delacroix's papers about the last case he'd ever taken, but she hadn't destroyed them, either.

CHAPTER TEN

"WHAT WAS THAT ALL ABOUT?" Charly asked as Jax got into the car.

You're pregnant.

Jax tossed the small plastic bag of herbs into Charly's lap. "She wants you to drink a cup of tea made out of this every morning until it's gone."

"Tea? What for?"

With child.

"To build your strength up or something." Very carefully, because her hands were shaking and she didn't want Charly to notice, she inserted the key into the ignition and turned it. "It's some kind of restorative."

"What do you suppose is in it?" Charly opened the bag and lifted it to her nose, taking a cautious sniff. "Smells like peppermint."

In an interesting condition.

"I think that's to disguise the taste of whatever else is in there."

"Wolfsbane?" Charly guessed. "Eye of newt?"

Jax, honey, you've got a bun in the oven.

"I have no idea," Jax said, her eyes on the rearview mirror as she backed out of the parking space. "She didn't say."

"Well, I'm not drinking it. I don't care if it smells like peppermint or not," Charly said, lifting her hand to her mouth to stifle a yawn. "Don't tell Marie."

"I won't," Jax promised, but her sister was already asleep.

Jax pushed the accelerator closer to the floor and headed toward home.

It took less than ten minutes to maneuver the little Mercedes through the streets of the small downtown area of Bayou Beltane and onto the road leading out to Delacroix Farms. Along the way Jax tried to remember the exact date of her last period and failed. She knew more about her horses' reproductive schedules than she did her own, but when a woman had no reason to keep close track, precise dates became unimportant.

Was she due in a few days? Next week? Last week?

Until she could get her hands on a calendar, she wouldn't know for sure.

She thought she should probably try to get her hands on one of those early pregnancy test kits, too.

Although both the local Winn-Dixie and Gleason's Rexall Drug Store undoubtedly stocked such an item, she passed them by without stopping. Even if she hadn't had Charly in the car with her, she wouldn't—*couldn't*—have stopped. Five minutes after she walked out of either place with a brown paper sack in her hand, the news would be all over town that Jax Delacroix had purchased a pregnancy test.

She'd have to go to Covington. Or Slidell. Yes, Slidell was a much bigger town. No one would know her there. She could probably pick up a pregnancy test at some out-of-the-way drugstore and be assured of total anonymity. Maybe there was a clinic she could visit, too. One of those urgent-care facilities where you didn't need an appointment. It would be reassuring to have a doctor's opinion to back up what she was sure would be the negative results of the pregnancy test, assuming medical science even had a test that could detect a pregnancy the first week after conception.

Not that she actually *believed* she was pregnant. Oh, no. It was just that she wanted to make sure she wasn't before she gave in to the welter of feelings that had swamped her at the first mention of the word in connection with herself.

But first she had to get rid of Charly.

"Wake up, honey." She reached over the console and shook her sister's shoulder. "We're home."

"Already?" Charly stretched and yawned, then stretched again.

Jax had to clench her hands around the steering wheel to keep from opening the door and pushing her out. She got out on her own side instead and hurried around to the passenger door.

"Let's get you inside." She reached down and put her hand under Charly's elbow, practically lifting her bodily from the seat. "What you need is a nice long nap."

"Oops. Wait a minute. I dropped my tea."

"Leave it. You said you weren't going to drink it, anyway."

"Yeah, but I can't just leave it out here. What if Marie—"

"Here." Jax picked it up and shoved it into her hand. "Now, let's get you inside before you pass out."

"I'm not going to pass out, okay? And slow down, would you? You're making me dizzy again."

Jax forced herself to moderate her pace. "I'm sorry. I just wanted to get you into the house before you—"

Charly shot her a blurry, narrow-eyed glare, daring her to say it.

"You're awfully pale," Jax said instead. "I'll feel better when you're lying down."

"I will, too," Charly admitted, which was a measure of

how much the day's excursion had taken out of her. Charly hated admitting to any weakness.

Jax got her into the house with a minimum of fuss after that, holding her elbow all the way to the sofa. "Here, let me help you with those," she said, bending over to pull Charly's sneakers off. "Lift your legs up on the sofa...that's it." She pulled the afghan over her sister's shoulders.

"Would you brew me a cup of Marie's tea?" Charly asked. "I think I could use some strengthening, after all."

Jax clamped her teeth against the scream of impatience that rose to her lips and went to make the tea. "Boil, dammit," she muttered at the kettle, vowing to buy a microwave for her cabin—right after she bought the pregnancy test.

By the time the tea was brewed, Charly was fast asleep.

Jax set the delicate Wedgwood cup and saucer down on the coffee table next to the sofa and tiptoed out of the room, thankful not to have to come up with an excuse for why she was leaving again, so soon after coming home.

She had just curled her fingers around the handle of her car door when she heard someone call her name. Stifling a scream of frustration, she turned to face the distinguished white-haired man making his way toward her down the path from the main house. "Grandfather," she said, forcing herself to smile. "Can I do something for you?"

"Jacqueline, my dear," he said pleasantly. "You could take a few minutes to visit with an old man, if you would," he said. "That is—" he glanced at her hand resting on the handle of the car door "—unless you have somewhere you must be right away?"

Jax snatched her hand back. "No, of course not. I was just going into town to, uh, get some tea for Charly. If you need me for something, it can wait."

"Excellent, my dear." He crooked his elbow, offering it to her with a courtly gesture. "Walk with me, will you?"

Jax curled her hand around his forearm and let herself be drawn along beside him. He walked quietly for several minutes, ambling toward the racetrack as if he were just out for a casual stroll and had merely wanted the company of his eldest granddaughter. But Jax wasn't fooled. He might look like a sleepy-eyed country gentleman with his snow white hair and cardigan sweaters, but Charles Delacroix was still as sharp as a tack. He seldom did anything without a purpose. Jax knew that whatever the reason he'd sought her out, he'd get to it in his own good time. He often used the tactic of silence, waiting for some unwary soul to fill it and incriminate him or herself. Jax had learned to wait him out.

She strolled along beside him, neither hurrying ahead nor lagging behind, for all the world as if she had nothing better to do and nowhere else she wanted to be.

They ended up leaning on the fence circling the quarter-mile track, watching the exercise boys breeze two of Beau's three-year-olds, before Charles spoke again.

"Beau tells me he's thinking of entering Hot Shot in the Bayou Stakes," Charles said.

"Yes, he mentioned it to me, too. I don't think he's made up his mind, though. The race isn't until next fall, so he has plenty of time to decide."

"Still, the sooner he starts the filly on a special training regime, the better his chances will be if he decides to enter her."

"Oh, I think he's started Hot Shot's training. Beau wouldn't leave a thing like that to chance."

"Perhaps not," Charles agreed. He fell silent again, his eyes on the two young horses circling the track. "I hear you've been seeing quite a bit of the Taggart boy."

Jax nearly swallowed her tongue at the unexpectedness

of his comment. Her relationship with Matt was the *last* thing she would have ever thought her grandfather would ask her about. "We've, ah...we've been out a few times, yes."

"Is it serious?"

Was the possibility you were carrying a man's child serious?

"In what way?" she asked carefully.

Her grandfather slanted a look at her from under his snowy brows. "There is only one way in which a relationship between a man and a woman can be serious, Jacqueline," he chided gently.

"We've only been, ah...seeing each other for a couple of weeks, Grandfather. There hasn't been enough time to decide if we're serious yet."

"Hasn't there?" he said, and left one of his silences for her to fill.

Jax refused to fill it. She wanted to tell him that it was none of his business. That she was thirty-two years old, not sixteen, and her private life was just that—private. But the habits of a lifetime were too deeply ingrained. Being impolite to her grandfather was impossible.

"We're not engaged or anything, if that's what you're asking," she said finally. "We're just dating."

"High school children date each other, Jacqueline. You and Matt Taggart are adults. You've both been married before."

"So?" she said warily.

"You should be able to tell within a relatively short period of time whether there is the potential for a serious relationship."

"Why?"

"Why what?"

"Why are you interested in whether or not Matt and I are involved in a serious relationship?"

"You're my granddaughter. I'm naturally interested in your happiness."

She stared at him, using his tactic of silence on him.

"There's been talk," Charles said finally. "I'd hate to see your reputation tarnished."

"Talk?" she sputtered. "My reputation... Tarnished..."

"You're a Delacroix, Jacqueline. And an Olympic gold medal winner. That makes you a role model, especially in this community. People, young women, look up to you. You have a duty to your position."

"My position? What the he—"

Her beeper went off.

"Oh, for crying out loud, *now what?*"

Peg was in labor.

JAX WAS ON HER KNEES, checking the position of the foal, when Matt arrived.

He approached Peg's stall quietly, making no unnecessary noise, waiting silently just outside the door until Jax had withdrawn her hand from the mare's vagina and moved back against the wall next to Bear, out of the range of any stray kicks.

Peg was not generally a kicker. In fact, she had never kicked anyone, but like her human counterpart, a mare in labor was not to be trifled with or underestimated. The pain could turn her mean in a heartbeat.

"Everything okay?" Matt whispered.

"So far, so good," Jax whispered back. "Her water broke a few minutes ago. All we can do now is wait for the contractions to begin."

Within another few minutes, they did.

The rotational contractions began first, as the mare's body began to roll the foal over for delivery. A short time later, the expulsive uterine contractions, meant to push the baby from the womb, started. The foal's tiny front hooves emerged, one slightly ahead of the other, in the staggered position that indicated all was going well. And then Peg faltered and began to show signs of restiveness. She kicked out abruptly and got to her feet—causing Jax and Bear to move quickly in the other direction—then just as abruptly lay back down again, only to struggle to her feet once more.

"The foal isn't turning," Matt said.

He opened the stall door, stepping inside as Bear moved past him to the outside. Too many people hovering around her would only make the mare nervous and complicate matters even further. That was why pregnant mares were kept in a separate barn; there was less noise and less activity to upset them. The lights were kept low and distractions held to an absolute minimum.

"Let's give her a few minutes to work it out on her own," Matt said, putting his hand on Jax's arm when she would have gone forward to assist. "She's not in any trouble yet."

Peg repeated the process a few more times, getting up, turning around, then lying back down again, without any appreciable progress. The foal's front feet remained the only part of the baby that had made the passage through the birth canal.

"All right. Let's take a look," Matt said.

Jax knelt at the mare's head to hold her, stroking her neck to keep her calm while Matt checked the position of the foal.

"She's trying to turn it to the left," he said, tacitly informing Jax of what he meant to do.

Very gently, with the utmost care for the fragility of both the unborn foal and the mare's delicate tissues, Matt grasped the foal's legs above the fetlock joint and crossed the right one over the left.

"Here it comes," Jax said, meaning the next contraction.

Very gently and slowly, his movements precise to the

inch, Matt twisted the foal's legs in a sort of corkscrew motion, helping Peg to roll her baby into position so she could push it out. When the contraction was over, he rested, breathing along with Peg, still holding the foal's legs to keep it from rolling back as they waited for the next contraction to begin.

"That's it, girl. That's it. You're doing fine, sweetheart." His soft Louisiana drawl was barely more than a whisper, soothing, hypnotic, calming. "Give me another one, now. That's it. Just a couple more. Come on, girl. Come on."

Peg labored hard for twenty minutes more, her whole body straining to expel the foal. When it came, it came in a rush, the force of it sending Matt backward with a lapful of newborn foal in his arms. He struggled to a sitting position, being careful not to injure the new baby or jostle it so much that its back legs slipped outside of its mother's body.

The mare was in a post-foaling fog, resting quietly, her head down, exhausted by the ordeal she'd just gone through. Having the foal's back legs remain inside her somehow seemed to contribute to this "hypnotic" state. The longer she could be kept quiet, the better it would be for both mother and baby. She needed the recovery time to regain her strength, and the longer the umbilical cord remained attached, the better it was for the foal. Peg would signal her readiness for the next step in the process by standing up, which would break the cord. Until then, the only thing her human attendants could do was sit very still, say nothing and wait.

Matt looked up, across the back of the exhausted mare. "It's a boy," he mouthed silently when Jax's gaze met his.

She was crying.

"WHAT'S THIS ALL ABOUT?" Matt asked gently, wiping at her damp cheeks with his fingertips, trying not to let his increasing uneasiness show.

She'd been crying for the last twenty minutes, the big, fat tears rolling down her cheeks like summer rain on magnolia petals while he sat there on the floor of the stall, watching her, helpless to do anything to soothe her until Peg surged to her feet and released them all from the need for absolute silence.

Jax had risen with her, stroking the mare's nose, crooning a few words of praise before turning to fall softly to her knees beside the colt. She ran her hands over him almost reverently, smoothing and stroking him, her tears falling on his already wet coat, until Peg became impatient and knocked her out of the way with a forceful butt of her head.

Bear had reentered the stall then, coming in to take over and do what had to be done for the mother and her newborn.

Matt had taken Jax by the arm and led her out of the foaling barn.

"Sweetheart, what is it? Try to tell me. I can't help you if you don't tell me what it is."

"H-h-he's s-so b-beautiful," she said, which was no answer at all.

Matt did the only thing he could do. Ignoring the unmistakable evidence of the birth process still smeared all over both of them, he took her in his arms and held her tightly.

"Okay, sweetheart, cry it out," he murmured, stroking her hair as if she were Amy's age. "Howl, if you want to. We'll figure out what's wrong later."

Jax curled her fingers into the fabric of his shirt and did exactly that.

She felt so wonderful, and so awful, all at once.

She'd given up all thoughts of a home and a family of her own years ago, managing, somehow, to convince herself that she hadn't ever really wanted them, anyway. And she'd done a pretty good job of it, too. She'd almost believed it. For ten long, lonely years she *had* believed it.

And then Matt had come into her life.

Matt, with his gentle voice and gentler hands.

Matt, with his strong body and stronger principles.

Matt, who made her tremble and quiver and burn for his touch.

Matt, with his two wonderful children.

Matt, who'd made her pregnant.

Pregnant!

She didn't need any early pregnancy tests or doctors to tell her it was so. Like Marie, she knew. The minute the word had been spoken, out there on the sidewalk in front of Rick's Café, she'd known it was true, despite her protests to the contrary. It had taken the miracle of birth—seeing it, feeling it, as Peg strained to bring new life into the world—before Jax could finally admit it to herself. But it was true. She knew it, deep inside, on some instinctive, inexplicable, infallible level that defied all logic. She didn't need tests. She *knew*.

She had conceived a baby with the man she loved.

It was the culmination of all her dreams. The thing she'd given up wishing for but had never stopped hoping would happen. Everything she had ever wanted, ever wished for, ever dreamed of, was right in front of her.

A home.

A husband.

A family of her own.

A baby.

Only…how was she ever going to find the words to tell him he'd been trapped into fatherhood again?

Maybe it would be best to start with something just a little less earth-shattering.

Jax lifted her tear-streaked face from his chest and looked up at him. "I love you," she said.

"It's okay, sweetheart, everything will—" He stopped cold, realizing what she'd said. "Say that again," he ordered, just to be sure he'd heard it right.

She smiled tremulously through her tears. "I love you," she said again, and hoped that would be enough to make it right.

CHAPTER ELEVEN

THEY WERE GOING to New Orleans for the weekend, after all.

Jax fairly flew up the path to her cabin, happiness and excitement sizzling through her veins, with only the tiniest cloud of doubt to mar her joy. She hadn't told him yet, but she would.

Sometime this weekend, when they were alone and the mood was just right, she'd tell him she was going to bear him a child.

And he'd be happy about it.

He'd have to be happy about it.

Because he loved her.

He'd said so.

Standing there, outside the foaling barn, both of them smeared with streaks of blood and goo, he'd ordered her to repeat the words, and then gave them back to her in that slow, sweet drawl of his.

"I love you, too, sweetheart," he'd said.

And then he'd kissed her, right there out in the open, in front of God and everybody, taking his time about it, doing a thorough job, leaving her breathless and aching and as giddy as a schoolgirl who had just won the heart of the most popular boy in high school. The news would be all over Bayou Beltane by nightfall.

He loved her!

And surely a man who loved a woman would be happy to know she was going to have his baby.

She grabbed on to that thought, holding it close to her heart as she mounted the steps to her cabin and pushed open the door.

"It's over," Shelby said. "I know it's over. And damn it, *I don't care!*"

"Yes, you do care," Charly said reasonably, "or you wouldn't be acting like this."

"Shelby?" Jax said as she stepped into the room.

Shelby turned to look at her oldest sister. Her posture was unnaturally stiff, her slender shoulders braced as if to ward off a blow. Tears glittered in her eyes, making them look like rain clouds on a stormy day.

"Shelby, honey, what is it?"

"I talked to Travis."

"And?"

"And he said if I couldn't manage to get down there for all four days, then I might as well not bother to go at all."

"Oh, Shelby." Jax reached out, offering comfort, but Shelby moved away.

She wasn't finished raging yet. "He's just being so damned unfair about this! I tried to explain about the caseload at work, and how Granddad is counting on me to keep it all together until things level off, but he didn't want to hear it. He's had a grudge against the family from day one, and he resents the fact that I have obligations to it that I can't and won't disregard. I don't care what he thinks Granddad was involved in way back before God was born, he's just plain wrong! He *admitted* he was wrong."

"A grudge about what?" Charly asked, her nose twitching at the scent of a mystery. Her injuries may have slowed her down physically, but they hadn't dulled her instincts one iota. "What does he think Granddad was involved in?"

"He doesn't think he was involved in anything now," Shelby said.

"But he thought he was involved in something once," Charly persisted. "What was it?"

"It isn't important. Really. It involved an old case of Great-grandfather Hamilton's and one of Travis's relatives, who's been deceased for a very long time. He thought Granddad might have known something about it, but he didn't and he doesn't, and that's the end of it."

"Except that Travis is still holding a grudge."

"No, Travis is *not* holding a grudge," Shelby said in exasperation. "He's being a pigheaded, selfish, irrational jerk."

"And you love him, anyway," Jax said.

"Yes, dammit! I love him, anyway." She looked up at her oldest sister through watery eyes, as if just realizing she was in the room. "What happened to you?"

"What happened to... Oh." Jax looked down at her filthy riding breeches and rumbled blouse. "Peg O' My Heart just delivered a foal, sired by True Blue. Prettiest little bay colt you've ever seen. I've entered him in the stud book as True Heart."

"No," Shelby said. "I mean what happened to *you?* You're—" she shook her head "—incandescent."

Jax hesitated. She felt selfish and unloving and just plain disloyal, being so happy when Shelby was so miserable, but she couldn't help it.

She was in love.

And she was going to have a baby!

"Matt and I are spending the weekend in New Orleans."

IT DIDN'T TAKE JAX LONG to pack for the weekend; a couple of simple dresses for day, something a little more elegant for evening, nightclothes, a few toiletries and she was done. There was one more thing she had to do, though, before she could consider herself ready for the weekend that lay ahead.

She might know, deep in her heart, beyond any doubt, that she was pregnant. But she still wanted scientific proof of it before she told Matt he was going to become a father for the third time.

The drugstore in Covington carried half-a-dozen different early pregnancy tests. She bought two. They both came out positive.

While Jax was locked in the bathroom of her cabin, taking her pregnancy tests, Matt was at home, packing for the weekend jaunt to New Orleans in a haze of indescribable joy and abject terror. He was getting ready to spend the weekend with a sweet, beautiful, exciting, wonderful woman and yet...

Three weeks ago—hell, *less* than three weeks ago—he'd been hesitant to ask her out on a date because he wasn't sure he was ready for another relationship.

An hour ago he'd told her he loved her.

And meant it.

But he still didn't know where all this was headed.

If it was just himself to consider, he could let it coast along and enjoy the ride for as long as it took to figure it out. But he had Amy and Jeff to think of. What if they fell in love with her, too? Amy was already more than halfway down that road; she'd developed a severe case of hero worship that could blossom into love with very little provocation. And while Jeff was a tougher nut to crack, he *was* just a little boy, one who'd been deprived of a mother's love at far too young an age. He was acting out now, but with enough exposure to Jax, he'd eventually come around.

And if Matt's children did give their hearts to her and it didn't work out, what kind of father would that make him? If he had it in his power to save them from hurt and didn't, what did it say about his priorities as a parent? He had a responsibility to make sure of a future with Jax *before* he put his children's emotional health at risk. A responsibility he'd already played fast and loose with. This weekend was his chance to rectify that.

This weekend he and Jax would get a few things straightened out, lay down a few ground rules, make some plans. It was all good and well to be in love, but there had to be some order to it, some natural progression they could all count on. This wild, out-of-control feeling scared the hell out of him.

If they couldn't figure it out, or plan for the road ahead, well... If it came down to a choice between Jax and his children...

He paused, his hand in the air, arrested in the act of stuffing a clean polo shirt into his overnight bag.

He didn't want to have to make that choice.

So maybe he knew exactly where he was headed, after all.

THEY HAD DINNER at the Court of Two Sisters instead of Galatoire's. It was less formal but just as charming, and more important, it was within easy walking distance of their hotel. By mutual consent they agreed to skip the evening of jazz at Toni's Chanson Triste. This weekend was just for the two of them. They didn't want to share it with anyone. After a light supper of grilled sole and chilled white wine, they strolled hand in hand back to the hotel, hung out the Do Not Disturb sign and locked the door.

The room was small but luxurious, done in shades of cream and blue, with a king-size bed and tall French doors opening onto a traditional wrought-iron balcony that overlooked the street below. At any other time they might have gone outside, to linger on the balcony, sip a Pernod and watch the people pass by. Matt closed the doors instead, pulling the long curtains across them to further shut out the world.

"Alone at last," he said, turning to her with an exaggerated leer.

Jax glanced at the bed. "It's got a real mattress. Box springs, too. And satin sheets. I checked before we went out."

"Well, then...what are we waiting for?"

He crossed the room in three quick strides and picked her up, whirling her around in his arms. She shrieked and grabbed at his neck, only to have her hold broken when he tossed her down on the bed. He threw himself on top of her, catching himself on his hands and knees, lowering his head to nuzzle the tempting curve of her neck, tickling her with his eyelashes until she giggled and tried to squirm away.

He felt lighthearted and happy and carefree in a way he hadn't felt in years—or maybe even ever—as if he'd mainlined an entire bottle of champagne.

"Have I told you lately that I love you?" he growled, nipping at the curve of her elegant chin.

Jax stuck out her lower lip. "Not in the last thirty minutes," she replied with a pout.

"I love you," he said, and kissed the corner of her mouth. "I love you." The other corner of her mouth was treated to the same sweet gift. "I love you."

"I love you, too, Matt," she whispered. "I love you, too."

Tell him now, she thought.

But she couldn't.

She was too afraid of what his reaction would be.

"Kiss me," she said instead, ignoring the little voice inside her that warned it would only get worse the longer she waited.

He lowered himself onto her, fitting his hips between her thighs, and kissed her...and kissed her...and kissed her.

The little voice faded into the background where she could pretend it didn't exist.

At least for the rest of the night.

The long, glorious night.

She'd tell him tomorrow.

But tomorrow came, and she didn't tell him.

They awoke late. Matt ordered room service while Jax showered, and they ate it on the balcony in thick terry-cloth robes, doing the people-watching they'd neglected to do the night before. Later that morning, after breakfast and love-making and another shower, they wandered the French Quarter like a couple of out-of-town tourists, admiring the talents of the street artists in Jackson Square, enjoying the music, laughing at the clowns and mimes who worked the crowds. They went back to the hotel after a late lunch at the Gumbo Shop and made love again, in the bright clear light of day, with the long glass doors to the balcony standing open and the music of the street floating in. They ordered up room service instead of going to the bother of getting dressed to go out to dinner that night, then made love again while their seafood creole cooled on the plates.

They couldn't get enough of each other, couldn't get enough of kissing and touching and looking into each others' eyes as they slowly, slowly...oh, so slowly and sweetly brought each other to completion once again.

The next morning, while they were lying naked in bed together, on their sides, staring into each others eyes like two baby owls, dreading the time when they would have to get up and rejoin the world, she finally gathered her courage together.

"Matt, I—"

"Jax, will—" he said at the same time.

"You first," Jax said, seizing at any excuse to postpone her news.

"No, you go ahead," Matt urged. "Ladies first. What were you going to say?"

"I…" She closed her eyes. "Oh, God, I don't know how to say this."

"Say what?" He reached out and smoothed her hair behind her ear. "Go ahead, sweetheart. You can say anything to me. What is it?"

Jax hoped that was true. She drew in a deep breath and opened her eyes. "I'm pregnant, Matt."

Matt went stock-still. "What did you say?" he asked very carefully, as if he thought he might not have completely understood what she'd said.

"I'm pregnant."

He jackknifed to a sitting position, as if he'd been savagely yanked upright by unseen puppet strings. "Pregnant?" he said softly, as if he wasn't familiar with the word.

She nodded against the pillow. "Yes."

She watched his eyes, watched him calculate and conjecture.

"It's yours," she said quickly, needing to get that in now, before he asked the question.

"Assuming that's true," he said, cutting her to the quick with the quiet words, "how could you know so soon? It hasn't even been three weeks."

"I just know." She put her hand over her bare stomach, shielding it. "Marie saw it first and—"

"Marie *saw* it?"

"She…reads auras," Jax said, realizing how ridiculous it sounded even before his eyes widened in disbelief. "I know it sounds crazy, and we tease her about it all the time, but it's the truth. You've got to believe me." She sat up and reached out, putting her hand on his arm in entreaty.

He looked down at it silently.

She removed it and reached for the crumpled satin sheet

at the foot of the bed, pulling it up to her breasts like a shield. "I'm not just going by what Marie saw," she told him. "I took a pregnancy test. Two of them. They both came out positive. There's no doubt I'm pregnant. None at all."

"I believed you that night in the van when you said you were on the Pill."

"I never said I was on the Pill. I said I couldn't get pregnant."

He just looked at her, not saying anything, waiting for the punch line.

"I was wrong," she said.

"Obviously."

"Matt, I'm sorry. I never meant for this to happen, but it did and I—"

He was suddenly furious.

Blindingly, blazingly furious.

"Sorry?" He pushed her down onto the mattress, holding her there with his hands at her shoulders. They weren't gentle now. "Sorry! You lied to me. Used me. Tricked me into making love to you—" even in his anger he couldn't bring himself to call it anything else "—without protection so I'd believe your cock 'n' bull story. And then you have the gall to say you're *sorry!*" He pushed against her shoulders as if trying to thrust her away from him, using the motion to propel himself from the bed. "Just what the hell are you trying to pull?"

"Nothing! I swear to you, Matt. I'm not trying to pull anything. If you'll just listen to me for a minute, I can explain. I wasn't trying to trick you. I thought I was infertile. The doctors said—"

"What good will explanations do now? You're pregnant. And you're claiming I'm the father. What's there to explain? It's the oldest scam in the book."

"Scam?"

"The fabulous Jax, darling of the international equestrian world, society deb from Bayou Beltane, got herself knocked up in Europe and came home to find someone to pin it on and give the little bastard a name."

"Matt!" She looked at him, horror and hurt in her eyes. Tears welled up and spilled over. "That's not true. You know that's not true."

He knew it wasn't. She would have been showing by now if she'd been pregnant when she came home from Europe. He would have been ashamed of himself for saying it if he wasn't so furiously angry.

And so damned scared.

And so crushingly disappointed. In her. And himself.

It was happening all over again! He'd given in to his hormones, letting his cock do his thinking for him and...*wham!* A broadside, right to the heart.

The last time this had happened, he'd ended up married before he even knew if he was really in love, tied to a woman he barely knew except in the physical sense. At twenty-three, a mistake like that was almost...*almost*...excusable. At thirty-three, there was no excuse for it at all. And there was no road out, except the one he had taken before.

Which had led straight down the aisle.

Into a marriage that never evolved into what a true marriage should be.

At least there had been honor in it, if nothing else. He'd done the right thing.

Matt gave a weary sigh as the anger died out of him, leaving only disappointment in its wake. "Get up and get dressed," he said as he turned toward the closet for a robe. "We'll go see about getting a license as soon as you're ready."

"A license?"

"That's what this is all about, isn't it? Marriage?"

Jax knelt there in the middle of the bed, the sheet pressed to her naked breasts, and stared at him with a horrified look on her face.

She'd wanted marriage, yes, but not like this. Not as penance for his sins. Not because he'd been ''trapped'' into doing the honorable thing.

Again.

She wouldn't do that to him.

She wouldn't let him do it to himself.

She loved him.

And, dammit, she'd never let herself be used that way again! She wasn't a brood mare.

Jax got up off of the bed, the sheet wrapped around her like a toga, and faced him across the width of the hotel room. Her eyes were dry now and clear as a mountain lake under snow.

''While I am fully aware of the honor you do me with your gracious proposal,'' she said formally, ''I'm afraid I can't accept it.''

''You can't accept it?''

Jax shook her head. ''No.'' She swept past him without another word, heading for the safety of the bathroom, where she could cry in private.

He wrapped his fingers around her upper arm. ''What the hell do you mean, no?'' he demanded. ''Explain yourself.''

She lifted her chin, haughty as a queen.

He felt his gut tighten.

''No,'' she said. ''A negative term, signifying refusal. No. I won't marry you.''

He just stood there, staring at her with a look of blank astonishment on his face.

''Let me go, please. You're hurting my arm.''

He loosened his hold fractionally but didn't let go. *''Have you lost your mind?''* he roared.

"I don't know what you mean."

"Do you have any idea—any idea at all?—what's going to happen about five months from now when you start swelling up like a ripe pumpkin if we're not married well before then?"

"I imagine there will be some gossip." Jax twisted her arm out of his grasp and moved away from him. "But gossip doesn't bother me," she lied.

"*Some* gossip? The whole damn town will be buzzing with the news. You think you can't go out to dinner now without causing talk? Try doing it wearing a maternity dress and no wedding ring. Your pretty little ears will be burning from here to forever."

"For heaven's sake, Matt, listen to yourself. Good Lord, you sound just like my grandfather!"

"What does your grandfather have to do with this?"

"He cornered me on Friday, just before Peg went into labor, to talk to me about us," she said. "He's worried about my reputation, too. People are talking, he says. I think he's afraid I'm in danger of being labeled a scarlet woman."

"I don't know about the scarlet woman part," Matt said. "But he's right about your reputation. People are already talking about us. This will just be the icing on the cake as far as the gossips are concerned."

"Oh, for crying out loud! This isn't the fifties, Matt. It's the tail end of the nineties. All kinds of people have babies without benefit of matrimony these days. Movie stars, politicians..."

"I don't know any movie stars who live in Bayou Beltane, do you? And while I'll admit you're probably the closest thing we've got to royalty, you're a Delacroix, for God's sake, not the princess of Monaco! You're expected to act like a Delacroix." He drew in a deep breath, obviously struggling for reason. "What do you think your aunt

Mary would say if you insisted on having that baby on your own?"

That gave Jax pause. "I'd be sorry to disappoint her," she said, and it was all too true. "But I can't live my life to please other people."

"What do you think your father would say?" Matt persisted. "To you *and* to me? He'd probably come after me with a shotgun—after Beau beat me to a bloody pulp for not doing right by you. And I wouldn't blame them one damn bit!"

"So now we get to it," she said. "It's your reputation you're worried about. Not mine."

"Hell, yes, I'm worried about my reputation! I've lived in Bayou Beltane all my life, and I intend to keep on living there. My kids live there. I don't want them hearing gossip about how their daddy trifled with Jax Delacroix and then refused to marry her."

"I'll make sure everyone in town knows that I'm the one who refused to get married. I'll put up a billboard on Main Street, if that's what it takes. Will that satisfy you?"

"No, that will not satisfy me, dammit! Getting a wedding ring on your finger before my baby is born will satisfy me."

"Well, I'm sorry. That isn't going to happen. I won't marry you just because I'm pregnant. I won't trap you into doing the right thing by me, charming as that sounds. You've done the right thing. You offered marriage. I refused, so you're off the hook. End of story."

"It isn't the end of the story," Matt insisted. "And I'm not 'off the hook,' as you so eloquently put it. That baby you're carrying is mine. He or she will be half brother or sister to Amy and Jeff. That makes it my responsibility, whether you marry me or not. A *lifelong* responsibility. A baby's not something I can walk away from. Ever. If you have my baby, then we're bound together forever, no two ways about it."

"If?" Jax went very, very still. "Are you..." She swallowed and tried again. "Are you suggesting what I think you're suggesting?"

"I don't know. What do you think I'm suggesting besides marriage?"

She licked her lips so she could move them. "Abortion."

"*No!*" he said, horrified. "What the hell gave you that idea?"

"You said *if* I had your baby we'd be bound together forever. That it would be a lifelong responsibility. One you wouldn't have if I...if I got rid of it. It would solve a lot of problems, for both of us," she said carefully. "No gossip. No scandal. No shotgun wedding."

"No baby," he growled, and strode across the room, grabbing her arm again. "I swear to God, Jax," he said fiercely, "if you try anything like that, I'll skin you alive and feed you to the gators. I swear I will." He shook her. "Tell me you didn't mean it."

"I didn't mean it." Her voice was low and fervent. "I want this baby, Matt. I didn't think I'd ever have children, and I didn't deliberately get pregnant, no matter what you believe, but now that I am, I want this baby so much it hurts. I want to hold it in my arms and nurse it, and rock it to sleep, and see it grow up. I want it to grow up in Bayou Beltane. I want it to know you and Amy and Jeff. I want—"

"Then marry me and you can have all that."

"And what will you have?"

"The very same," he said.

"Another wife who *trapped* you into marriage," she said. "Another responsibility you didn't ask for and don't want."

"You didn't trap me. Not deliberately. I shouldn't have said that."

"It happened, though, whether I meant it to or not. I'm not going to force you to pay for my mistake."

"Dammit, Jax."

"I won't marry you, Matt."

"Dammit, Jax. I love you. You're pregnant. You have to marry me."

"Too late." She smiled sadly. "I might have believed you if you'd said it before."

"I did say it before." He wrapped his arms around her, clamping her arms to her sides to keep her from slipping away from him. "I said it over and over and over."

"You didn't know I was pregnant then."

"What the hell difference does that make?"

"It would have made all the difference in the world to me, Matt."

CHAPTER TWELVE

MATT CURSED HIMSELF six ways from Sunday as he sat on his back porch with an ice cold can of Coors pressed to his swollen eye, and still couldn't think of anything bad enough to call himself. He'd been a fool. A cad. A blind, stupid, pigheaded ass. He cringed with shame every time he recalled his part of the conversation in that hotel room with Jax.

Tricked me into making love to you...

The oldest scam in the book...

Knocked up.

Give the little bastard a name...

You're pregnant with my child. You have to marry me...

Hell! No wonder she wouldn't talk to him.

He'd accused her of lying, called her a tramp and implied that the only reason he'd asked her to marry him was because she was pregnant. She'd left him at the hotel, refusing to stay in the room with him, refusing to let him drive her home, and had taken a taxi all the way back to Bayou Beltane. His last sight of her had been through the grimy window of the taxi as it pulled away from the hotel, her soft magnolia cheeks paper white from the shock of his harsh words and her pretty eyes all red from crying.

His only excuse for his unforgivable behavior in that hotel room was the irrational fear that had gripped him when she made her announcement. He'd felt like a cornered animal, willing to gnaw its own leg off to get free. He'd ended up gnawing on his own heartstrings, instead. And found out it hurt a whole lot worse than mere physical pain.

His suffering didn't cut any mustard with her, though. Or with her family. He'd found out in short order that Justin Delacroix's offspring might scrap and squabble among themselves, but they circled the wagons when someone else attacked one of their own.

Beau had been the first to confront him, rushing to his sister's defense like any good brother. Jax apparently hadn't said anything specific, but Beau knew that whatever had happened was bad *because* she wasn't talking, and he fully intended to beat the snot out of the man who had trifled with his twin sister and made her cry.

"I gave you the benefit of the doubt when I saw you necking with my sister on her front porch," Beau said furiously, "because I could see that she was kissing you back. And that day in the barn, I knew you two had been doing more than checking up on Peg. But Jax is a grown-up and I figured it wasn't my place to interfere. I didn't like you taking her to New Orleans for the weekend, either, but that was her decision, too. But now you've stepped over the line, Taggart, and I'll be damned if I'll stand by and watch you use her. Jax deserves better."

Matt was feeling guilty enough to let Beau take a couple of free swings at him—hence the swollen eye—but he'd refused to turn the confrontation into a bloody brawl. He wanted all his body parts in working order when he finally convinced Jax to give him another chance. *If* she gave him another chance...

"Just stay the hell away from my sister," Beau snarled, and stalked away, unable to continue to hit a man who wouldn't hit back.

The female of the species, Matt decided after that, were a whole lot meaner than the male. More vindictive, too. As far as he could tell, Jax's sisters weren't going to be satisfied with anything less than his head on a platter. Preferably with an apple stuffed in his mouth to show the world exactly what he was.

Jax's youngest sister answered the door the day he went to throw himself at Jax's elegant feet and beg for forgiveness for being such an insensitive pig.

"Jax isn't here," Charly said, her gray eyes as cold as glaciers beneath her spiky fringe of silky black bangs. "And she won't be here in the future, either."

"I have to see her," Matt said.

"I'll be back in uniform pretty soon," Charly informed him, ignoring his plea. "And when I am, you'd better watch your back whenever you go into Slidell because I'll be doing my best to find a reason to throw your sorry butt in jail, even if I have to violate your civil rights to do it. Do I make myself clear?"

"As glass," Matt said through his teeth. "Where's Jax?"

"Like I said. She isn't here."

"Will you at least tell her I stopped by?"

"She *knows* you stopped by, Taggart. That's why she's not here."

"*I have to see her, dammit!*"

"Not a chance. I don't know what you said to her, or what you did, but you made her cry. And I've never seen Jax cry like that, not even when that slimy ex-husband of hers was making her life miserable. She doesn't want to see you again. *Ever*," she said, and slammed the door in his face.

Shelby Delacroix threatened him with a restraining order if he ever tried to come near Jax again. "I can do it, too, don't think I can't," she warned him. "My father's a judge, remember. And if he won't do it, I have other connections. Some of them aren't nearly as savory as my father," she added ominously.

Sweet Marie didn't say a word. She just sent him a voo-doo doll with one pin through its heart and a second lodged cruelly in another, rather more delicate portion of its anat-omy.

Give her a hard time, and you answer to all three of us.

Obviously, that hadn't just been a pretty figure of speech.

The older Delacroix had so far managed to restrain them-selves from joining the fray, but Matt figured it was only a matter of time before her father or her uncle Remy, or both, appeared on his doorstep with a shotgun and a preacher.

He was almost looking forward to it.

If that was the only way he could get her to marry him, he was willing to walk down the aisle with a shotgun in his back, and sort out the particulars later. At least that way she'd be married to him, even if she wouldn't unbend enough to listen to his apology until their twenty-fifth wed-ding anniversary.

He loved her, dammit!

And what's more, she loved him.

She'd said so.

She was just too mad right now—and too hurt—to re-member that she'd ever felt anything other than contempt toward him.

One thing puzzled Matt, though.

In all the charges against him, amid all the slurs on his character and ancestry, no one had mentioned the baby.

No one.

Not one word.

He could only suppose she hadn't told them, letting them think something else had caused their sudden split. He won-dered just what in hell she thought she was going to do three or four months down the road when she couldn't get those slim-fitting little riding pants of hers buttoned anymore. People were going to start asking questions, especially her father.

And maybe *then* Justin Delacroix would finally pull out that shotgun and give Matt the chance to do right by his daughter.

The plan had merit, except that Matt didn't want to wait three or four months for his chance to explain why he'd acted like such a damn fool and to beg her to forgive him. He wanted her back *now*.

In his arms.

In his bed.

In his life.

Forever and ever, amen.

He bided his time, staking out what he considered the weakest link in the Delacroix defenses, as well as the best source of information. He headed into New Orleans and Marie Delacroix Henderson's aromatherapy shop, waiting outside until after the last workman left and she was alone.

Inside the shop, the smell of newly sawn wood and fresh paint mingled with myriad scents of fragrant oils. It was almost enough to make a man dizzy.

Marie looked up from some potion she was mixing as the bell above the door tinkled a welcome, the beginnings of a smile on her face. It disappeared abruptly when she saw who her visitor was. "I'm closed, Mr. Taggart," she said, and deliberately turned her back.

"Aw, come on, Marie, have a heart," he pleaded. "Haven't I suffered enough yet?"

She turned her head slightly, just enough to see him over her shoulder. "Do you think you have?"

"No," he admitted with a hangdog look. "I deserve every bit of punishment she wants to dish out. But I don't think I can take much more."

Something in his answer pleased Marie. She turned around and faced him. "What do you want?"

"Can you help me get in to see her? If I could just talk to her, I could explain."

Jax had moved up to her old room in the big house, making it doubly difficult for him to get near her. He might think about kicking in the door to her little cabin, but the huge wooden door on the big house, with its oval, leaded-glass insert, was another thing entirely. Besides, a goodly portion of her immediate family lived in that house, and they had him outnumbered.

Marie crossed her arms in a way that let him know he would have to convince her of the worth of his intentions before she would lift a finger to help him. "Why should I help you do anything?"

"Because I love her. Look at me. Jax said you can read people's feelings or something. Look at me, and you'll see I'm telling the truth."

Marie looked, but it wasn't necessary; a blind man could see that Matt was in love with her sister and suffering mightily because of it. It radiated off of him in waves. "I'd like to help you, Matt," she said at last, "but I honestly don't think she's ready to see you yet."

"When? When will she be ready?"

"I don't know. You broke her heart, you know. She puts up a good front, but Jax's heart is very fragile. It was broken before and never mended completely. Until the baby."

Matt felt lower than a worm.

He felt like pond scum.

He felt like crying.

"Why hasn't she told anyone about the baby?" he asked.

"Why do *you* think she hasn't?" Marie countered.

He was afraid to think about it. There was only one way, as far as he could see, for her to go on living in Bayou Beltane, remain unmarried and still avoid bringing scandal down on him and her family. And she'd promised him she wouldn't do that. He had to believe she wouldn't, or he'd lose what was left of his mind. Besides, she wanted that baby. If he knew anything—which, obviously, he didn't, or he wouldn't be in this fix—he knew that. Jax was hungry to be a mother, now that the chance had presented itself. He didn't have a clue as to why she hadn't said anything; after all, it couldn't stay hidden for long.

"Don't worry. She isn't planning on getting an abortion," Marie said, reading him as easily as if he'd spoken his fears out loud.

"What, then?"

"She's moving away from Bayou Beltane. Away from Louisiana."

"Where? Back to Europe?" That seemed the most logical choice to him, given her recent background. "Florida?" Her cousin, Annabelle Delacroix Rowland, lived someplace in Florida. "Aspen?" Her mother lived in Aspen. "Where?" he demanded when Marie just shook her head each time.

"She's arranging to take a job out in Los Angeles," she said.

"Los Angeles, California?"

"That's the place. She's going to set up a training program for some Hollywood bigwig who wants to help finance the next Olympic equestrian team."

"Why California?"

"From what I gather, it's as far away from Bayou Beltane as she can get and still be in the United States."

"You can't let her move to California," Matt said frantically. "She only just found her way home."

"I'm glad you realize that." Marie stared at him for a minute or two, her misty blue eyes sharp and considering.

He felt as if he were being probed by one of those seeing-eye gizmos on *Star Trek: The Next Generation*.

"All right," Marie said finally, seeing whatever it was she needed to see. "I'm going to cut you some slack. But it you misuse the information I'm about to give you, I swear, I'll—'' she searched through her mind, trying to think of something horrible enough ''—I'll put a hex on you that will shrivel you up like a piece of beef jerky.'' The direction of her gaze left him in no doubt as to what portion of his anatomy she meant to shrivel if he crossed her.

Although he didn't believe in that sort of hocus-pocus in general, right then, at that minute, he was totally convinced she could do exactly what she said she could.

''That's how it works,'' she said with an evil little smile. ''If you think I can, then I can.''

''Do I have to sign something in blood?''

''No, your word will be enough.'' She gave him one of those probing looks again. ''I'll know if you lie.''

''I promise I won't misuse whatever information you give me,'' he said, and crossed his heart. ''Tell me.''

''Did Jax ever tell you anything about her first marriage?''

''Only that she and her husband couldn't have children. His fault, obviously,'' he added.

''Not according to the Martins and their doctors. It was Jax who was defective.''

''Defective?'' Matt snarled, insulted on Jax's behalf.

''In reality, the problem was probably with the two of them together,'' Marie said. ''Greg had a child with the woman he kept here in New Orleans. And Jax didn't have any trouble conceiving with you. Some things aren't meant to be.'' She shrugged. ''And some things are.''

''Her husband kept a woman on the side when he was married to her?''

''More than one. Greg goes for the trashy, flashy kind, and he likes them in multiples. Tight clothes, big hair, little brains and lots of exposed cleavage.''

''Then why in hell did he marry Jax?''

"He and Mama Martin wanted a brood mare. And none of those trashy types would do."

"A brood mare?" Matt frowned, not liking the sound of that at all.

"Jax had the right bloodlines. The right pedigree. And the right connections. Her marriage brought all that into the Martin family fold. Or so they hoped. Jax was just a means to an end. She was supposed to produce the Martin heir—who would, not so incidentally, also have some claim on the Delacroix strongbox through his mama. When she failed to conceive on schedule, Greg and his mother made her life miserable."

"Why didn't somebody do something?"

"Nobody knew. Jax was the oldest, the shining example to the rest of us. Saint Jacqueline, we used to call her...and we weren't always nice about it, either, I'm ashamed to say. As far as she was concerned, the failure of her marriage was hers alone, and she had to live with it. And she did, for almost four years. She might still be married to him—Jax is nothing if not stubborn—"

"Tell me about it," Matt muttered.

"But he suddenly up and petitioned for an annulment."

"Annulment? How the hell do you get an annulment after four years of marriage?"

"He claimed Jax had misled him about her ability to bear children, which he dearly wanted." Marie snorted inelegantly. "What he *wanted* was a long-legged debutante from Houston who refused to have anything to do with a married man."

"So he cut Jax loose, just like that."

"Just like that. It was probably the best thing he ever did for her. She might never have gotten out of the marriage otherwise. As it is, she carried a lot of scars away with her when she left. Not the least of which was the feeling that she was somehow defective because she couldn't conceive, and no man would ever want her because of it."

Matt suddenly felt as if he'd twisted a knife in his own gut. "And then I come along and propose to her *because* she's pregnant. A proven breeder."

"Got it in one, Sherlock."

"It didn't really have anything to do with her not wanting me to feel trapped."

"Oh, I'm sure that entered into it somewhere, but it wasn't the main reason, just a contributing factor. The bottom line is, Jax thinks you only proposed because you got her pregnant." Marie cocked her head. "And she's right about that, isn't she? You wouldn't have asked you to marry her otherwise."

"That's not true. I'd already made up my mind I was going to ask her to marry me while we were in New Orleans." He reached deep into the pocket of his Dockers, pulled out a small velvet box and flipped open the lid with his thumb, revealing a brilliant round opal surrounded by diamonds. "I bought this on Friday afternoon before I picked her up. I was going to wait until just the right romantic moment before I proposed. In fact, I was just about to pop the question when she told me about the baby."

Marie stared at him for a minute, openmouthed with shock. "You big dumb *jerk!*" she said finally. "Why in heaven's name didn't you just show her that instead of telling her she had to marry you because she was pregnant?"

He shrugged, looking like a whipped puppy with his tail between his legs. "I forgot."

"You *forgot?* How do you forget a rock like that?"

"Well, she sprang the pregnancy thing on me, and I reacted badly, and she started yelling and I started yelling, and then she said no, and I got stubborn and—"

Marie held up her hand, stopping him. "I get the picture,

so you can spare me the góry details, please. I'd rather not know any more than I have to." She shook her head, as if she still couldn't believe what an idiot he'd been. "I'm going into Bayou Beltane early tomorrow morning to gather medicinal plants with Desiree Boudreaux. We plan to go over to Rick's Café afterward for breakfast. Jax is supposed to meet Katherine Beaufort there tomorrow, too. She wants to sell some of those antiques she brought home from France before she leaves for California. I can arrange for those two encounters to happen at the same time, so if you show up around, say, nine-thirty, I think I can convince Jax to sit still and talk to you. After that it's up to you. And you'd better make it good because I won't run interference again."

"Thank you, Marie," he said sincerely, reaching to take both her hands in his. "You won't regret helping me. I promise."

"I'd better not regret it, or you will. Remember the beef jerky," she said sternly, and then gave in and grinned at him. The poor man was one lovesick puppy, for sure. She decided to give him a little extra help in his quest to win her sister. "Wait here a minute." She withdrew her hands from his and disappeared through a curtain of crystal beads hanging in the doorway that led to a back room. A few minutes later she returned, handing him a small stoppered vial made of pale amethyst glass.

"What is it?" he asked suspiciously.

"The base is jojoba oil. I've mixed in some basic love oils—rose essence, a little myrtle, some yarrow and orange blossom, and just a touch of henbane. The henbane would work better if you'd picked it yourself in the early morning, naked, but..." She shrugged.

"A love potion?" he said carefully, not wanting to offend her. But, good God, a *love* potion?

"A marriage potion," she corrected him. "Anoint yourself with it before you see Jax tomorrow."

"Anoint myself?"

"Rub a little on your pulse points. You know—your temples or the insides of your wrists and elbows. Just pretend it's cologne. And put this in your pocket." She held up a tiny nosegay of dried flowers tied together with copper wire and a green satin ribbon. "It's yarrow flowers and orrisroot, for getting and keeping love, with a little basil oil rubbed into the stems to cool tempers in case things—" Her eyes flared suddenly, then narrowed to fierce slits as she focused on something outside the window of her shop.

Matt twisted around to see what she was looking at.

Two young people stood on the sidewalk across the street from the shop, their heads close together in deep discussion, totally oblivious to the other pedestrians who had to step off the sidewalk to go around them. One of them was a tall, muscular young man in tight blue jeans, a white T-shirt and a black leather jacket, his long dark hair unbound and flowing over his shoulders. The other one was a teenage girl, about sixteen, with a petite figure and shoulder-length blond hair. She was wearing a cropped yellow sweater over a pair of snug-fitting blue jeans. A shiny metal ring pierced her exposed navel.

Marie put the bundle of dried herbs down on the counter and went to stand by the window. "It's Etienne Boudreaux," she said as Matt came up behind her. "I don't know who the girl is."

"Whoever she is, she's too young for him."

Marie's soft mouth twisted. "He's the kind who likes them young. They're easier to impress than girls his own age."

Matt slanted a glance at her. "I'd heard he was dating your young cousin."

"He is. Or was." Marie sighed. "Actually, I don't really know how things stand between him and Nikki."

"Maybe that—" he tilted his head toward the pair out on the sidewalk "—means they've broken up."

"One can only hope," Marie said. "It would save everyone a lot of worry all around if they have. For Joanna, especially. She's done everything she can think of, short of locking Nikki in her room, to break them up. But there's just no reasoning with a seventeen-year-old girl who thinks she's in love."

Matt gave a murmur of agreement, thinking of Amy at seventeen and the frightening possibility of her getting involved with a young thug like the one standing in front of Marie's shop. He wanted to rush out there, gather the young girl up and bundle her home to her family where she'd be safe. But it wasn't his place to interfere. He didn't even know who she was.

"He's getting angry," Marie said, a note of alarm in her voice.

Matt glanced over at her. "Do you want me to go out there and break it up?"

"No." Marie shook her head. "No, they're just arguing. And I doubt she'd thank us for interfering, anyway."

Still, neither one of them moved away from the window or took their eyes off of the two kids. The argument escalated as they stood there watching. The two voices grew progressively louder, the girl's becoming so shrill that it was possible to make out a word now and then.

Someone named Lucy figured prominently in the discussion. Nikki's name was mentioned, too. The young blonde didn't like Etienne dating the two other girls, and, apparently, Etienne didn't give a rat's ass what she liked.

"That's it, then," the girl screamed. "I've had it." She turned and flung herself away from him. "It's over."

The boy reached out and grabbed her arm roughly. "It's

not over till I say it's over, *ma 'tite chatte*," he purred menacingly.

"I'm not your little cat!" she snarled, and tried to yank away from him.

Etienne lifted his free hand and backhanded her across the face.

Matt growled, low in his throat, and charged out of Marie's shop. Stranger or not, he wasn't about to stand there and watch a young girl get smacked around by some walking hormone with an attitude.

"Take your hands off of her, Boudreaux."

Etienne looked up toward the sound of the voice. "This isn't any a'yor business, old man," he said insultingly. "Me an' my girl here are jus' havin' a li'l discussion, is all." He brushed the back of his hand along the girl's reddened cheek, as if he hadn't just hit her there. "Ain' that right, honey?"

His words were a bit slurred. Matt wasn't sure if that was an unfortunate habit of speech, or if the kid was drunk. It didn't matter either way. Etienne Boudreaux was going to take his hands off of the girl voluntarily, or Matt was going to make him do it.

"Let her go." Matt's voice was low and soft, threatening only in its quiet intensity. "Now."

The boy hesitated for a moment, his eyes calculating as he judged Matt's height and weight and capability for violence. Matt stared back at him, waiting. He could see the exact moment when the young punk decided that whatever he might gain from a direct confrontation wouldn't be worth it.

"You want her, you can have her." He released the girl's arm with an exaggerated gesture, palm out, fingers wide spread, and backed away. "She's gettin' to be to be more trouble 'an she's worth, anyway."

"Etienne," the girl said pleadingly.

"You had your chance with me, *'tite chatte*," he said insultingly, "an' you blew it."

The girl stood there for a moment, watching him walk away, a bewildered look on her young face. Her left cheek was still red from the slap Etienne had dealt her. The other was paper white. Tears glittered in her eyes. Matt couldn't tell if she was frightened, embarrassed or angry. Or some combination of all three.

Marie, who had followed him out onto the sidewalk, took a step forward. "Are you all right, honey?"

The girl stepped back, out of reach, and shook her head. "Yeah, sure," she insisted. "Everything's cool."

"You can file charges against him for hitting you, you know," Matt said softly. "We'd be glad to go to the police station with you and tell them what we saw."

"It was just a slap," the girl said. "No big deal. Really."

"Would you like to call someone to come and get you?" Marie asked. "Your parents?"

The girl recoiled. "Not my parents."

"A friend, then?" Marie suggested. "My shop's right across the street." She gestured toward Heaven Scent. "You could call from there."

The girl hesitated a moment longer, looking back and forth between Matt and Marie. She looked pitiably young and uncertain. "Okay, yeah," she said finally. "I guess I could call this girl I know."

Marie reached out and touched the teenager's shoulder, slipping an arm around her when she didn't back away. "You come on with me, then, honey. We'll go on over to my shop and call that friend." She glanced up at Matt as they stepped past him. "I'll see you tomorrow. Nine-thirty, at Rick's. Don't be late."

CHAPTER THIRTEEN

AT NINE O'CLOCK the next morning, Matt was sitting in his van in the parking lot behind the building next door to Rick's Café, wondering if he'd put on too much of Marie's "marriage potion"—he smelled like a damned plug-in air freshener!—and wishing he smoked. He'd never been so nervous in his entire life—not during his final exams at Texas A&M, not while speaking his wedding vows with Livvy, not when his children were born, not the first time he'd had to put down a horse. Never.

Nothing in his life had ever made him shake and sweat like the thought of losing Jax for good.

He believed Marie had meant exactly what she'd said to him last night. If he messed it up this time, she wouldn't help him again. And it was a damned sure bet none of the other Delacroix would, either. Jax would move to California, taking their unborn baby with her, and he'd never see either of them again.

The thought alone made him shake with fear.

He couldn't stand it a minute, not even a *second* longer...but he did, waiting until exactly nine-thirty, as instructed, before pushing open the front door to Rick's.

With the breakfast crowd long gone and the lunch crowd not due to begin arriving for a couple of hours yet, the small café was nearly empty except for a few people at the counter...and the women grouped around the big table near the back of the room.

Marie dominated the scene, looking like a gypsy soothsayer as she sorted through the packets of plants and herbs spread out in front of her. Desiree Boudreaux, looking even more gypsylike with her wavy gray hair gathered back in a bright scarf, sat close by her side, head bent, fingers busy, as she pointed out various properties of the native herbs in her soft, musical cadence. A pretty, sun-streaked blonde in khaki shorts and a rumpled T-shirt sat on Marie's other side, peering over her shoulder as she listened to the discussion. Charly and Shelby Delacroix were sitting on the opposite side of the table, watching him over cups of steaming coffee and a plate of sugar-dusted beignets. Jax was nowhere in sight.

Matt shuddered. He knew a setup when he saw one. A smart man would have turned tail and run. But Matt wasn't a smart man. He was a man in love.

"Ladies," he said politely, wary but determined as he made his way across the tiled floor to the back of Rick's Café.

Marie looked up.

Desiree stopped talking.

The blonde turned her head, glancing at him over her shoulder.

Five pairs of feminine eyes were now staring at him, as if their owners were contemplating the most painful and permanent way of removing his manhood.

Matt stood his ground, waiting.

Charly Delacroix unbent first. "Well, I'll say this for you, Taggart." She grinned approvingly. "You've got guts."

"What he's got is a hell of a lot of nerve," Shelby Delacroix said. "That's an entirely different thing."

"Shelby," Marie said, her tone carrying a note of censure. "We agreed."

Shelby sat back in her chair and crossed her arms over her chest. Her glare told Matt exactly what she thought of whatever agreement the sisters had made, but she offered no further protest.

"Where's Jax?" Matt asked, getting right to the point.

"You remember Kendall, don't you, Matt?" Marie said pleasantly, reminding him of the social niceties. "Uncle Remy's new wife?"

"Yes, of course." He sketched a brief nod in the blonde's direction. "How are you?" he inquired politely, as if he were really interested in her answer.

Everyone in the room knew he wasn't. His gaze had already drifted past Kendall, searching the place. Rick, on duty behind the kitchen counter, nodded at him. The waitress plucked the coffeepot off of the warmer with one hand, picked up a cup and saucer with the other and started forward.

"I'm doing just fine. Thanks for asking," Kendall said with a little smile, ignoring his distraction. "It's been a little difficult adjusting to life in such a small town. Everyone knowing everyone else's business and all," she added, tongue-in-cheek.

But Matt was past picking up on subtleties. "Well, that's nice. Glad to hear it." He looked back at Marie. "Where's—"

"Can I get you anything besides coffee?" the waitress asked as she approached the table. "Orange juice?"

"What? Oh, no. Nothing, thanks."

"You can warm mine up, if you would, please," Shelby said.

The front door of the café opened as the young waitress was topping off everyone's cups.

Matt whirled around to face his destiny.

It was Katherine Beaufort, the antiques dealer from New Orleans.

Matt turned back to Marie without even saying hello to

the newcomer. "I thought you said Jax was coming with her," he accused.

"I said Jax would be meeting her here," Marie corrected him. She rose from her chair, her hand extended in greeting. "Ms Beaufort, how nice to see you."

"Katherine, please." The two women shook hands.

"Would you like a cup of coffee?" Marie asked the newcomer. "It's made with chicory, but we can get you something else if you like. Tea, maybe? Lucy..." She raised her hand, gesturing at the waitress. "Bring us another order of beignets, please. And a cup of...?" She looked at Katherine.

"Chicory coffee will be fine," Katherine said.

"Another cup of chicory coffee for Ms. Beaufort."

Matt ground his teeth.

"Please, sit down, Katherine," Marie said, shooting a censuring glance at Matt as she pulled out a chair for their guest, letting him know that, as a Southern gentleman, *he* should have performed that service. "Jax should be along any minute."

"I'm really looking forward to seeing the antiques she wants to sell," Katherine said. "From what she told me over the phone, it sounds as if she has some exceptional pieces. Mostly seventeenth century French, she said. As well as some early Victorian."

"Jax does have exquisite taste," Marie agreed.

Matt nearly screamed in frustration.

Where the hell is Jax?

He wasn't aware he'd spoken the words aloud—shouted them, actually—until everyone in the café turned to look at him. The six women at the table regarded him with varying degrees of well-bred shock, but only Katherine Beaufort's was real. The other five harpies were laughing at him behind their hands.

He turned his back on them, figuratively speaking.

"I'm sorry," he said to Katherine. "I understood that Jax Delacroix was supposed to be meeting you here this morning. I have some business with her myself and I—"

The front door of the café opened again.

This time it *was* Jax.

Matt went stock-still, afraid to breathe in case he scared her away.

Everyone else in the room craned his or her neck for a better look.

Jax didn't notice anything amiss at first. "I'm sorry I'm late," she said as she moved into the shop, her attention focused entirely on the woman she'd come to meet. "I—"

She became aware of the unnatural silence in the small café.

The stillness.

The almost electric air of anticipation.

She turned her head, taking it in. "What's going…"

She went utterly still.

Her eyes widened.

Her soft lips parted, but no sound came out.

"Jax," Matt said, his voice aching with longing and love.

She took a half step back.

"Jax…sweetheart…" he said pleadingly, torn to the quick by her automatic retreat.

"No." She shook her head, putting a hand out as if to ward him off.

He grasped it in his. "Please, Jax, just listen."

"No." She tried to pull away and found herself trapped. For a moment she hesitated, unsure of what to do, afraid of making a scene…. And then something just snapped. It was as if the rest of the people in the café had disappeared into thin air.

"No!" she said, jerking hard in her effort to pull away

from him. "No, I won't listen. I won't go through this again."

"Jax, honey." Marie came around the table and put her hand on her sister's shoulder. "Just listen to him. Give him a chance to explain. He loves you."

"No!"

If she listened, she'd believe. And if she believed, he'd be trapped into another marriage he didn't really want, and she'd be destroyed by her love for a man who'd only married her because she was pregnant. She turned her head away from him, looking to her sisters for help and understanding.

"How could you do this to me? You knew I didn't want to see him. You all knew...."

"Let go of her." Shelby jumped up and grabbed Matt's forearm, trying to yank his hand away from her sister's. "I can't stand this. Just let go of her. She doesn't want to talk to you."

Matt ignored Shelby as if she wasn't there. "She has to talk to me."

"She doesn't have to do anything she doesn't want to do," Charly said. "This whole thing was a lousy idea. I'm sorry, Jax." She grabbed at Matt's arm from the other side. "Let her go, Taggart. She doesn't want to talk to you."

"She has to talk to me, dammit! *She's carrying my baby.*"

Stunned silence greeted his announcement.

Mouths dropped open.

No one knew what to say.

And then, Desiree Boudreaux stood up, pushing the chair back with her legs, and came around the table. She reached out, cupping both of her gnarled old hands around Jax's and Matt's clasped ones.

"A baby is an unbreakable link between two people," she said. "It is a bridge between families. No matter if you love or not, no matter if you marry or don't, the child is there and you must deal with the reality of the new life you have made. From the very moment of its conception, it depends on you both to be its champions and protectors, to think of what is best for it and to disregard any cost to yourself. This I know, from my own experience, to be the truth," she said with quiet, uncompromising conviction.

Every Delacroix there knew she was talking about her own son, sweet Uncle William, and what she had done for him. If she hadn't disregarded the cost to herself all those years ago, what might have happened to him? Where—and who—might he now be?

"For the sake of the baby you have created between you—" she squeezed their hands together "—talk."

ONCE HE HAD HER ALONE, out by his van in the parking lot behind the row of Main Street businesses, Matt didn't know quite what to say or where to begin. *I love you* hadn't worked for him before, but it was true, truer than anything he had ever said to her, and the words were clogging his throat, aching to be said.

"I love you, Jax. I know you don't believe that. I even know why you don't believe that but—"

"You know why?"

"Marie told me about your marriage to Greg Martin."

"She shouldn't have done that."

"No. She shouldn't have," he agreed, surprising her. "*You* should have."

Jax shook her head. "I couldn't."

"Why?" He reached out and took her hand then, encouraged beyond measure when she didn't pull away.

"I was ashamed," she said.

"Ashamed?"

"I wasn't enough for my husband. I couldn't satisfy him sexually, so he went to other women. I—"

"His fault," Matt interrupted, wanting to make that perfectly clear. "Not yours. You're woman enough for any man. I would think you'd have realized that by now, by my reaction. I can't get near you without wanting to make love to you. I want to make love to you right now." He pressed her palm to his groin for a brief moment, just long enough to prove his point, pulling it away before she had more than a chance to draw in her breath. "Any man who is a man would want you, Jax. Martin is a rutting pig who wouldn't know a real woman if he tripped over her."

"A real woman would have given her husband children."

"That's bullshit," Matt said crudely, angered that she would say such a thing. He'd had lots of pretty words planned, words meant to convince her of her desirability and his love, but they all flew right out of his head. He spoke from the heart, instead. "That's just plain bullshit. Dammit, Jax, I know your ex-husband and his mother did a number on your head. I know they beat you down and made you doubt yourself and your desirability. And I know it must have been hell for you, but, dammit to hell, *I'm not Greg Martin!*"

He cupped her face in his hands and stared down at her, as if the truth and strength of his feelings would seep into her through the touch of his hands and the heat in his eyes.

"I love you, Jax. I love everything about you. I love your elegance and sophistication, the way you move and sit and stand, the proud way you hold your head. I love the way you ride, with confidence and daring and grace." The words were low and soft and caressing, straight from his yearning heart. "I love the way you lift your left eyebrow when you're amused about something. I love the way you are with my children, your patience with all of Amy's questions, and your sweetness with Jeff, even when he's pushing you away. I love the way you respond to me when we make love, the way you always give me everything you've got, and that sweet little sound you make when you come. I don't know how else to say it, Jax. I love you. I want you to marry me more than I've ever wanted anything before in my life.''

"Then how come you didn't ask me until after you knew I was pregnant?''

Matt let her go and clenched his hands at his sides. "This doesn't have anything to do with whether you're pregnant or not!''

"But—''

"But, nothing! I reacted badly, all right? I admit that, and I'm sorry for it. More sorry than you can ever know. But for a minute, just after you told me, all sorts of feelings started tumbling around inside me. Old feelings that had nothing to do with how I feel about you. They took me by the throat for a minute and I acted like a...''

Marie's voice echoed in his ears. *You big, dumb jerk.*

He'd forgotten the ring again.

"Wait a minute. I'll show you.'' He stuck his hand into his pocket and pulled out the tiny, velvet-covered box he'd been carrying since the day he bought it. "Here.'' He shoved it into her hands. "It's for you. Open it.''

Slowly, her hands shaking, Jax opened it. A smooth opal surrounded by a halo of sparkling diamonds winked up at her from its bed of black velvet. "It's a ring,'' she said stupidly, staring at it.

"It's an engagement ring.'' He reached up and touched the tiny opal in her right ear. "I noticed you wear these a lot and I wanted to get you something you'd like.''

"When?'' she said.

"When what?''

"When did you buy this?''

"Before we left for New Orleans. I stopped by Hensen's Jewelry before I drove out to your place to pick you up.''

"Before? You had this with you *before* we left for New Orleans? You mean you were going to..." Joy strangled the words in her throat and brought tears to her eyes.

"I was planning to ask you to marry me," he said, watching her carefully for a reaction. "I was going to wait for just exactly the right romantic moment and then, well—" he shrugged uncomfortably, remembering some of the things he'd said to her in that hotel room in New Orleans "—things kinda went to hell in a wheelbarrow and I forgot I even had the ring with me."

She closed the box and handed it back to him.

He looked down at it. It had been his last line of defense, his last, best shot at convincing her, and she'd lobbed it back at him. Pain gripped his heart like a fist.

"Ask me now," she said.

He looked up at her, not understanding.

"Ask me to marry you now."

Relief drove him to his knees on the dirty asphalt behind Rick's Café. Love kept him there. He took her left hand in his.

"I love you, Jax," he said, staring up into her glowing face. "Will you do me the great honor of becoming my wife?"

"Yes, *please*." She dropped to her own knees in front of him and threw her arms around his neck, toppling him over backward, offering her lips, giving her all as she had from the beginning. "I love you, too, Matt," she said between kisses. "I love you so much. I'm sorry I didn't understand. That I was so pigheaded and afraid. I—"

He put his finger over her lips, stopping her apology. "That's over and done. We're starting fresh from right here. Deal?"

She pursed her lips in a kiss against his finger. "Deal," she said, and sniffed. "What's that smell?"

"Smell?"

"Roses and…" She sniffed again, deeply. "Other stuff." Her eyebrow slid up. "Is there a reason you smell like my aunt Mary's garden on a hot June day?"

"Marie made me wear it."

"Wear what? Perfume?"

"It's a marriage potion, all right?" He shrugged, his broad shoulders moving against the ground. His smooth-shaven cheeks were just slightly tinged with pink. "Marie thought I needed all the help I could get."

Jax—elegant, sophisticated Jax Delacroix—giggled. "I guess it worked, didn't it?"

"I guess," Matt said gruffly. And then he smiled. "You said yes. Now, where's that damn ring so I can make it official?"

Laughing, giddy with love and happiness, they struggled to their hands and knees, fumbling around on the ground looking for the little velvet box. Matt found it just behind the front tire of his van. They juggled the tiny box between them, nearly dropping it again before they got the ring out. Matt slipped it onto her finger and kissed it into place.

"Well, I wouldn't have believed it if I hadn't seen it with my own two eyes."

Still on their knees on the ground by the van, Jax and Matt turned as one to look at the speaker. Two middle-aged Bayou Beltane matrons in flowered dresses stood staring down at them, shaking their heads in amazement. The entire morning clientele of Rick's Café, including the cook, the waitress and the Delacroix sisters, stood behind them.

"Jacqueline Delacroix, rolling around on the ground like a common trollop," one of the matrons huffed. "Wait until her grandfather hears about this!"

THEY DECIDED TO TELL Jeff and Amy that afternoon, as soon as they came home from school. If they put it off any longer than that, there was a chance one or the other of the children would hear about their father's engagement from someone else. And nothing good could come of that happening.

Jax sat in the living room with Matt, waiting for the children to come home, her stomach tied up in knots. She didn't have any doubts about Amy. Well, not many, anyway. Amy made no secret of the fact that she adored Jax, and had always done so, nearly from the beginning but... She hadn't been looking at Jax as a potential mother. Her adoration might well change to something else when she found out her father was actually planning to *marry* "the fabulous Jax."

Jax had no doubts at all about Jeff's reaction.

He was going to hate the whole idea.

"How are we going to tell them?" Jax pressed her hands to her stomach and stared up at her husband-to-be. "*What* are we going to tell them?"

"We're going to tell them the truth," Matt said.

"The truth? All of it? About the baby and everything? But—"

"They're going to find out about the baby whether we tell them or not," Matt stated. "And it's best that it comes from us." He sat down on the sofa beside her and covered her hands with one of his. "Don't worry." He rubbed his thumb over the small bone in the back of her wrist. "Amy will be thrilled. And Jeff will come around. I promise," he said, hoping it was true.

He didn't know what he would do if it wasn't.

MATT CALLED HIS CHILDREN into the family room the minute they came in the back door. Patiently, slowly, calmly, giving them the courtesy of the truth, he laid the situation out for them.

"You're getting married?" Amy's little face lit up as if

she had a candle inside her. "To my daddy? Does that mean you're going to live here, in our house, with us?"

"Yes." Jax nodded. "That's what it means."

The child shrieked and threw herself into Jax's arms. "Can I call you Mommy?"

Jax caught her close, filling her arms with the child, cuddling her the way she'd been longing to do since that day in her office when Amy had first hugged her. She hadn't been completely sure, until just that moment, what Amy's reaction to the news would be. Relief and gratitude nearly overwhelmed her.

"Yes, you can call me Mommy, sweetheart." Jax blinked back tears. "You can call me anything you want to."

Jeff jumped to his feet. *"No, she can't!"* he roared, outrage etched on his young face.

He'd been sitting quietly, listening to his father's explanation of why it was important for the marriage to take place as soon as possible. He hadn't said a word, neither to ask a question nor voice an objection. He'd merely listened, staring at his father through his wire-rimmed glasses with an intense, focused expression on his face. Jax had begun to hope that maybe it would be all right, after all.

Now nine-year-old Jeff was flushed with fury.

"You can't call her Mommy, Amy." He reached out and grabbed his sister's shoulder, trying to yank her off of Jax's lap. "You can't. Our mom is dead."

Amy shrugged away from him and burrowed deeper into Jax's lap, holding on for dear life. "I know that, but Jax is going to be our new mom. I want her to be our new mom."

"No! I don't want a new mom." He lifted his gaze to Jax's. His eyes were full of anger, fear—and confusion. "I don't want you. I don't want your dumb baby, either!"

"Jeff," Matt admonished, rising from the sofa to put his hand on his son's quaking shoulder.

Jeff shook him off. "Why did you have to make a baby with her?" he demanded. "You already have two kids. Why do you need another one?"

"We didn't plan to have a baby, Jeff," Matt said. "It just happened."

"I thought grown-ups were supposed to be careful about not making babies unless they wanted to. That's what you said before. And now you have to get married because *she's* having a baby."

"No, son, we're not getting married because we're having a baby." He put both hands on Jeff's shoulders and turned his son to face him. "Jax and I love each other and we would eventually get married, anyway. The baby—your new little brother or sister—just means we're getting married a little sooner than we planned, that's all."

"But I don't want you to get married. I don't want a new mom. Or a new brother or sister. I—"

"I want Daddy and Jax to get married," Amy said, instinctively trying to smooth things over. "And I want a new baby, too. I think a new baby would be fun to have."

"That's because you're just a dumb little kid and you don't know *anything!*" Jeff wrenched himself out from under his father's hands and ran from the room. The sound of his bedroom door slamming reverberated throughout the house.

Matt started after him. "Jeff—"

"No." Jax reached out and grasped a handful of his pant leg, stopping him. "Let me talk to him," she said. She shifted Amy off her lap, setting the little girl on her feet, and rose. "I'm the cause of the problem. I've got to be the one to fix it. If I can."

She rapped softly on his closed bedroom door. "Jeff?" No answer.

She knocked again. "Jeff, I'd like to talk to you. Please."

She wanted, very badly, to reach down and turn the handle, letting herself in, but instinct told her that was a bad idea. It was his room. She'd already commandeered his house, his father, his family... She was the interloper. Strategy and good manners dictated that she wait for an invitation before she invaded any more of his territory.

"Jeff, please let me come in. I really need to talk to you."

Another twenty seconds of silence went by. "It's open," he said finally.

It was as much of an invitation as she was going to get. Jax turned the knob and went in.

Jeff was sitting at his desk in front of the window that overlooked the backyard. His posture was slumped, his arms folded across the polished surface, his chin resting on his forearm as he tapped softly on the glass wall of the terrarium that held pride of place among his books and notepads and a twelve-inch-tall rubber Godzilla. The tarantula in the terrarium appeared to be tapping on the glass from the other side, the movements of one long, hairy leg seeming to mimic the motion of Jeff's finger.

Jax sincerely hoped that the unhappy boy wasn't planning to turn the creature loose again. "May I sit down?" she asked politely.

Jeff shrugged, his narrow shoulders looking defenseless and vulnerable under the striped fabric of his T-shirt.

Jax took a seat on the edge of his bed and stared at his back, wondering how to start...what to say. Matt had said the best way to deal with children was with absolute honesty. Anything less was condescending, and kids—especially smart kids like Jeff—knew when they were being patronized or talked down to.

"Would you turn around and look at me, please?" she asked. "It's kind of hard to talk to the back of someone's head."

Jeff hesitated just long enough to make her think that he wasn't going to do as she asked before slowly turning around to face her.

"Thank you," she said, meaning it sincerely. Praying she could find the right words, she took a deep breath and began. "I know this is hard for you, Jeff. You hardly know me and here I am, suddenly telling you I'm going to marry your dad whether you want me to or not. If things had been different, if I wasn't going to have a baby—" she touched her hand to her stomach "—we could have waited until we all got to know each other better. But things didn't turn out that way."

"You could have waited for a long, long time but I still wouldn't want you to marry my dad."

"Don't you like me, Jeff, even a little?"

Jeff lifted one foot, crossing it over the opposite knee, and looked down, picking at the laces of his Converse high-tops. "You're okay," he said finally, in a tiny voice. His lower lip quivered slightly. "But you're not my mom."

"Oh, sweet—" She reached out her hand, then dropped it, sensing he wouldn't welcome her touch. Not yet. "I'm not trying to be your mom, or take your mom's place. No one could do that. But I'd like to be your friend, if you'll let me."

"I've already got lots of friends."

"I'm sure you do, but everybody can always use more friends. I could use another friend right now. Especially someone like you."

He just looked at her, his expression far too serious and suspicious for a nine-year-old boy.

"It's true," she said. "This is as scary for me as it is for you. I was married once, a long time ago, before you were even born, but it didn't work out and I had to get a divorce. I thought I'd never get married again. And then I met your dad and I fell in love with him, more in love than I've ever been with anybody before.''

Jeff *almost* rolled his eyes at that.

Jax hurried on, encouraged by that small sign. "And now we're going to have a baby." She touched her stomach again. "And that scares me, too."

"You're scared to have a baby?"

She'd caught his interest now; she could see it in the bright gleam of his eyes.

"Because it will hurt?" he asked.

"No, not that. Well…" *Honesty,* she reminded herself. "Maybe I'm a little afraid it will hurt, but mostly I'm afraid because I've never been a mom before. I'm afraid I won't know how to do it right, or I won't do a good job. A friend like you could help me with that."

"I could?" The look he gave her was patently skeptical. "How?"

"You know what a good mom is supposed to be like, how she's supposed to act, because you had a good mom. Your dad told me what a good mother she was and how she always knew just how to take care of you and Amy, and how proud she was of both of you. If you were my friend, you could teach me to be a good mom, too."

Jeff considered that for a long moment, his blue eyes intent as he stared at her through the lenses of his glasses. Jax felt as if he were looking all the way to her soul, and hoped to God he could see the truth. She *did* want to be a good mother to the baby she carried—and to him and his sister. She wanted it more than she'd ever wanted anything before in her life.

"Would I have to call you Mom, too, like Amy?"

Jax shook her head. "Not unless you wanted to. You could call me Jax, or Jacqueline." Her lips curved in a trembling smile. "You could even call me 'Hey, you' if you wanted."

Jeff did roll his eyes then. "I don't think my dad would like it if I did that."

"No, maybe not," Jax agreed.

They smiled at each other, a small smile—two potential co-conspirators sharing their very first confidence.

"Well, I guess I could call you Jax, then," Jeff said.

"ARE YOU SURE this is what you want, honey?"

Jax looked up at her father, surprise evident in her eyes. Justin Delacroix wasn't one to discuss emotions. He'd never been much for endearments, either. The last time she'd gotten married, he hadn't even seemed to notice anything was going on until it was time to walk her down the aisle. And even then, he had performed that particular duty in what seemed to her a perfunctory manner, as if his mind were elsewhere. It had always seemed to Jax as if his family was never as important to her father as the law was.

"Yes, Dad," she said, wondering why he was asking the question. "This is what I want."

"You don't have to marry him, you know. And you don't have to move to California, either. You can stay right here and have your baby."

The surprise in Jax's eyes turned to outright shock.

"It would be nice to have grandchildren around the place while I'm still young enough to enjoy them," Justin added, his tone almost wistful.

"But..." Jax's mouth opened and closed, like a fish gasping for air. "What about what people will say? The scandal?"

He waved it away as if it were of no consequence. "Don't worry about that. This family has endured worse scandals than an out-of-wedlock baby."

"But..."

Jax couldn't believe what she was hearing. Was this really her father, dismissing scandal with a wave of his hand?

"A good marriage, to the right person, is one of the most rewarding relationships two people can have," he said. "Your sister found that out at Christmastime when she married Lucas. Not that I want you to go running off to get married like she did," he warned. "If you really want to marry Matt Taggart, we'll do the thing up right, here at Riverwood with your family around you. If he isn't the right person, well...you don't have to marry him just to give your baby a name. The Delacroix name is plenty good enough for anybody."

"He's the right person, Daddy." Jax hadn't called him Daddy since she was a child. "I love him."

"Then be happy, baby." Justin Delacroix leaned down and kissed his daughter's cheek, a thing he hadn't done in years. "And hold on tight to what you have, no matter what happens."

JAX'S FIRST WEDDING had been all pomp and circumstance. She'd had eight bridesmaids, two flower girls and more than six hundred guests. There had been a small orchestra at her reception, which featured a full-course, sit-down dinner under white silk tents on the lawn at Riverwood. Her cake had been six tiers high, decorated with pink sugar roses and white marzipan swans. Her wedding dress had been a costly designer confection of snowy white satin and lace, with yards of fabric in the billowing skirt and a flowing tulle veil sprinkled with tiny seed pearls.

This time, her only attendant was her husband-to-be's seven-year-old daughter, and her only guests were her family and Matt's. Her reception would consist of a simple buffet brunch, followed by a homemade, two-layered wedding cake. Her dress was made of heavy ivory silk, with cap sleeves, princess seams and a ballet-length hem that flared gently around her slender calves. She wore a single magnolia tucked into her mass of dark hair and carried a bouquet of the same flower. Her earrings were opals, to match her engagement ring. The music would be provided by her aunt Toni and Toni's piano player, Pudge, from Chanson Triste.

Standing upstairs, just outside the door to her childhood bedroom, waiting for the signal to begin, Jax looked down at her daughter-to-be.

"Are you nervous?" she asked the child.

Amy shook her head. "No. Are you?"

"Yes," Jax admitted.

Amy tilted her head to peer up at Jax. "Why? Because you have to go down there in front of all those people?"

"Well, yes, that's part of it. But mostly…" Jax hesitated, wondering if she should voice her fears, then decided to tell the truth. She was always going to tell the truth from now on, especially where it concerned her emotions. Anything else only led to heartache. "You know I've never been anybody's mommy before," she confessed. "I'm afraid I won't be a good one, or that I'll make mistakes."

Amy didn't even have to think about that. "Jeff already told me," she said. "And we're both going to help you, so you don't have to worry. But Daddy wouldn't have asked you to marry us if you wouldn't be a good mommy, anyway," she said confidently. "An' it's okay to make mistakes sometimes. Daddy says everybody makes mistakes, but it's okay if you learn a lesson from them. Like when I stood up on the ropes, remember? That was a mistake. But it was okay 'cause I learned not to do it again."

The music started then—the piano first, then Toni's sultry voice singing the words to "Always."

Amy squirmed excitedly. "Do I look all right?"

Jax traced a circle with her finger. "Turn around and let me see."

Amy twirled, making the skirt of her bridesmaid's dress bell out around her. It was an Impressionist watercolor floral in pastel pink and the palest baby blue, with a white lace collar and a wide pink satin ribbon at the empire waist. A matching ribbon held her hair back from her face, and she wore shiny white patent Mary Janes and white anklets with a narrow frill of pink lace trim. Her miniature bouquet was made of baby's breath and pink sweetheart roses.

"You look absolutely beautiful," Jax assured her.

"Do you think Daddy will like it?"

Like Jax's wedding dress, the bridesmaid's outfit had been kept a secret, too.

"Your daddy will love it."

The music changed, the lyrics to "Always" fading out to be replaced by the opening notes of the traditional wedding march.

"Is that our music now?" Amy demanded.

"That's it."

Amy nodded and, clutching her bouquet in both hands in front of her, started down the stairs ahead of Jax, as they had rehearsed. Then she stopped and came back, carefully shifting her bouquet to one hand.

"You can hold my hand," she said, lifting her other one to Jax. "So you won't be nervous."

They walked down the stairs and into the front parlor, hand in hand. Matt and Jeff, dressed in nearly identical dark blue suits, stood waiting for them at the end of the long white runner that had been laid down to provide an aisle between the chairs ranged on either side of the room. Her entire family was present. All the people she loved. All those bound to her by blood or affection.

Beau, looking handsome as always, and just the tiniest bit self-satisfied, as if he had engineered the whole thing. Charly, in the one good black dress that was the only one she seemed to own. Shelby, just a bit wistful without Travis by her side. Marie and her new husband, Lucas, holding hands. Uncle Remy and his new bride, Kendall. Toni and

Brody. Her grandfather Charles and beloved Aunt Mary. Her father, looking uncharacteristically sentimental and misty-eyed. Odelle, who had had a hand in raising all the Delacroix kids, and her husband, Woodrow. Uncle Philip had fortunately been unable to attend, but Drew was there, sober as a judge and dashing as always. And the elegant Joanna with her pretty daughter Nikki, who was actually smiling for once. And sweet Uncle William, who was waiting up front to perform the ceremony. Matt's family was all there, too. His parents, Amelia and Henry. His grandparents and cousins, aunts and uncles, nieces and nephews.

Jax smiled at each and every one of them as she walked down the aisle with Amy's hand in hers.

She held her hand out to Matt as she approached him, the one holding her bouquet. He cupped her elbow in his palm, drawing her close, and gathered his son to him on the other side. And then the four of them—the bride and groom and their two young attendants—turned toward Father William and took their vows.

AFTERWARD, AT THE WEDDING brunch, after all the toasts had been made and the cake had been cut, Amy stood up on her chair and demanded the attention of the group.

"Jeff's the best man, an' he wants to make a toast." She motioned to her brother, imperious as a princess. "Stand up, Jeff. You can't make a toast sitting down. Okay, now, is everybody ready?" She looked around the room to make sure everyone was holding a glass high. She nodded at her brother. "Do the toast, Jeff."

Blushing a little, his eyes round and serious behind the lenses of his glasses, he raised his glass of sparkling apple juice. "This toast is to our dad," he said. "And to our new mom."

DELTA JUSTICE

continues with

SON OF THE SHERIFF

by Sandy Steen

He'd never stopped loving her.
But he didn't dare trust her...
After sixteen years, Annabelle Delacroix has
come home. And despite her past betrayal, Jake
Trahan wants her as badly now as he did then.
But it isn't until he meets Annabelle's son, Cade,
that he finally realizes the true extent of
Annabelle's deception...

Available in February

Here's a preview!

SON OF THE SHERIFF

DUMBFOUNDED, Jake simply stared at Philip.

"Now just a damn minute, Senator. I'm trying very hard—"

"To finally get your hands on the Delacroix money. That's what you've been trying to do all along, isn't it? Well, it didn't work sixteen years ago, and it's not going to work now. I intend to cut Annabelle out of my will. She won't get a dime!"

Jake swallowed the words he desperately wanted to say. This was Annabelle's father, and even though they were estranged at the moment, he knew that could change and he didn't want to say anything he couldn't take back later.

"I'm sorry you feel that way, Senator. And as far as the Delacroix money is concerned, I can't speak for Anna, but I can tell you one thing for certain. I didn't want your money sixteen years ago, and I don't want it now. All I care about is making your daughter happy."

"Oh, yes," Philip all but snarled. "Such a pretty speech. But you forget, I've heard it before. And I'm not any more impressed now than I was then."

"You're right," Jake said. "It's the same speech. And Annabelle's still the sweetest, most caring and honest person I've ever known. She's still the best thing that ever happened to me, and I was a fool to lose her. But the difference now is that I'm smart enough not to give up. Smart enough to fight for what I want. I love her and want to spend the rest of my life with her. And Cade."

Suddenly Philip's eyes sparked, and his mouth curled at the edges. "Yes, Cade. We mustn't forget about Cade."

Casually, he walked over to the set of three crystal decanters and liqueur glasses sitting on a silver tray. After removing the top from one of the decanters, he poured what appeared to be sherry into a glass.

Jake didn't like the sudden change in the senator's demeanor. One minute, he looked as if he were about to explode, and the next, he looked like the cat that had swallowed the canary. What in the world was going on with Delacroix?

"I haven't forgotten about Cade," Jake said. "He's a wonderful kid. Bright and compassionate. I hope someday he'll come to think of me as a father." Jake didn't know why he was saying this to Delacroix, except perhaps that since he hadn't stood up for loving Anna all those years ago, he somehow needed to make up for it now.

Philip sipped at his sherry. "So you think Annabelle is honest and caring, do you?"

"She is."

"She's a liar."

There was a sofa separating him from the old man, and it was all Jake could do not to vault across it and choke the hell out of Philip Delacroix. He clenched his fists at his sides. "I'll send one of my men back out here to take your statement," he said flatly and started for the door. "I think it would be better—"

"She cheated you, Jake."

At that, Jake stopped and turned. "Senator Delacroix, at the moment the badge pinned to my shirt is the only thing keeping me from smashing in your face. But I'm warning you, don't push me."

"Ask her."

The look in Delacroix's eyes was so sadistically gleeful it made Jake's blood run cold. Had the old man gone crazy?

"Ask her what she took from you sixteen years ago. What little secret she's been keeping all this time."

The hair stood up on the back of Jake's neck and fear knotted his stomach. A small voice of warning told him to run. Leave before he regretted staying. He hated himself for forming the question in his mind, let alone voicing it. "What are you talking about?"

"I'm talking about the boy. I'm talking about Cade."

"What about him?"

"Haven't you wondered why Rowland divorced her? Why he never contacts Cade?"

Before Jake could respond, Philip, still wearing the same sadistic grin, raised his glass in salute. "Fifteen years too late, but what the hell. *Congratulations, Daddy. It's a boy.*"

Coming in August 1997!

THE BETTY NEELS RUBY COLLECTION

August 1997—Stars Through the Mist
September 1997—The Doubtful Marriage
October 1997—The End of the Rainbow
November 1997—Three for a Wedding
December 1997—Roses for Christmas
January 1998—The Hasty Marriage

COLLECTOR'S EDITION

This August start assembling the
Betty Neels Ruby Collection. Six of the
most requested and best-loved titles have
been especially chosen for this collection.
From August 1997 until January 1998,
one title per month will be available to avid
fans. Spot the collection by the lush ruby red
cover with the gold Collector's Edition banner
and your favorite author's name—Betty Neels!

Available in August at your favorite retail outlet.

HARLEQUIN®

Take 4 bestselling love stories FREE

Plus get a FREE surprise gift!

Special Limited-time Offer

Mail to Harlequin Reader Service®

3010 Walden Avenue
P.O. Box 1867
Buffalo, N.Y. 14240-1867

YES! Please send me 4 free Harlequin Intrigue® novels and my free surprise gift. Then send me 4 brand-new novels every month. Bill me at the low price of $2.94 each plus 25¢ delivery and applicable sales tax, if any.* That's the complete price and a savings of over 10% off the cover prices—quite a bargain! I understand that accepting the books and gift places me under no obligation ever to buy any books. I can always return a shipment and cancel at any time. Even if I never buy another book from Harlequin, the 4 free books and the surprise gift are mine to keep forever.

181 BPA A3UQ

Name	(PLEASE PRINT)	
Address	Apt. No.	
City	State	Zip

This offer is limited to one order per household and not valid to present Harlequin Intrigue® subscribers. *Terms and prices are subject to change without notice. Sales tax applicable in N.Y.

UINT-696

Ring in the New Year with

New Year's Resolution:
FAMILY

**This heartwarming collection of three
contemporary stories rings in the
New Year with babies, families and
the best of holiday romance.**

Add a dash of romance to your holiday celebrations
with this exciting new collection, featuring bestselling
authors **Barbara Bretton, Anne McAllister** and
Leandra Logan.

Available in December,
wherever Harlequin books are sold.

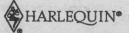

KEY TO MY HEART

Unlock the secrets of romance just in time for the most romantic day of the year— Valentine's Day!

Key to My Heart
features three of your favorite authors,

Kasey Michaels,
Rebecca York
and Muriel Jensen,

to bring you wonderful tales of romance and Valentine's Day dreams come true.

As an added bonus you can receive Harlequin's special Valentine's Day necklace. FREE with the purchase of every *Key to My Heart* collection.

Available in January,
wherever Harlequin books are sold.

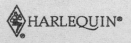

WELCOME TO *Love Inspired* ™

A brand-new series of contemporary inspirational love stories.

Join men and women as they learn valuable lessons about facing the challenges of today's world and about life, love and faith.

Look for the following January 1998 Love Inspired™ titles:

Night Music
by Sara Mitchell

A Wife Worth Waiting For
by Arlene James

Faithfully Yours
by Lois Richer

Available in retail outlets
in December 1997.

LIFT YOUR SPIRITS AND GLADDEN YOUR HEART with *Love Inspired* ™!

Steeple
Hill™

LI198